I0788408

THE ULTMATE SACRIFICE

THE ULTMATE SACRIFICE

A NOVEL BY

ANTHONY FIELDS

WAHIDA CLARK PRESENTS PUBLISHING, LLC.

This is a work of fiction. Names, characters, places, and incidents either are the product of the author's imagination or are used fictitiously, and any resemblance to actual persons, living or dead, business establishments, events, or locales are entirely coincidental.

Wahida Clark Presents Publishing
134 Evergreen Place
Suite 305
East Orange, New Jersey 07018
973-678-9982
www.wclarkpublishing.com

The Ultimate Sacrifice
ISBN 13-digit 978-1-944992-21-7
ISBN 10-digit 1944992219
Library of Congress Catalog Number 2010926073
    1.   Urban, D.C., Hip-Hop, African American, – Fiction

Cover design and layout by Oddball Dsgn
Book design by Oddball Dsgn
Edited by JPC

Printed in United States

.DEDICATION.

This book is dedicated to my mother, Deborah Ann Wiseman, who departed this life on August 5, 2008. Shedding tears does not stop the constant ache in my heart. I never got the chance to tell you I love you before you went away. So I say that now and hopefully you'll hear it. I LOVE YOU, MA! Rest in peace, baby girl.

*In loving memory of Deborah Wiseman
(March 29,1953 – August 5, 2008)*

.ACKNOWLEDGEMENTS.

First and foremost, all praise is due to Allah, the creator of all the worlds. When all people fade away, He is always there. I pray that one day Allah makes me a better Muslim. A better father, uncle, brother, lover, friend and overall person.

I have to say a few words to the woman who stood by my side for the majority of this bid-Lashawn Wilson. True love is hard to find, but I've found that in you. I have loved you since the first moment I saw you 17 years ago. As the years go by and our connection is tested more and more, just know that I love you more than my own life. You are a wonderful mother, a beautiful woman and a true testament to that old school love. Your resilience inspires me and your strength impresses me. I only have a few more years to go. Stick around for awhile and it will all be greater later. I love you. And no, the character named Shawnay is not you. Her similarities are purely coincidental. I love you. Give my love my love to the girls.

To my children-Kevin Grover, Destinee Wilson, Aniyah Fields and Amari Fields, I love each and every one of you with all my heart. Daddy will be home one day. Just know that everything I am is you. Everything I do is for you all. I love ya'll.

To my stepmother-Gloria Mason, your support is so special to me. When I was home, I never understood just how much you meant to me. I took you for granted and I'm sorry for that. You are the embodiment of real black love. The way you stood beside my father until his dying day has endeared you to me forever. You epitomize strong black womanhood and I pray that Allah sends me a wife who is just like you. I love you Poochie with all my heart.

To Toni, how could I go an further and no thank you for everything you have done to further my literary career. You single handedly made my name relevant again. For all the work you did and will do in the future- I am eternally grateful. For putting my MySpace page together to creating my email address, you have helped me a great deal and you did it unselfishly and unconditionally. For your advice, your wisdom, knowledge of the business, your shoulder that I leaned on, your phone I blew up, your mailbox I filled up and for your constant trips to the post office for me-I thank you with every part of my being. You are a beautiful lady inside and out. Thanks for putting up with me when no one else would. My success is your success, so strap on your seat belt, we're about to take a ride. And a special shout our goes out to the whole O.O.S.A. family. A thousand thank yous Toni.

To all the female friends that have crossed my path during this bid and at least attempted to hold me down-thank you. To Kim Thompson, Sunnie Simms, Tameka Maddox, Eno Oduk, Shoneel Reed, Nacheshia Fox, Naomi Smith, Ladawn Duncan, Angelina Scott, Philicia Boston, Tashia Gardner, Annie "Sherry" Battle, Tina Grover, Lakia Ransom, Damika Ward and Stephanie Fields. In what every way, you touched my life-Thank you.

To both the Wiseman and Fields clans. Whether you supported me or not. This one is for the team. Special thanks to Toi Wiseman for everything. To Tonya Gilliam, Deborah "Lee-lee" Wiseman, Deangelo and Dre, this is also for all the ladies at the nursing home, support the brother. This is for everybody in D.C. jail that love Buck. "In the Blink of an Eye" is even better.

This book is also dedicated to my father Thomas "Bucky" Fields, who passed away in 2005. I miss you Pop. I wish that you could be here to see your boy blow up. It ain't the same without you here. You planted a seed in me when I was young that took 28 years to blossom, but it did Pop. I did it. I finally made it. You were right when you said that I was special. My every success is for you. Rest in Peace.

To all the good men around the country in the Feds from D.C.-Keep y'all head up, To Nehemiah Hampton-El, Antone White, Eric Hicks, George Foreman, Cochise Shakur, Randy Shaw, Jayvan Allen, Gregory Wright, Marvin Jackson, Joseph Ebron, Pushead, Kay-Kay, Dave Battle, Raphaek Parker, Lil Donny, Sean B., Tony Coleman, Larry Moe, Mike Lucas, Cardoza Simms, Henry "Lil-Man" James, Khalif A. Mujahid, Moe Best,

Izzy, Jew-Baby, Tariq, Ned C., Doodie, Rell, Griff, Poochie, Eric Gordon, Wendell "Scoop" Juggins, Derron McMillan, Dock Roach, Kenny "KP" Williams, Pinball, Jontay Robinson, Bay-newt, Crank, Nu-Nu, Bam and Boo Alford, Deon O., Larry W., Bushwack. Lavelle H., Cortez Gatlin, Eddie Mathis, Peaches Ma-this, Ronald "Pimp" Fleming, Detroit Bam, David "Coo-Wop" Wilson, Antwan Ball and everybody that didn't tell on them Congress Park dudes. Steve from 10th Place, Antoine Lewis and Rosco Smith (RIP).

To all the good men in Pollock U.S.P. with me. I'ma hold us all down. To Reggie "Champ" Yelverton, Twim Moe, Styles, La-La, Zeke, Big Shaq, Dontay Kidd, Freaky Smooth, Whistle Pop, B.F., Big E, Gumsmoke, Dickie, Dollar, LB, Sharp hands, Andy, Scoop and Cain, The Whole B-more Mob-Player, Ache, Mike, Lil Bee, Hay, Vito, Reggie and the others, to AirRon Davis, O.G,Rome, Marvin Sanders, Reggie Blunt, Foxy, Youngboy Lee, Lips, Khalid, Boo Joyner, Primetime, Mansoo, Nut, Curt, Nelson, Muslim Mike, T-Mac, Sandy, J. Baker, Gogom A.D., T.J., Black Junior, K.C., Poonie, Terry, Vicious Bob, Big Play Ray, Twin, Marthell, Redds, OldMan and others.

Next, I'd like to thank all the people that gave up on me in the middle of the struggle. All the people who counted me out and said that I'd never amount to much-Thank you all. You mo-tivated me to succeed even while at the lowest point of my life. I'd like to shout out all the people in the literary game that slammed the door in my face, threw away my mail, talked bad about me and tried to beat me. You know who you are, there's no need for names.

I need to shout out the hood authors that keep it funky in every book. Kwame Teague, K'wan, Quentin Carter, Paul John-son, Leo Sullivan, Jason Poole, Al-Saddiq Banks, Seth Ferranti, Eyone Williams and Mike Sanders.

A special thank goes to Teri Woods for publishing my first book **Angel** and never giving me the props I deserved. Thank you to Crystal Perkins and Cyrstell Publications for bringing GHOSTACEKILLAZ to the people. Your company was too small to really push that book, so I ain't mad at you because it didn't do well.

Out with the old and in with the new is what I always say. So I'd like to thank Wahida Clark and the whole WCP Team for allowing me to be a part of the family. Wahida you believed in me and my struggle from day one and I respect you and your hustle. Get that money, sista girl. To Eyone Williams-I respect you slim and your pen game is sick! Keep doing what you doing and keep your head up. To Jason Poole- I appreciate the plug homie. I loved Victoria's Secret, Larceny and Convict Candy.

To all the stores in D.C. that keeps us outfitted in the fly stuff-HOBO, SHOOTERS SPORTS, MADNESS, SOLBIATO, HUGO BOSS, JOTO SPORTS, WE R ONE, MCHUNU, OMERTA SPORTS AND I.S.O. ORIGINALS. To all the bookstores, venders and dot.coms-thanks for your support.

To the whole D.C. - hold us down. We'll be back one day. To all my friends at MySpace-hold me down. To become a friend, my info is *www.Myspace.com/AnthonyFields* . To all the people I forgot to mention, charge it to the fact that my brain is not what it once was. Some I left out on purpose. Be sure to check out my next bestsellers, **ULTIMATE SACRIFICE 2** & **IN THE BLINK OF AN EYE**. Let me know what you think of my work.

I can be reached at this address:
Anthony Fields #16945-016
USP Pollock
PO Box 2099
Pollock, LA 71467

ONE LOVE,
Buckey Fields

.PROLOGUE.
BEAUMONT PENITENTIARY

ANTONIO AMEEN FELDER

Looking at the clock on the wall, it read 9:45 a.m. We had twenty minutes before the next move. I put one foot up on the second level of the railing on the top tier and leaned on it. Oblivious to the conversation going on around me, my focus was on the dude standing by his cell on the bottom tier. Keith Barnett was engaged in a conversation with a Mexican Mafia gang member. Standing about six foot one in his blue Bob Parker prison decks, I sized Keith up to weigh about 200 pounds. His low cut curly temple taper blended perfectly with his beard. The dark ink from his heavily tattooed forearms stood out against his light brown skin. As if on cue, he looked up at me. Our eyes held each other for a few seconds. He gave me a head nod and then went back to his conversation. Every time he smiled at the Mexican, something inside me caught fire. I watched him finally go into his cell. I thought for a second about going to get him in the cell, but decided against it. Five minutes later, he came out with a bag in his hand and headed to the shower room.

"C'mon. He's in the shower room." I announced to Boo, Umar and Lil Cee and then walked calmly across the unit to the shower room.

The dude was just stepping into his shower shoes as we entered. He watched us closely as we approached.

"You from D.C., scrap?" I asked him.

"Naw," he lied.

"So how'd you get a 007 number?" Boo added.

"I caught my case in D.C., but—"

"Your name Keith?"

"Naw. My name is Abdul Wa—"

He never got the chance to finish his sentence. I hit him with a three-piece combination that flattened him. "Boo, you got the sheet?"

"Yeah," Boo replied, pulling pieces of a ripped up bed sheet out of his pants.

"Get his bitch ass up so I can tie his wrists to this pipe right here."

Boo handed me the strips and then helped Umar and Cee lift Keith Barnett's body off the floor. I doubled each strip and tied both of Keith's wrists to the pipe. They let him go. He now hung suspended from the low hanging pipe.

"Wake him up," I said and looked at Boo.

From his pocket, Boo pulled out a white sock with a combination lock inside of it. He cocked back and swung it through the air. The lock made contact with Keith's head. Blood appeared instantly and ran down his face.

"A-A-R-R-g-gh!" Keith groaned. "Wha...What I...I...do?"

"You came to the compound, nigga. That's what you did. Didn't somebody tell you that we don't do rats in Beaumont?" Boo said venomously. "Then you gon' lie and say you ain't from D.C. and your name ain't Keith."

"Hot ass nigga! What's your name, nigga?"

"Abdul—"

Whack!

"You from D.C., ain't you?"

"I'm fr—"

Whack!

Boo was in a zone. He was a man possessed.

"Lie again, nigga and I'ma keep puttin' this lock on yo' ass. Your name Keith Barnett, ain't it?"

"Y—y—yeah!" Keith mumbled.

Whack! Whack! Whack!

"Hold on, ock," I said, getting Boo's attention. "He makin' too much noise when you hit him."

"Man, fuck that nigga!" Boo said. He turned his attention back to Keith. "Nigga, why you tell on your man?"

"My…my mother… made me tell."

"Your mother made you tell?" I repeated. "Hit his bitch ass again, scrap."

Boo swung at Keith again. *Whack!*

"*A-r-r-gh!* Don't hit me—don't hit me—no more! Please!" Keith begged. "The kids. They threatened to take…my kids. My baby mother—my mother—I had to. They said I had to—" A stain appeared in the middle of Keith's khakis and spread down his leg. He had pissed on himself.

"Cee, you and Umar go out in the common area and wait for Khadafi." I glanced at my watch. "He should be coming in on the move in five minutes. Tell him we got slim in here. Umar, don't let nobody come in here. If somebody tries, tell 'em we cleanin' up in here."

"I got you, ock." Umar replied. Then he and Lil Cee left the shower room.

"P—p-please d-d-on't hurt me no more! P-p-please!" Keith stuttered.

"We ain't the one you gotta beg, nigga. He'll be here in a minute."

I looked at the doomed man hanging from the pipe and smiled. He could plead for his life all he wanted. There would be no sympathetic ears for his pleas to fall on. The man coming to CB unit was coming for one reason and one reason only— to kill.

.CHAPTER ONE.
LUTHER KHADAFI FULLER

I stood at the door of my unit waiting for the next ten minute move. As soon as I heard the beep before the announcement, I was out the door. As I moved across the pound (or yard), I was on a serious mission. Nobody approached me or said what's up as I marched to Unit CB. I was going to bring this nigga a move. Keith Barnett's rat ass had to go! My word is my bond. I told my man Mousey if I ever saw that bitch-ass nigga, it was over for him. As fate would have it, he showed up on the compound a couple days ago. Since then, I haven't been able to catch the nigga. Today was my lucky day.

I can't understand for the life of me why niggas still snitch when the Feds don't give a fuck about your well being. They put you straight in harm's way. As soon as you get off the stand, they will send you right to the same prison with the same niggas you told on. If I didn't know any better, I would think they hated snitches too. Either that or they crazy, cause niggas gon' pay one way or the other for their deeds.

Keith must have thought niggas would look the other way since he's a "Muslim" now. Please! I won't ever forget how as soon as the heat came down, he lifted his skirt and showed his thong. The Feds grilled him about the double murder him and my man did in Southeast, D.C. and he started singing like a bitch. It's cool 'cause I'ma make a man out of him during his last few moments of life.

When Keith came to the pound, he came in the disguise of a Muslim. Rat niggas always come to jail and become Muslim for protection. They want to hide out amongst one of the strongest organized groups inside the prison walls. I guess he assumed since he switched his name up, wouldn't nobody know it was him. I don't care if he was "The Imam," he would still get it! I'll deal with the brothers when the time comes.

I'ma Muslim myself and the brothers know how I get down. That nigga ain't gettin' no free pass just because he done found religion, even if it happens to be my own faith. If I was Christian, I'd still nail his ass to the cross. It's just that simple. He should've had a miraculous conversion before he took the witness stand. In the world I live in, the penalty for treason is death— signed, sealed and delivered by me.

Killin' ain't shit to me. I've been doing it for years. I caught my first body at thirteen years old. I would have continued to kill if these people hadn't locked me up when I was sixteen. That was nine years ago and here I am ready to kill again.

I walked into CB unit and was met by my men, Umar and Lil Cee. "What's up with y'all?"

"Ain't shit, ock. Ameen and Boo got slim in the shower room," Umar responded.

"What's he saying in there?" I asked but really could care less. His time was up no matter what he said.

"He talkin' about his mother made him tell." Lil Cee said. "He says that they threatened to lock his baby mama up and take the kids."

"Fuck his mother!" I spat while walking toward the shower room.

At the entrance to the showers, I told Lil Cee to post up outside the door and make sure that nobody tried to come in. "Hit the door if the C.O. comes this way."

When I walked into the room, I saw that Keith was tied up and hanging from a pipe. His face was a bloody mess. "Damn, what y'all do to him, cuz?"

Boo looked at me and smiled. Then he produced a bloody sock. "I put that lock on his ass, moe. I been wantin' to do that to a nigga forever."

I looked at Ameen, who was just standing there looking strong as shit in a wife beater, prison khakis and boots. He hated rats just as much as me, so he just nodded his head as if to say, "Do what you gotta do."

Keith looked up at me and tried to speak, but his words came out incoherent. It didn't matter anyway, because the need for words had long passed. I wasn't trying to hear shit. I pulled the ten-inch shank out of my waistband. Then I grabbed the bloody sock from Boo. I took the lock from it, balled it up and forced it into Keith's mouth.

I stabbed him in both of his eyes and said, "See no evil." Then I hit him in both ears. "Hear no evil." The sock was in his mouth so I couldn't stab him in the mouth to finish off the "Speak no evil," so I just plunged the knife into his chest repeatedly. I watched the life leave his body. I felt exhilarated. I was like the exterminator killing a rodent. When I was sure he was dead, I untied the cloth that binded him to the pipe. His body dropped with a loud thud and his lifeless limbs sprawled out at my feet.

I looked at all three of my men and said, "I'ma show these Texas niggas how to kill a rat D.C. style." I pulled out my latest purchase from the Aryan Brotherhood, a small homemade ax. "Umar, go get me one of those green duffel bags I saw out there by the steps."

Umar returned with the bag, only to see Keith's foot flying off.

"What the fuck?" he yelled.

He looked at me like I was crazy. I looked back at him and shrugged my shoulders. It took thirty minutes to fully dismember Keith's body. Seeing all the blood, tissue and cartilage made me hack even harder. I missed my calling. I should have been a butcher.

"This nigga trippin' like shit," Ameen said.

I snatched the green bag out of Umar's hand and stuffed all the body parts into it. Then I secured the bag shut with some metal clamps at the top. I dragged the heavy bag over to the corner of the room and then disrobed down to my boxer briefs. I balled up my bloody clothes and handed them to

Ameen. "Get rid of these and bring me some institution shit to put on."

Everybody left the room as I stepped into the shower and turned on the water. I grabbed a bar of soap and lathered myself up, feeling better than I had in years. I had just committed another murder and it didn't faze me one bit. I stood there in the hot water and thought about my life. I thought about the things and people I loved and my eventual release from prison. I thought about how all of my life I always felt alone, even when surrounded by friends. I glanced over at the green bag and laughed. The thing I found amusing was that I stood not even five feet away from a dismembered corpse and suddenly I didn't feel alone at all.

Early the next day, I was awakened out of my sleep by my celly, Reggie "Champ" Yelverton. "Dirty Redds, get up, slim!"

Champ was the only person who still called me by my nickname. I had told him on several occasions to call me Khadafi, but he said he couldn't remember. I always let it go because Champ was punch drunk from fighting in the ring for years. "What's up, cuz?" I asked, wiping sleep from my eyes.

"They must be getting ready to shake down or something." Champ stated while standing at the cell door, looking out." It's about forty police in the block. Lieutenants, the captain, a rack of muthafuckas. Hold on, they looking up this way."

"Let me see." I jumped off the top bunk and went to the cell door. Champ wasn't exaggerating. There had to be at least fifty cops in the unit. The captain, a middle-aged, balding, fat Mexican named Garcia, glanced up at my cell and I knew what time it was. "Aye, cuz, they coming to get me. They might shake the cell down, so put everything up real fast."

"They comin' to get you? How you know that?"

Champ wasn't in the loop, so he had no idea I killed the dude the day before. "Trust me, cuz. I know. Just give them all my mail and pictures 'cause I probably won't come back out.

Give them my cosmetics too. Put my lucky dice inside the powder bottle. You can keep all the food and stamps. I know you tryna make parole, slim, so I left you out of everything. I didn't want them to be able to put you with nothin'. I don't know when our paths will cross again, but it was definitely a pleasure being around you. I hope you make it out."

Champ was seasoned enough not to ask any questions. But as I waited for the cops to get to my door, I questioned myself. *What went wrong? What could they have? Who had they spoken to? What mistakes had we made?* I was brushing my teeth in the sink when I heard the knock on the cell door. "Fuller, we need you to back up to the door and stick your hands out of the food slot, so we can cuff you."

Slowly, I got dressed and then did as the C.O. said.

Champ nodded his head at me and I nodded back. "One love, cuz. Death before dishonor."

"Death before dishonor," I heard Champ say as the door opened and I was led out of the unit.

.CHAPTER TWO.

AMEEN

Looking out the window of my cell, I saw Khadafi being led across the field in handcuffs. He was being escorted by a team of officers in full riot gear. It didn't take a rocket scientist to figure out what was going on. They were rounding us up. When I left Khadafi in the shower room, I took the bloody clothes to my cell and methodically cut them into strips. Then I flushed the strips and the gloves down the toilet. The knife that was used to kill the dude, I got rid of that, too. The ax, Khadafi took with him.

Me and Umar cleaned up most of the blood on the floor and let the shower water wash the rest down the drain. All the while, the bag with the body parts was still there in the same spot where Khadafi had left it. I wasn't fucking with that bag under no circumstances. In fact, nobody did.

While conducting the four o'clock count, the cops realized that an inmate was missing. After a massive search of the unit, the bag of body parts was discovered. We've been on lockdown ever since.

Something inside me told me that they were coming to get me, so I prepared myself to go to the hole. I wondered who else they had snatched besides Khadafi. I knew my stay in the hole would be for the long haul, but fuck it. I'm tired of Beaumont anyway. It's time to shake the spot. Ever since they shipped my men, Tone, Black Rain, Chico and Buck to the other prisons, the spot been on some shit.

I could've stayed away from the murder, but I chose not to. Khadafi is my man and I didn't want to let him see the dude

Keith alone. When he first told me who Keith was and what he wanted to do, I felt him all the way. I can't stand a rat myself.

As we tied the nigga up that morning and Boo whopped him with the lock, my mind kept racing and my memory kept showing me Eric. Eric Frazier was my childhood partner that gave me up to save his ass. And the messed up part about it all is that I put myself in harm's way for him. We were both up at Congress Park hustling in the projects. Eric loved to fuck all the young girls. I was tryna stack that money. Fucking a rack of them hoodrat broads wasn't my thing. Besides, I had a good girl at home. Shawnay was my boo. We had been together since we were both fourteen. We had two daughters, Asia and Kenya. My family was my world, I would never jeopardize that.

That is, until I decided to go to bat for Eric. Eric was my partner in crime since I started doing crime. When my father would come home drunk, he'd beat me, my mother and my two brothers. I always ran away to Eric's house to escape. We ate Ramen noodles off the same fork. He and I were more like brothers than the two I shared a house with.

Eric got into it with a dude named Quincy over a broad. Eric beat him up. Later that night the dude came back and brought Eric a move. When I heard the gunshots, I came out the building and saw the dude chasing Eric down the street. I reacted instantly. I ran out into the street and made the hunter the hunted. Moving off of pure emotion, I chased Quincy down, stood over him and crushed him.

It seemed like everybody in the hood, including Eric, saw me commit the murder, but nobody came forward to tell on me. Apparently, Quincy had burned a lot of bridges in the hood. When it was all said and done, the person who ended up taking the stand against me was Eric. The man I jeopardized my life for, pointed me out in court and demonstrated for the jury how I stood over Quincy when I killed him. I gave myself to save Eric's life and he betrayed me. I was sentenced to fifty years to life for felony murder while armed. I've been in jail for seven years and every day that goes by, I lose more and more of my connection to my girl and daughters.

So helping kill Keith was my release of frustration. Every time Khadafi plunged that knife into his body, all I saw was Eric. I wanted to kill him myself, but I couldn't deny Khadafi his glory. He said it was his destiny, so who am I to get in the way of that?

I walked over to the cell door and hollered across the tier. "Goody?"

"Yea, moe?" he answered.

"They just took Khadafi across the yard. I wonder what for."

"I don't know, moe, but they snatched Lil Cee early this morning. I think it's about that hot nigga gettin' killed in the unit."

I played Goody off. "Fuck that nigga. He should've been killed a thousand times. We gonna be locked down for months messing with that new warden."

"They coming back this way, moe. It looks like they coming up here."

I already knew they were coming back for me. I was ready, properly bagged up and everything. Somewhere along the way, something had gone wrong. A base hadn't been covered. They were coming for us too soon. I slammed a couple of pouches of tobacco and waited for what I knew to be coming. Ten minutes later, the food slot on my door opened.

"Felder, step to the door, turn around and cuff up," a pink-faced lieutenant said.

"Cuff up? For what?" I asked.

"Just cuff up, Felder. You'll find out why, when you get to the S.H.U."

I cuffed and let them take me to the Special Housing Unit.

.CHAPTER THREE.

VERNON BOO DAMMONS

They didn't let any of us go into cells with each other. It was the old divide and conquer tactic, but we were all too sharp for it. But to our surprise, when the prison came off lockdown, they let us rec together. Once we were all outside in the rec cage, I noticed that Lil Cee was missing.

"Didn't they grab Lil Cee, too?" I asked to make sure that I wasn't trippin'.

"Yeah, they grabbed him. From what I heard, they grabbed him first," Ameen said as he dropped down and did burpies.

"Did somebody get word to him to come outside?" Umar asked.

Khadafi stood up from doing a set of push-ups and said, "I asked that C.O. Baker, what range Charles Gooding was on. He told me that ain't no C. Gooding locked up in the S.H.U. We're the only ones on this investigation. Lil Cee's bitch ass is gone."

"Gone where?" I asked.

"He ain't on the compound, that we know for sure. He probably over in the Medium or the Low. He's the reason we're in the S.H.U. That ain't hard to tell."

I was genuinely messed up at what Ameen said. He had to be mistaken. Lil Cee couldn't be a witness against us. "Naw, moe. I ain't going for that. Lil Cee been pushin' that knife and holding it down since Oak Hill. He ain't never told on a mutha-fucka before. Why now?"

"If I ever catch his ass, I'll ask him that right before I kill him," Khadafi said. "This beef we on is death penalty shit. Cee ain't got but three years left. He cracked under pressure and told on us. This shit is some real shit."

I thought about what Khadafi said and got quiet. *Death penalty*. I never knew that shit. I thought about the fact that I go home next year and silently cursed myself for being stupid. How had I allowed myself to get caught up like this? My whole mood changed instantly. I was up shit creek with no boat, paddle, or life jacket. "Did the people say anything to y'all?"

"The S.I.S. nigga, Lieutenant Neal, told me that somebody in CB unit saw me in the unit on the move. He said their tape confirms that. Plus his confidential informant said I went into the shower and killed Keith. That's all they have," Khadafi said.

"Did he show you any of what the tape caught?" I asked him.

"Naw, but he tried to tell me that y'all were telling on me and I better save myself. The basic bullshit."

"Did you say anything?" Umar interjected.

Khadafi gave him a look so wicked that it scared me.

"Cuz, don't ever in your life ask me no sucka-ass shit like that. Do it look like I said something? Am I in a cell with Lil Cee somewhere?"

"I didn't mean—"

"I don't care how you meant it, cuz," Khadafi exploded. "Just don't mean it no more. Ain't no cameras in the shower room. They ain't got shit on us. Everybody gotta stick to the script. We ain't did shit. Cee can't tell them what he didn't see. That's why they snatched us all. They don't know who killed Keith."

"Y'all niggas chill out," Ameen said as he wiped sweat off his head. "We don't need to be at each other's throats right now. Let's just lay back and ride the waves. They'll show us their hand before we throw ours in. It's a poker game right now. We gotta keep our cards close to our chests and not let them bluff us. Let's see what happens in a few weeks."

That made a lot of sense to me. Ameen always said the wisest shit. I became a little more optimistic about the outcome of the case. And Khadafi had made a valid point as well.

Cee couldn't say who killed Keith because he wasn't in the room.

My mood brightened and I decided to do some burpies with Ameen. I couldn't let myself stress out about the things I couldn't control.

.CHAPTER FOUR.

HAROLD UMAR HOWARD

After offering my morning prayer, I laid on my bunk and pondered my predicament. Here I am, scheduled to be released in thirteen months after doing a six-year bid for selling coke, and now I'm deeply embedded in a murder investigation. I never even knew that Khadafi was gonna kill the dude. I thought he was just gonna stab the dude and that's it. When I came into the room and saw the chopped up body parts, I almost threw up, but I held it in. That was some shit straight out of one of them scary movies. I still see that shit in my dreams.

We've been in the hole now for about ninety days and they still haven't told us anything. "It's a waiting game," Ameen says every day that we go outside. I'm tired of waiting. The anxiety is killing me. I need to know what's happening. Ever since this shit happened, I've been sleeping less and not eating proper. I've lost about fifteen pounds off of my usually chiseled frame.

I feel like I'm just as gangsta as the next man, but this institution murder got my head fucked up. I've done a rack of foul shit in my life, but the older I get, the wiser I become. I've changed a lot in the five years I've been in jail. I owe most of it to Islam. The rest I credit to myself. I'm determined to become a better person.

"Howard?" a voice called out through my door.

"Yeah?" I responded. I stepped to the door.

"The lieutenant would like to speak to you," the C.O. said.

What the fuck did he want with me? Didn't I refuse to talk to them on every other occasion? I thought long and hard for a minute. What could it hurt to hear the man out? And the suspense was killing me. Maybe I'd learn something. "Give me about ten minutes and then come and get me. I'll be ready then."

I woke up my celly, Joe Ebron, and told him where I was going and why. I didn't want anything to seem sneaky about my move. I didn't need to be under suspicion by my men. I was handcuffed, pulled out of the cell and taken to the Lieutenant's office. SIS Lieutenant Neal sat behind a desk with his eyes glued to a folder in front of him. As I walked in he glanced up at me and said, "Have a seat, Howard. Inmate Howard, what's your first name and your fed number?" the lieutenant asked.

"Harold. 13776-007."

The lieutenant opened a file in front of him and read something. After a brief moment of silence he said, "I'm glad you decided to come and see me. Howard, I only want to help you."

"Well, let me out the hole, then. And off of this bullshit investigation."

"I'm afraid I can't do that, Howard. I've got a tape that shows you and Fuller entering a shower area in CB unit moments before a guy was killed in there. That tape also shows you exiting that room alone two minutes later. Inmate Gooding is standing at the entrance as the lookout man. You returned to the shower area holding something under your arm. We can't actually make out what it is. It may have been the knife used to kill Barnett, or it may have been the instrument used to dismember the poor guy. Which was it, Howard?"

I looked at the lieutenant like he was crazy and kept quiet.

"Well, I'd wager and say that it was the green bag that Barnett's mutilated body was found in. That's accessory to murder one, kid. Automatic life in prison for you. It says here that you are scheduled to be released via good time credits on June 7, 2008. That's a little over a year away. Do you really wanna miss that date, Howard? Are you ready to do life in prison for somebody else? We know why Barnett was killed. He was killed because he assisted the government in convicting his co-defendant, Michael "Mousey" Carter. Am I right?"

I found a spot on the floor and stared at it. I never acknowledged anything that he said. I was still stuck on the life in prison part.

"You can sit here and act like you don't hear me all you want. But at trial, you'll have to answer or take the fifth. The jury will convict you for sure then. We know everything about the murder and why it happened. What we don't know is who actually killed the guy. Or did all four of you kill him? You wanna help yourself out by answering that for me?"

I remained completely silent.

"No? Okay. Just let me say this: Fuller is scheduled to be released in eight months, Dammons in ten. Do you think that they are gonna stand firm on this beef? Somebody is gonna break and they are gonna give you up. Your chance to cooperate then will be gone. Think about what I'm saying to you, kid. Save yourself from yourself. When you're ready to talk, just get one of the officers to call me."

Everything that the lieutenant said to me I relayed verbatim to Ameen, Khadafi and Boo. Ameen paced the rec cage for a few minutes. Then he said, "Let me tell y'all something. This shit we going through is real. You ain't gonna wake up one day and all this is gone away. They ain't got much, but any prosecutor worth their law degree can paint a picture to a jury using that tape to convict us. I'm facing the death penalty if we go to trial and lose. By the way, that boy's people been in the papers calling for somebody's head. They'll get mine. Somebody has got to step up and take the beef. They know we were in that room and they got Lil Cee. Ain't no sense in bullshittin' each other. This shit don't look good for us. We need to make some hard decisions and make them now."

"Decisions like what?" Khadafi asked with a confused look on his face.

"All three of y'all go home in the next eight to twelve months. If these people indict y'all, y'all stuck like Chuck. I'ma take the beef."

"I can't let you do that, cuz." Khadafi stated emphatically. "This is my beef. Keith told on my man, not yours. I killed him, not you. You saying anything right now?"

"Naw, scrap. You saying anything?" Ameen replied. "Them people don't know all that shit you just said. I'm already fucked up in the game. I gotta do forty-two years before I see the board. I got thirty-five years left before they give me a five-year hit. I'm washed up, scrap. If I cop to the body, all they can do is give me thirty more years at the most. What the fuck is thirty more years when I'll probably die in here anyway? Either way, I'm finished." He looked around at each of us. "There ain't no way that I'm gonna let all of us go down on this body. I need y'all out there on the streets. Who's gonna look out for all of us as we rot away in Florence, Colorado? Nobody! That's why I'm gonna take the beef and free y'all."

"You'd really do that for me, cuz?" Khadafi asked with tears in his eyes.

"I'd do it for any one of y'all. But at the moment, it's for all of y'all. Y'all gotta be true to the game, respect the code and remember death before dishonor. And take care of my family. That's all I ask."

I was too emotional to speak and so was Boo. Khadafi was openly crying. Ameen hugged each one of us in turn and said, "I'ma tell Lieutenant Neal that I killed Keith and that y'all ain't have nothing to do with it." To Khadafi, Ameen turned and said, "You are the first to shine. Make a way for Boo and Umar. Then send me some loot and a rack of them Internet freak pictures. Then go and hit my daughters and their mother off. Promise that you gonna take care of my family."

"I promise you that, cuz."

"I love y'all niggas for real, but don't ever cross me," Ameen warned.

"Never that," we all said in unison.

"They gonna put me on a three-man hold, so we probably won't rec in the same cage no more. Just keep y'all mouth closed and go home. Do the muthafucka out there for big Ameen. Insha'Allah. I'll see y'all again before y'all leave."

Ameen hugged us all again and then walked over to the front of the rec cage. "Aye, C.O., can you call and tell Lieutenant Neal that Antonio Felder would like to see him as soon as possible? It's important."

"Okay, Felder," C.O. Estrada said and walked into the S.H.U. building.

"Remember, scrap, take care of my family. I guess this is my destiny, huh?"

Before Khadafi could respond, two officers came to the cage and pulled Ameen out. Once they were gone, Khadafi turned to me and said, "That nigga is a real gangsta. I swear on my mother's grave, when I get outta here, I'ma crush Lil Cee's mother and his baby sister. Then I'ma find the nigga Eric that snitched on Ameen and crush him."

When I got back to my cell, I felt like an enormous weight had been lifted off my shoulders. I didn't know whether to laugh or cry. What I did know was that my love and loyalty for Ameen would never die. I could never forget the selfless act he had committed. He had just made the ultimate sacrifice.

.CHAPTER FIVE.

KHADAFI

8 Months Later

"We are now making our descent into Ronald Reagan National Airport. Please fasten your seat belts. It is seventy degrees in our nation's capital with clear skies. Thank you again for choosing American Airlines..."

As the plane came to a complete stop on the runway, I wasn't really sure of what I felt. I was finally back in the city that bred the cold-blooded killer in me. It was a good feeling to be finally freed from my cage and it was time to let the streets know I was back. I don't know if the queasy feeling in my stomach was anxiety, but it did a drum roll as I stepped off that plane.

Walking into the terminal was crazy. Too many people for me. They were moving so fast in every which direction. I had to tell myself to be easy. This ain't the joint where I had to watch everything and everybody. I felt like a fish out of water trying to gasp for air, but I knew that it would take me no time to adapt to my freedom. I walked in search of an exit, but there turned out to be several. At one exit there was a bank of telephones. Kemie knew what time my plane arrived, so she had to be in the area somewhere. I silently hoped that she had done what I asked her and brought what I needed with her. I picked up the phone and dropped coins into it. Kemie answered on the second ring.

"Hello?"

"Where you at?" I blew into the phone.

"Baby, I'm at the airport. Where are you?"

I glanced around for some identifying mark, a sign, anything. "I'm at the front and I see a sign saying Ground transportation. There's a big white shuttle van that says, "Fields Transportation Company" on it, sitting in front of the entrance. There's a beige Ford truck parked behind it. That's all I see. People are everywhere."

"Don't worry, baby. I'ma find you. You wearing the clothes I sent you?"

"Of course."

"You shouldn't be hard to spot then. Come outside and stand on the curb so that I can see you. I'ma circle this whole airport until I find you."

"Did you holla at my uncle like I told you to?"

"Baby, I got you. I went and picked that up yesterday. Why you want it or need it is beyond me. But yeah, I got it."

"Good. I'll see you when you find me. One love."

"Boy, don't one love me. That's that fake-ass New York shit that you say to your men. I'm not one of your men. I'm your woman. Tell me you love me."

I broke out smiling. I couldn't even fake like what Kemie had said wasn't real. I had to respect her gangsta. "You sure right, boo. I love you."

"That's better. I love you, too." Kemie disconnected the call. I laughed to myself again, picked up my bag and went outside. A candy apple red Nissan Altima coupe pulled in front of me with tinted windows. I watched the car closely as the passenger window came down. "You waiting for somebody, sexy?" It was Kemie.

I walked over to the car as she climbed out. We embraced and kissed for what seemed like an eternity. I finally pulled my face from Kemie's and said, "Baby, let's continue that kiss later. Right now I have to pay somebody a visit." I gave Kemie the address as we got into the car.

I was familiar with the Fairfax Village area in Southeast, Washington D.C. and from what I could see, nothing had really changed. The 3900 block of S street sat behind a small shopping center off Pennsylvania Avenue. As we cruised slowly down the street, I scanned both sides for the address I was looking for. *3931...3935...* "Stop right here. That's it right there."

"What? What's right there?" Kemie asked.

"Let me out right here. Drive down to the end of the street and park. Wait for me there and keep the car running," I said as I opened the door.

"Boy, what the hell are you about to do?"

I shut the door on her words. I didn't have time to listen to that shit. I owed somebody my life and I intended on blessing them. I stopped in front of the red brick row house. Yeah, this is it 3937. I kissed the paper. Niggas be slipping when they hand out their family address.

Even though I had only seen the face once or twice by photo, I knew exactly who I was looking for. I rung the doorbell and waited. Seconds later I heard a female voice say, "Who is it?"

"It's Dontay. Is Lil Charles home?"

The door opened and a woman that looked just like Lil Cee appeared. Dressed in a floral print dress with curves for days, I knew it was the woman I'd come to see. "Charles is not here, baby. He's in—"

"Are you his mother?"

"Yeah, that would be—"

I never gave her a chance to finish her sentence. I raised the gun I had hidden down by my thigh and shot the lady in the face at point-blank range. She never even knew what hit her. I climbed up on the front step and stepped over her fallen body. All Lil Cee used to talk about was his little sister. There she was playing by herself in the living room. She looked up at me. *Aw, she's a cute little thing.* She can thank her telling-ass brother when she see him again. Too bad they will never meet alive. *BOOM! BOOM!* Playtime was over.

On the way out the door, I pumped two more bullets into Lil Cee's mother's head. "See if your hot-ass son can go and tell that," I whispered.

Even though I knew that Lil Cee's family was innocent, they had to pay the price for his betrayal. Now every day that he wakes up, he'll know that what he did was against the rules. So his family paid the ultimate price. His mother and sister's life for Ameen's.

"What the fuck did you do back there, Khadafi?" Kemie asked me as soon as we were a mile away from the scene of the crime. "Who did you just shoot?"

I never said a word. Kemie caught the hint that I didn't want to discuss it, so she drove in silence all the way to the hotel where she had a room reserved. As soon as we got in the room, the questions started again.

"Did you hear what I said in the car? Who did you shoot?"

"Mind your business, lady. Nosy people get it, too." I rapped as if I was DMX. "No questions right now, boo. Let's finish that kiss we started earlier. C'mere."

Kemie walked slowly over to me and at that moment I truly recognized that she was a bad muthafucka on all levels. Her Juicy Couture outfit looked like it was designed with her in mind. The outfit was beige and brown and it matched her hazel eyes and the blond tips of her dreads. Her shoe game was proper as well. Chanel sandals never looked better on a set of toes. The French manicure on her toes had me geeking to fuck her. When I held Kemie close to me, my dick got as hard as stone.

The fact that I hadn't had sex in years didn't make me overly excited. I wanted to be patient and methodical with my seduction. I slowly kissed all over her face. I kissed her eyes, her forehead, her ears and her neck. Soft moans escaped from her mouth as I unzipped her jacket and pulled it off her body. Her shirt went next. Braless, I felt Kemie shiver slightly as my mouth found her nipples. I carefully sucked on her left nipple until I felt that the right one would feel left out. As I breastfed like a newborn baby, I reached down into Kemie's pants. When

I felt the print of her pussy, precum shot out of me. Her panties were soaking wet. Kemie gyrated her hips to the rhythm of me rubbing her clit.

My dick was brick hard and threatening to bust loose from the Solbiato sweat pants I was wearing. As I put two fingers inside of Kemie's pussy, I could feel her moisture. Then all of a sudden I heard her say, "Shit, shit, shit." I knew then that I had hit that spot. Just as I stepped up my exploration game, I felt Kemie's fingers tugging impatiently at my sweats. "Not yet," I whispered and moved her hands away.

"Please, baby, fuck me! Please fuck me! I want that dick in me right now. Stop fucking teasing me and give me that dick!"

I ignored Kemie's pleas. Instead, I kissed down her stomach and pulled her pants down. She stepped out of her pants legs, one at a time. I got on my knees and licked her navel, then her pelvic area. The lightly shaved hairs on her pussy peeked out of the sides of the thong panties she wore. I pulled those off, too. As my face found the center of her, I felt Kemie using one foot to kick off the Chanel sandal on her other foot.

"Leave your heels on, boo," I whispered.

I dropped down even further and kissed her toned legs. I bent completely and licked each one of her toes. I licked up her thighs and stayed there for a few minutes. I read in a Smooth magazine somewhere that women love that shit. My mouth watered for that pussy so I attacked it with vigor. A few minutes later, I was rewarded by Kemie coming in my mouth. Her hands locked in my braids and I felt her legs shake violently. I didn't stop there, though. I started at the bottom of her pussy and licked my way to her clit. I had to use all my neck strength to back up a little before Kemie suffocated me in the pussy.

"P-p-p-l-l-l-e-e-a-a-s-e-e stop! I-I-can't-take…it…n-n-o-o-more! I-I'm c-c-cu-u-m-m-ming a-g-g-ain! O-o-o-oh shit! O-o-o-oh-h…..I-I-I'm-m-m……Shit!"

I locked on Kemie's clit and shook it like a pitbull, as she came for the second time. I put my face in the pussy and moved it all around. I was so turned on that I had pussy juice all over my face.

Kemie grabbed me by my shirt and pulled me up off my knees. She pulled my shirt over my head and then my wife beater t-shirt. I leaned on the table for support as Kemie licked me all over. She reached inside my pants and grabbed my dick. She pulled my pants halfway down and freed me from the restriction of my briefs. Then she put her head game down something wicked. I felt the stirring start at my toes then rush to my dick. I wanted to stop her from sucking further, to prolong the moment, but it wasn't meant to be. I came in tidal waves. The release was mind boggling because it felt totally different after so many years of doing it myself.

Kemie's mouth continued to slide on and off my dick as she gulped several times and swallowed my seeds. *Where the hell had she learned that trick? She wasn't doing that when I left ten years ago.* I dismissed all further thoughts as I got caught up in the moment.

So far, Kemie had won the first round of our championship fuckfest, but I was determined to win the later rounds. When my dick got hard again, I put Kemie on the bed on all fours and entered her. The pussy was so warm, wet and snug that I had to slow my pace down to keep from cumming too soon. After a while, I threw caution to the wind and started beating the pussy up. Kemie screamed and shouted so loud I was sure that somebody would call the police.

"Baby, quiet down some," I whispered to her.

"I can't help it," was all that she said and then buried her face in a pillow. As I thrust that nine-inch dick in her repeatedly, the pillow did nothing to muffle her cries and screams. I stood straight, grabbed Kemie's waist and penetrated her deeper and deeper. The doggie style position was always my favorite because it brought the punk out of a thorough bitch. Watching my dick slide in and out of Kemie had me on cloud nine. Her caramel-colored ass cheeks jiggled and bounced with my every thrust. I licked my middle finger and tried to ease it into her ass as I continued my assault on the pussy. Every time

Kemie scooted up and tried to run from the dick, I grabbed her hips and pulled her right back to me.

"Talk that slick shit now that I'm right here," I demanded. "Take that dick like a big girl. I thought you said you were a real bitch? Pop that slick shit now, real bitch. I can't hear you, boo. Talk to me."

"U-u-u-g-g-g-h-h-h! Fuck! Fuck you, nigga! Fuck you!"

"Fuck me?"

"No-o-o-o, baby. Fuck me! Shit yeah, fuck me!"

I poked my chest out and felt like the Incredible Hulk. After about ten more minutes, I came deep inside of Kemie. I smiled a wicked grin and felt good about the fact that I had definitely won round two.

.CHAPTER SIX.

KEMIE

The words to that song "Smoking Cigarettes" kept playing in my head as I puffed on a Newport. I know, I know. It's a nasty habit and not fit for a bad bitch like me. But I had to smoke one tonight. I always smoked me one whenever my nerves got rattled. And right now my libido is jumping and my nerves are shot. I woke up after a short nap and turned on the TV. I watched the late night news on *City Under Siege* Fox 5 News and saw that a forty-one-year-old mother named Charlene Gooding and her three-year-old daughter were shot and killed in their home.

Usually, murders such as those in the nation's capital wouldn't have even fazed me at all. We have so many brutal murders here in D.C. that everybody is immune to the violence. But what did catch my attention was the time they were killed and the address. Charlene Gooding and her daughter were killed around 11:43 a.m. at 3937 S Street in Southeast. I was never the brightest person in my math class. I didn't need to be to do simple math. After I added and subtracted a few things, it was plain to me that the man lying next to me committed those murders. That's what he needed the gun for. And that's why I heard all those gunshots as I sat down the street. I thought he was gonna just threaten or rob somebody, but committing murder in the first thirty minutes of your arrival home from prison, now that's some wild shit.

I asked him what he had done back there and he avoided my question. I could've pressed the issue, but that would've made him lie to me and I didn't want that. My mother named me Rekemie Bryant, not Damn Fool Bryant. I knew Khadafi was guilty. After he killed those people, the nigga calmly jumped in the car with me and rode to the hotel, never saying a word. I was an accessory to a double murder and didn't even know it.

Now, I know everyone would probably say, "Girl, get the hell away from that nigga. He crazy." But you know what? I can't get away from him. I don't want to. He just came home from doing ten years flat, day for day. He never folded and he never gave up. That's gangsta! I love that nigga with all my heart and soul. And the way he put that dick on me a few hours ago.....leave who? Let me say this, good dick comes a dime a dozen and I have a dollar. Add some good dick with a clean bill of health, then multiply that by the deep feelings involved and what you get is priceless. I can't go anywhere. I refuse to let one of these tramp-ass bitches have my man. So one of them dirty asses can give him that HIV shit? Not gonna happen.

Me and Redds were like peanut butter and jelly. We just clicked, mainly because we were going through the same shit. Both our parents were on drugs and we were practically raising ourselves. I had gotten used to him skipping school. He hated school. But when he didn't show up for the whole week, I knew something was wrong. Even though he never allowed me to go to his house, I still knew where he lived. So after school that Friday, I went over there. I didn't even have to knock on the door because it was cracked open. Luther sat in the middle of the living room. The house was reeking; it stunk so badly. When he finally spoke, he told me how these dudes came in and killed his mother over a drug debt she owed. He sobbed as he replayed the horrid details to me. He watched the entire thing from the closet where he was hiding. All he kept saying was he should have helped her. When he said he was going to kill them and everything they loved, I believed him.

He blamed himself for his mother's death. I felt terrible. I didn't know what to say. I hugged him while he cried. He kept saying, "I'ma murder them niggas."He swore on his mother's grave.

I stared into his eyes and it was like seeing him for the first time. To be so young, what I saw in his eyes was old and evil. I truly believe that Redds lost his soul at that point right there. Now as I think back on it, I don't really know if I believed what he said or not. But I hugged him as he cried and we formed a bond that has never died.

So I can't leave him. I didn't leave him then and I can't leave him now. I was there to console him every time grief overwhelmed him. We became more than boyfriend and girlfriend; we became soulmates and best friends.

Redds went to live with his father and that brought us even closer. The distance made our hearts grow fonder and we talked on the phone for hours every day. Redds was raised into the game by his uncle's partner named Damien Lucas. Damien taught him how to fight, shoot dice and everything he needed to know about guns and drugs. But most of all, he taught Redds how to kill. Luther got his nickname Redds because of the complexion of his skin, his freckles and his sandy brown hair. But after Damien was finished schooling him, Redds became so vicious and heartless, everybody started calling him Dirty Redds.

One thing about our relationship, Redds told me everything. He told me about the day he killed his favorite pitbull for losing a fight. He told me about the day he saw one of the dudes that killed his mother. He was thirteen years old at the time and gaining his hood reputation more and more daily. One of the dudes that killed his mother was named Rick. Word on the street was that after killing Margaret Henderson, him and his accomplice, Moody, left the city for a while. When they came back, Rick had the nerve to come back to Capers Projects. Redds told me how he felt when he first saw Rick, about the rage that built up inside him. He explained to me, in vivid detail, how he hid in a smelly garbage dumpster for hours until Rick came out of a nearby crack house. Redds said he crawled out of the dumpster and surprised Rick. He said Rick didn't even know who he was. Redds shot Rick then stood over him and emptied the gun in his face.

A year or so later, the second man involved in his mother's murder came home from Lorton. Moody had done two years on a parole violation. Redds caught him riding shotgun in a car with a female. Redds said he pulled up alongside their car and when they stopped at a light, he hopped out and shot Moody repeatedly in the head and face. The whole neighborhood had witnessed the brazen killing. I thought with that done, my boyfriend would chill out, but I thought wrong.

I turned sixteen February 3, 1997 and I gave myself sexually to Redds for the first time. I always promised him the pussy when I turned sixteen and believe me, boyfriend was there bright and early to collect. We went out to eat, saw a movie and then did what we had to do. That shit hurt like hell, but I sucked it up. I bit my lips, his lips, the pillow and scratched his back up, but we got it done. After that night, we did it like rabbits, fast and often. Our sex strengthened an already solid bond. I lusted for him every day as he ran the streets like a wild man.

During the summer of 1997, Damien Lucas got killed. His body was found on Stanton Road by a creek. An eighteen-year-old woman was found dead with him.

Redds went crazy. Damien and his uncle Marquette were like fathers to him. Word got back that Damien was killed over a $1,000 debt that was owed to him. It was also said that Damien's friend, Theodore, set up the killing. That in itself had really crushed Redds because he believed in loyalty and friendship. That day, Redds went and got a tattoo. On his chest he had the words "Please God Protect Me From My Friends. I Can Handle My Enemies" permanently etched into his skin. Two days later, Redds caught Theodore in his father's barbershop, and despite Luther Sr.'s pleas, he killed him.

At sixteen years old, my baby got arrested and was charged as an adult for first degree murder. After a brief trial, Luther was given a five to fifteen year, Youth Act. I was devastated, but at the same time, I knew what type of lifestyle my man lived. I knew that going to jail was all a part of the game.

All throughout Redd's bid, I was there for him. I did the letters weekly, the visits, the collect and prepaid calls, the phone sex, naked pictures and all that to the fullest. I held him down like I was supposed to. Now, don't get me twisted. I did me on the side as the years went by. But I was discreet and most importantly of all, I handled his business, so he stayed happy. The money orders never stopped and he never asked me how I got them. We lived and survived under the "Don't ask, I won't tell" rule.

I have been with that man through everything. When Lorton Correctional Complex in Lorton, Virginia closed its doors and sent him to Waverly, Virginia, I was there. When Waverly sent him to Greenville, Virginia, I was there. When Greenville sent all of its D.C. prisoners to the Feds, I was there. I flew once a month to Atlanta U.S.P. to see my baby. When he stabbed somebody there and they sent him to Beaumont Penitentiary, I packed my bags and flew to Texas.

In Texas, Redds converted to Islam. Now, that shocked the hell out of me. I didn't even know the boy believed in God. That move almost separated us, though. I was ignorant to Islam and Muslims. All I knew then was that some Muslims had crashed planes into the towers. Redds ended up breaking it all down for me and I understood a little better. I told him it wasn't for me, but I understood his reasons for embracing it. He accepted the fact that I was gonna die a good ol' sinful Christian woman.

Redds changed his name to Khadafi and refused to answer anybody who still called him Redds or Luther. He had read a book about the life of the Libyan dictator Muammar Gaddafi and chose that name to honor him, but changed the spelling. It was hard for me in the beginning, but over time Khadafi stuck. It became second nature to call him that.

Even if ten years in prison didn't quell his desire to kill people, what can I do but support my man? I watched him grow from Luther to Redds, from Redds to Dirty Redds, and from Dirty Redds to Khadafi. I don't care what people call him or what he calls himself. All I know is I love him no matter what— unconditionally and 'til death do us part.

.CHAPTER SEVEN.

KHADAFI

"Niggas bleed just like us/Picture me being scared of a nigga that breathes the same air as me/Niggas bleed just like us/Picture me being shook, we can both pull burners and make the muthafuckin' beef cook."

"Ain't nothing promised to no man in this world, nephew," my uncle said while using a remote to turn down the Life After Death CD playing in the car. "The Bible says that every man shall taste death, but fuck that shit. Me and you nephew, we gon' live forever. In these parts, ain't no muthafucka tryna give a nigga shit. I'm the same way, nephew. Don't get me wrong. I'm glad that you're home and all that shit, but I ain't gonna make a bad hustler out of you. I know you tryna eat, though. Feel me? I could throw you a few dollars and a fish dinner right now, but then you will have only eaten for one day. But if I show you how to fish and take you to where the fishes swim at, you can feed yourself for a lifetime."

I leaned all the way back in my uncle's Benz and nodded my head at what he had just said. His metaphors didn't go over my head. I knew exactly what he was trying to say. In less words, he was telling me that I wasn't going to live off of him and that I'd have to earn my keep. I was officially back in the jungle, one animal against many. To survive, I had to live by the jungle creed. I had to kill my food to eat. But what my uncle didn't know was I preferred it like that anyway.

Keeping my eyes on the restaurant on the corner of Southern Avenue, I pulled the Glock .40 from my waist and put it in my lap. The clip was full, the double action proper, so I was ready to eat. I turned my head and looked at my uncle as he spoke.

"This nigga here…" Marquette started to say but stopped to fire up his blunt. "…he the type of nigga that will nut up and buck on a pistol about that cash. So you gotta smash him off the break. Words will get you nowhere. See that champagne-colored Bentley Continental GT, sitting over there?"

I spotted the expensive sports car and nodded my head. "I see it."

"The drugs and money are in the trunk of that car right now. All you gotta do is get the keys out his pocket. You can either wait until he comes out here, or you can go in there and get them. You decide."

Instead of answering, I got out of the Benz and adjusted the black nylon mask to cover my face. I knew the layout of the White Corner restaurant from the many times I had eaten there in the past. In ten years the place hadn't changed at all. The restaurant being small worked in my favor. But the door chimes that rang when anyone came in the door, worked against me. The chimes would alert everybody in the restaurant of my entrance. The mask would cause instant pandemonium. Theoretically, it would be easier to get the dude outside, but there would be witnesses.

"Fuck it!" I said to myself and just ran into the restaurant. I heard a muffled scream as I spotted my target. Fat Sean Bundy had just lifted his fork to his mouth, when he looked up and saw me. His fork slipped from his hand as he tried to shield himself from death. He must've thought that his arms could stop bullets. I got up on him and hit him in the face twice. Quickly, I rifled through his pockets until I found the keys. People were running out the door. I just followed them out. Upon my approach, the Bentley doors unlocked and the car started automatically. I was startled at first, but as I climbed in the Bentley, I calmed down. I put the car in gear and pulled away. From the rearview mirror, I could see my uncle's midnight blue Benz pull off right behind me.

The designated breakdown spot was in our hood. We met up in an alley down Capers. I popped the trunk of the Bentley.

"All I want is the heroin, nephew. You take the bag of money and do you. Take the car somewhere and make sure you wipe it down first. The streets gon' be fucked up about fat boy getting crushed like that. He was down with some serious niggas uptown, but fuck 'em. His team is gonna body some shit about that nigga. He was their meal ticket. I heard that nigga told on them P street niggas back in the day. He supposed to have been dead." I watched as my uncle unzipped one of the large black duffel bags. A smile stretched across his face. He grabbed the bag and slung it over his shoulder. "This will be me, here." He nudged the other bag in my direction. "This one is yours, nephew."

I peeped inside the bag and was shocked to see so much money. My adrenaline started pumping and I got excited. My uncle walked in the direction of his car and I followed him. "Get rid of the car. Wipe it down and bounce," he said. "Go somewhere and chill out for a few days. I'ma call you tomorrow."

"A'ight, Unc." We embraced.

"Welcome home, nephew. I love you, slim," my uncle said. Then he got in the car and pulled off.

I walked up the alley to the Cadillac DTS my uncle bought me earlier and locked the money in the trunk. I drove the Bentley to the area where the stadium was being built for the Washington Nationals. It was the perfect place to abandon the car. After wiping it down and leaving the keys in the car, I jogged back to the projects, my Cadillac and my money. I finally felt like I was truly free.

My aunt Mary opened her home to me once she found out I was home. That's where I went to count the money. I had the whole basement to myself, so I spread the money all over the bed and just laid on it for awhile. Then I started to count it. An hour later, I was at $157,000 dollars and still had several stacks left to count. On the TV, BET was playing a video by Playaz Circle featuring Lil' Wayne. I stopped counting momentarily and rapped along with the song.

"The beat is so hot... the flow is ice cold/hit the Gucci store like honey I'm home/I'm on my shit/I need a pamper on me/toilet paper on the side for example homie...."

"Luther! Come and get the phone!" my aunt shouted down the stairs.

I told her ass not to call me that shit, but I knew she'd do it anyway when she laughed at me and said, "Your mama named you Luther. I'ma call you Luther."

I ran upstairs and picked up the cordless phone. "Hello?"

"What's up, boo?" It was Kemie.

"Ain't shit. What's up with you?"

"You. I haven't heard nothing from you all day. I'm about to come and get you," she said.

"Look, give me about an hour to finish what I'm doing and then I'ma come and scoop you."

"Scoop me? Scoop me in what?"

"My uncle copped me a Caddy today, but tomorrow you and me are going to cop us both something new."

"For real, baby? 'Cause God knows I need a new car. When are you coming to get me?"

"In an hour or so like I just said. I want you to do something for me anyway," I said as I walked back to the basement.

"Something like what?"

"You trust me, don't you?"

"Of course."

"Well, you'll see when I pick you up. Let me go so I can finish what I'm doing. I'll call you when I'm on my way."

"Okay, baby. I love you."

"Bye Kemie." I clicked the phone off and went back to counting my money. Get your money little duffel bag boy.

"Why we gotta record this?"

I ignored Kemie's question as I struggled to understand the directions for the camcorder and its tripod stand. I hooked everything up and was almost ready to roll. "I've been fantasizing about us making our own movie for years. When I was locked down, I used to look at all those fuck books and lust for you. I wanna do all the shit I been fantasizing about and then watch us. Why? Are you scared to fuck me on tape? You got something to hide?"

Kemie stood up and removed her Dior top. "Hide? Nigga, what I'ma be hiding? You saying anything? And as far as me being scared, you got your girl fucked up. I ain't never scared. I just don't want you showing my goodies off to your friends like the dude did Winter in the *Coldest Winter Ever*."

"That was a book. This is real life."

"Shit. That's probably the same thing Ray J. said to Kim Kardashian before he fucked her on tape and then sold it all over the Internet."

I had to laugh at that. I almost forgot how truly funny Kemie could be. By the time I had the camera turned on and adjusted to capture the whole room, Kemie was dressed only in a red thong. She looked so good, I had to stop and just stare at her for a minute.

I went to jail and left a young girl behind. Ten years later I came home to a woman. I couldn't get over how good she looked. The caramel skin that glowed, the white teeth, the M.A.C. lip glossed lips, the sparkle in her hazel eyes, the flat stomach, the plump ass, small breasts, pretty toes and a pussy so fat, it looked like she had a pair of socks stuffed in her panties.

"What?" Kemie asked. "Why are you staring at me like that? I feel like a steak and cheese sandwich. You got that look in your eyes that the cartoon characters be havin' when they hungry. People start looking like chicken legs and hot dogs and shit."

I laughed again. Kemie was exactly what I needed after a hard day's work. "I feel like I'm inside a dream and I'm scared I might wake up. I can't believe I'm really free and in this room with you. It doesn't seem real. I dreamt about you for ten years, holding you, kissing you, wanting you."

Kemie walked over to me and kissed me all over my face. She had tears in her eyes. She dropped to her knees and pulled my zipper down. "Is the camera on?" she asked.

"Yeah, it's on," I replied.

Kemie pulled out my dick and kissed it. "I'ma give you something to dream about for the next ten years."

She put my dick in her mouth and relaxed the muscles in her throat. When her lips reached the base of my dick, I heard her gag a little, but she kept on sucking. All I could do was grab her dreads and hold on for dear life. I loved the way I was feeling and everything, but I ain't gon' lie. I was fucked up in the head at the same time. Why? Because Kemie's head game was crucial and when I went to jail she wasn't even sucking no dick! That's crazy.

.CHAPTER EIGHT.

KHADAFI

The money in the duffel bag totaled over 360,000 dollars. That allowed me to kick my feet up and lay back for about a week. I used that time to get my affairs in order. I went to a female that my uncle knew and secured a twenty-four month lease on a townhouse in Takoma Park, Maryland. I dropped 25 Gs and paid the rent up for two years. I gave Kemie 50 Gs to furnish the spot and make it more like a home. Then I went and traded her Altima in and copped us both trucks. I got the big boy Range Rover in charcoal gray fully equipped. Kemie got the Land Rover Discovery in candy apple red.

We went shopping in New York. Kemie put me down with all the fly shit like John Varvatos, True Religion, Chip and Pepper, Cavalli, Rock and Republic and 7 for All Mankind.

It was fun watching her pick out and try on all the different outfits. "I can't hop out of the Land Rover looking like anything," she reminded me as she copped outfits by Bob Mackie, Michael Kors, Marc Jacobs, Hermes, Alfred Fiandaca, Dolce & Gabbana, Chanel and Christian Dior. Her shoe game really set my bank roll back. Two Christian Louboutins, two Jimmy Choos, three Max Azria pumps, two pairs of Gucci sandals and two Louis Vuitton tennis shoes cost close to $10,000 dollars. After everything was all said and done, I had spent a little less than $200,000. I never wanted to go back to being broke so I vowed to never let my bank go below 250 Gs.

Now that I had partied and bullshitted a little, it was time to go back to work. The next piece of money that I came up on would go directly to Ameen's baby mother, Ameen, Umar and Boo. I called my uncle when I got back home and hoped that he had another lick for me. He did.

"This nigga Poo is one of them cruddy niggas, nephew. Thirsty all the way to the end. He be coppin' keys of heroin and coke dirt cheap. The nigga is getting so much money, he feelin' himself," Marquette said, frowning. "You know I be fuckin' with that blow mostly, but every now and again, I'll cop me some coke to flip. I copped five bricks from this nigga, straight twenty-five a brick. I got to my spot and found out that every brick was cut with 100 grams of isotol and then recompressed. Petty-ass nigga was tryna win all the way around the board. I called this nigga and screamed on him about the bullshit he pulled. Bitch nigga didn't even deny it. He gon' tell me that he'd make it up on the next one. I wanted to smash his stupid ass, but I figured he'd be worth more to me alive, than dead. Feel me? Today it's time for the next one."

We sat in my Cadillac and staked out the apartment building in Hillcrest Heights. "This is his little chill spot. I used to meet him here to do business. I talked to him about twenty-five minutes ago and he was in there. That's his black Lexus truck right there, so I know he's still in there. His girlfriend Keisha was in there with him, when we talked. But I heard him telling her to go to the store and get some stuff. That's why I rushed you to get here. Her car is not out here, so she still at the store. She's the key, nephew. You gotta surprise her and get her to let you in the apartment. You know what to do after that."

When a tan Jaguar sedan pulled into the parking lot a few minutes later, I heard my uncle say, "That's her right there. Go in the building through the door right there and beat her to the fourth floor. She's going to apartment 402."

I slipped out of the Caddy and disappeared into the night.

The mask was still on top of my head as I stood in front of apartment 401 and acted like I was going inside. I heard the elevator door open and out stepped a bad ass broad with long black hair and Asian features. She was holding two plastic bags in her hands as she talked into a Bluetooth head piece. Just as she put the key in the door, I spun on her and put the chrome Desert Eagle .45 in her face. She stared directly into my eyes and I suddenly realized I hadn't lowered the mask onto my face.

"Don't make a sound or I'ma push all your pretty shit back," I told her as I pulled the mask down over my face. "Open the door calm and cool as if I wasn't here. All I want is the drugs and the money from Poo. This ain't got nothing to do with you. Nod your head if you feel me."

I could literally see the fear in her eyes as she nodded her head. "Good. Now remember, I got this gun in your back. You try anything, you gon' be the first to die. Don't get killed over your boyfriend's shit. When we get inside the apartment, call out to Poo and I'll take it from there."

Inside the spot, I saw that the living room was empty.

"Poo, come here!" Poo's girl shouted.

"I'm still busy in the kitchen. Bring your ass in here."

I kept the gun on his girl as she led me to the kitchen. I stood behind her and watched Poo cook coke in a large Pyrex glass pot.

"Did you get the Ziploc bags I asked for?" Poo asked before looking up and seeing me. "What the —." He dropped the egg beater in the pot.

I aimed the gun at him and said, "Don't move again, cuz. Or I swear to God, I'ma put your noodles all over that sink back there. Get your ass on the floor, slow, and lay all the way down on your stomach. Turn the palms of your hands up." After he laid down, I continued. "I want the coke and the money, cuz. Then I'ma leave. If all I get is this pot, somebody gotta die 'cause I'ma be mad then. One of y'all tell me where the shit is that I came for."

Poo spoke up. "The other half of that brick in the pot is on the table. In the bedroom, there's a box in the closet with fourteen keys in it. Ain't no money in here, though."

I gave Poo the I-ain't-bullshittin' look and said, "You wanna die today over some money that you can make back? If I take your life, you can't get that back. Don't be stupid, cuz. If I gotta tie y'all up and look for it, I'ma kill both of y'all. I'ma kill you for lying and your girlfriend for not talking some sense into you."

"He gotta safe in the bedroom." Poo's girl said with no hesitation. "It's behind the plasma TV on the wall."

"Do you know the combination?" I asked her. She shook her head no. "Give her the combination, cuz. You got five seconds ...... 1 ....2 ..."

"It's 35-20-31-05," Poo mumbled.

Fifteen minutes later, I got into the passenger seat of the Cadillac. I had a bag of money and a bag of coke. I even took the pot with the coke cooking in it.

"How'd it go, nephew?" Marquette asked me as he started the car and pulled off.

My adrenaline was still pumping and I needed to catch my breath. "It went a'ight. I had to kill one of them, though."

"That bitch nigga Poo bullshitted with that shit, huh?"

"Naw, I killed the bitch, not Poo."

"Why'd you do that?" Marquette asked me, confusion written all over his face.

"She saw my face in the hallway before we went in the apartment. I had to kill her. Shorty was a pretty muthafucka, too, cuz."

The money that I got from Poo was some short shit. It was only $92,500, but what the fuck? It was free. I can't complain. I put $70,000 with the 180 I had put up and exhaled. I was back at my minimum bank roll balance and that was cool for the moment. I got up early the next morning and went to the Western Union. I quick cashed all three of my men $6,000 a piece. Then I went shopping for the clothes that I was sending Boo to come home in. I copped my man some Hugo Boss shit and the new Gucci high-top tennis shoes. My last stop of the day was to the post office to mail off the package of clothes.

I was excited about my partner coming home. Hanging out with my uncle was cool, but I knew that our connection was purely based on blood. Inside, he was nothing like me. And the fact that he was using me to get rich wasn't lost on me. I'm hip to the game. The way I looked at it, we both needed each other. I needed him to show me where the money is and he needed me to take it. I love my uncle with all my heart, but I'd never fully trust him. So, Boo coming home was a blessing because at least I knew I could trust him.

.CHAPTER NINE.

MARQUETTE

Everything happens for a reason. I believe that and I live by that. Just as things were starting to get a little rough for me financially, what happens? My crazy-ass nephew comes home from prison. The timing was perfect. I was messing up money on a major level and the dudes I depended on to look out for me threw me the most shade. True enough, I'm a degenerate gambler and I get high a little bit, but so what? Let the one amongst us who is without sin and character flaw cast the first stone. None of them muthafuckas could toss a pebble.

What a lot of people don't know about small cities like D.C. is that a small circle of dudes control 95% of the drug flow into the city. If you are associated with them niggas, you're good. If not, your name ain't worth the paper your birth certificate is typed on. To fall out of grace with these dudes is like suicide if you're a hustler. They are the kind of dudes that are real superstitious and sticklers for the rules. If somebody violates their rules, he or she becomes an outcast and is ostracized.

I broke one of their sacred rules and they found out about it. Apparently, one of the No Holds Barred Crew bitches that I was fucking, was also fucking a few of the big boys and divulged my secret. When I first heard about the talk of me getting high, I was like, "what the hell are they talking about me for?" Then I got mad and said, "Fuck 'em." I struggled to make ends meet for a while. Then my nephew showed up. Like I said earlier, everything happens for a reason. I directed my anger at those who turned on me, together with the fact that my nephew is a natural born killer, and decided to get rich while eliminating the competition. By siccing my nephew on them niggas, I win on all levels. Right now, I'm just targeting the cruddy niggas. But in a few weeks, we are going after the big boys.

That raw that nephew got up off of Fat Sean was the best dope I'd had in years. One of the major rules of hustling is "never get high off your own supply." I was raised by the game with that rule always in my head. I fucked around and got with a bitch from Atlanta and started popping pills. I was so gone off this bitch that before I knew it, she was shoveling coke and dope up my nose during sex.

I let a bitch turn me out. That's the part that fucks me up the most. Now, I live with that every day as I hurl, nod and scratch myself into a blue funk. I never get high around people I know. I've been hiding my addiction for about two years now. My girlfriend Lijah said something to me that broke my train of thought. "What you say, boo?" I asked.

"I said what do you wanna order? I'm getting the shrimp scampi, a salad and a raspberry ice tea."

"Get me the stuffed chicken ravioli and a side order of fried calamari. And an ice tea too," I told her. I looked at my watch and wondered what was keeping my nephew. Picking up my cell phone, I dialed his number. Khadafi answered on the second ring. "Where you at, young boy?" I asked. "I told you to meet me at the Olive Garden on Powder Mill Road at two o'clock. It's fifteen after."

"We pullin' in the parking lot right now. Kemie was giv....Ooow! Why you do that?"

I heard his girlfriend in the background saying something, but I couldn't make it out. Then I heard my nephew laugh.

"Aye, Unc. I'ma be walkin' in there in a minute."

"A'ight, nephew. I'm gone." I hung up the phone.

After everybody at the table finished their meals, I told Lijah to take Kemie outside. I needed to holler at Khadafi alone. When they were gone, I shot my spiel. "It's almost time to step our bat up, slim. The niggas we been hitting are in the minors. In time we gon' go at the major leaguers."

"Whenever you ready, let's get money. You line 'em up and I'll knock 'em down. In twelve to twenty-four months, I'm tryna be out in the suburbs somewhere, playing on my laptop and investing my millions. A smart nigga knows that he can't eat on these streets forever, so I gotta make sure that me and mine don't starve in the future. What's next on the agenda? I gotta good man coming home that I need to put on his feet. What's up?"

I love it when a good plan comes together. Nephew is ready to kill and rob anybody I give him. And he don't give a fuck. "I gotta lick lined up for you. This nigga got that bread, for real. He came home about three years ago and blew up. That bitch Angel that used to move all that work in the city, she some kin to him. She put him down with Carlos Trinidad and 'em. Them niggas ain't around no more, but he still plugged in some kind of way. I cops from him on a regular," I lied. "His name is Money. I'ma put you down with him when the time is right. But, for right now, we gon' deal with this nigga Big Dawg. This nigga is the man uptown. He got all the dope moving like fish dinners. His dope is cut with morphine base, so it gives the user two habits instead of one. A morphine habit and a dope habit. This nigga been gettin' money for a while, nephew. It's time for him to pay his dues."

"Big Dawg, huh?"

"Yea, that's what they call him. The nigga like six-four and 280 or something. He was a star football player at Dematha back in the day. He went to Grambling College down south and fucked his back up. Big Dawg been in the city gettin' the money ever since."

"All it takes is a few pounds of pressure to kill a nigga that big. Tell me some more about him."

For the next ten minutes or so, I ran the goods down to my nephew. He promised to holla when he was ready and we both bounced. I went straight home and took me another blow and let my girl suck my dick 'til her jaws hurt. The dope keeps my dick hard as steel, but it messes with my ability to bust a nut. Her mouth felt good on my dick, so I laid back and enjoyed the ride. For a minute, I thought about telling her that I wasn't going to cum. But then I thought, *fuck it* and I let her do her. One day, I'ma stop getting high. But today is not that day.

.CHAPTER TEN.

KHADAFI

Damn! My brand-new Nike boots had blood on 'em, but what the hell. That's the way the cookie crumbles sometime, especially when you bustin' heads. When I got up close to inspect the damage to my boots, I noticed that I had dried blood and some gray looking dried mucus on my pants leg. How the fuck had I gotten brains and shit all over myself? Hadn't I laid Big Dawg's face on the ground before I blew his shit wide open with the .45? I thought back on how I caught and killed my latest victim...

I caught Big Dawg inside a strip club called the Skylark on New York Avenue. Inside the club, I sat at the bar and sipped on a fruit drink. The Skylark was one of them small, seedy strip clubs where the dancers did anything for the money. It was a little hard to keep an eye on my target because of my voyeur side that had me openly staring at niggas fucking the strippers right on the floor all around me. I turned down ten lap dances and five aggressive offers to "fuck the shit outta me."

I had caught a helluva break already because the Skylark had very little security and no one patted me down when I came in, so I had the four fifth on me. Big Dawg fondled a few bitches but never really indulged in the overt acts displayed all around him. For most of the afternoon all he did was make it rain all over the strippers. I kept glancing at my watch because I knew I had to pick up Boo from the bus station.

Impatience was starting to creep up and overtake me. But just as I was about to abandon my plan and come back for Big Dawg another day, he did me a favor. Tipsy and feeling himself, he walked to the back of the club. A voice in my head screamed "restroom." I jumped off the barstool and made a beeline for the bathroom. It ended up being all the way downstairs, which was better for me. I crept in there and spotted Big Dawg's legs and feet at the bottom of a stall. I pulled out the .45 and walked up on the stall. I kicked the door in. Big Dawg's eyes grew as big as saucers when he saw me and the pistol. After promising to spare his life, he told me about some drugs and some money. I took his cell phone, keys and his driver's license and threatened to kill him if he was lying. He swore he wasn't.

"I don't want you to follow me upstairs and try no hero shit, so get your big ass on the floor. Don't pull your pants up. Leave 'em down. As a matter of fact, don't reach at all. Just get on the floor."

Big Dawg did as I demanded. I listened to the music blasting upstairs and knew that gunshots would go unheard. Laying on his stomach, ass up and face down, he begged me not to kill him. I could've fucked his big scared ass if I was on ass, but I wasn't. I couldn't let him live after he saw my face, so I calmly blew his muthafuckin' brains out. When I saw that he shitted on himself, I got mad and kicked his head.

That's how I got blood and shit on my boots and pants. It was the kick.

I scanned the bus terminal for Boo. At a little past 7 p.m., I spotted him getting off a bus. He still looked exactly the same. Dreads that hung down his back and skin the color of milk chocolate. I reached inside the Chrysler 300 and blew the horn. Boo flashed a big smile and walked over to me. We embraced.

"How was the trip?" I asked.

"Long as shit and boring. I slept through most of it."

"You should've flew. You would've been home."

"You know how I feel about them geeking ass airplanes, slim. I don't fuck with them joints at all. It would be just my luck for that joint to crash while I'm on it. I'm cool on all that."

"What's up with Ameen and Umar?"

"They straight. They send their love and respects. We all got the money you wired. That was good looking out. And I love this Hugo Boss outfit, slim." He smiled. "I feel good as a muthafucka to be out here."

As we got into the car, I told Boo not to touch anything. "This joint is hot. I gotta make a move right quick. Are you tryna roll with me? Or do you want me to drop you off somewhere and scoop you later?" I looked into Boo's eyes and let my silence speak for itself. Boo wasn't green by a long shot. He figured out what I was saying.

"I'm rolling with you, slim."

I smiled and threw him a mask to put on when the time called for it.

"We can do this all night, cuz." I told the man tied to the lamppost on 16th and Green Street. "This is the perfect place to kill a nigga, cuz. That money you just picked up ain't worth dying over. Don't be stupid. Bravery will get you nowhere but dead."

When the dude didn't say a word, I smacked him upside the head with my gun. I asked him about the money again. Still, he refused to talk. I lost it a little and pistol whipped him like a runaway slave. Bleeding profusely, he whimpered like a sick puppy.

"If it's Big Dawg that you're afraid of cuz, don't be. He's the one that gave you up. He told me you'd be in Butler Gardens, picking up money and at what time. He told me you'd be pushing a black Suburban. So I'ma ask you one more time, cuz, about that money. I know there's a stash spot in the truck. Where is it?"

"The st-a-a-s-s-h sp-o-o-t-t," he stammered, "is under the third row seat. A panel in the floor will open up when you hit the gas door release button and the brake simultaneously two times. P-p-p-l-l-ease, don't kill me. I just run errands."

I looked at Boo. "Go and see if what he says is true, cuz. The gas door button should have a picture of a gas nozzle on it."

Boo jumped in the truck.

"Did Big Dawg really put y'all on me?"

"Yeah. He begged for his life and gave up yours to save his."

"Did it work? I-I-I m-mean did he save his own life?" the dude asked.

Before I could respond, I heard Boo say, "I got the money, slim."

I turned back to the dude on the lamppost. "Do you see the spots all over my boots?" I asked him and pointed at my feet.

The dude squinted his eyes and tried to see what I was pointing at. "Naw, I can't see it. What is it?"

"That'd be Big Dawg's brains and blood." I untied the dude. "Get down on your knees and look at my boots again. Go ahead. I ain't gon' do nothing to you. Do you see that other stuff on my boots?"

Like an idiot, the dude leaned in close and inspected my boots. "Do you see it?" I asked again.

"What am I looking for?" he asked.

I aimed the .45 at the back of his head and fired. *Bok! Bok! Bok!* "Your brains, bitch nigga."

Inside the Chrysler, Boo asked me, "Why did you kill him, slim, when we already had the money?"

"Because he made me go through all that shit to get it when he could've just gave that shit up. I hate when niggas do that shit."

"Do you really have a nigga's blood and brains on your boots? And who the fuck is Big Dawg?"

"Yeah. Before I put that nigga back there brains on my boots, I crushed Big Dawg. I crushed him about thirty minutes before I scooped you. And I'm fucked up because I just bought these joints," I said, pointing to my boots.

"Slim, you burnt out like shit."

"Tell me something I don't know. There should be $250,000 in that bag. We gon' break it down five ways— 50 for me, you, Ameen and Umar."

"That's four ways. You said five."

"We gotta give my uncle $50,000 since the dude had already dropped the drugs off. You cool with that?"

Boo looked at me like I was crazy. "Of course, I'm cool with that. I ain't never had 50 thousand dollars in my life. I appreciate it, slim."

"Don't even sweat it. That's what friends are for. Welcome home, cuz."

.CHAPTER ELEVEN.

BOO

It seemed like the smell of smoke had permeated not just my clothes, but my skin, too. After watching Khadafi douse the Chrysler with gasoline, I couldn't figure out why we both were just standing there watching the car as it blazed. Khadafi seemed to be mesmerized by the burning metal and eventual explosion. When the car's frame had finally burned itself out, he told me why he stayed to watch the car burn.

"Cuz, do you remember what I told you in the rec cage after Ameen made that sacrifice for us?" Khadafi asked me.

"Of course, I remember."

"What did I tell you?"

The look on Khadafi's face gave me the creeps.

"You said that you were gonna kill Lil Cee's mother and sister. Then you said you were gonna find the dude that told on Ameen and kill him."

"I kept my word, cuz. I sent y'all the newspaper article about Lil Cee's family after it happened and that dude Eric died today."

"How you know that?" I asked.

"He was in the trunk of the Chrysler."

"Get the fuck outta here. You telling me that we been riding around all this time with a body in the trunk?"

"Who said anything about a body?"

"You did. You just said that the dude Eric was in the trunk."

Khadafi nodded. "He was."

"I'm lost, slim. Tell me what you said again."

"I told you the car was hot. I stole it after I put that hot-ass nigga in the trunk. The car belonged to him. He was alive, but tied up and gagged in the trunk, all while I crushed the dude Big Dawg, picked you up and killed the dude on Green Street. He wasn't a body because he was still breathing through it all. He just died when the car burned and exploded." Khadafi had a wicked grin on his face. "I stayed to watch it because I wanted to make sure that he died a terrible death. A bullet would've been too quick a death. I wanted him to suffer. He deserved to die a fiery death."

And just like that the conversation was over. With a bag slung over each of our shoulders, we walked until we eventually caught a cab to Khadafi's house out in Maryland. Hands down, Khadafi was the most ruthless nigga I knew. After chopping that dude's body up in Texas, I thought I had seen the extent of what his madness could be. I thought he'd never top that, but I was wrong. He drove around in a car that he carjacked, with a man bound and gagged in the trunk, as he killed two people and picked up a friend. Then he ended the day by setting the car on fire with the man still in the trunk. He watched the man literally burn to death. That beat out the Texas situation, hands down.

True to his word, Khadafi gave me 50 Gs and dropped me off at my grandmother's spot, which is where I am now, trying to wash away the smell of smoke from my body. My grandmother knew that I was coming home today, so she had my daughter, and my girl Sanaa, waiting for me when I got there. They smothered me with hugs and kisses. Then we sat down and ate a meal. As my grandmother tried to bring me up to speed on everything that was happening in the neighborhood and beyond, I only half listened. The other half of me was still in that abandoned lot watching the car burn. I tried to imagine what choking and burning to death felt like, but I couldn't.

"Damn, girl, you got some good ass pussy!" I exclaimed as I laid on top of Sanaa.

"It's all yours, baby. This your pussy," she whispered back.

"Oh...it's mine now, huh?"

"It's all yours... Ooooohhhh yes, it's yours, Boo."

I grabbed Sanaa's feet and pressed them all the way back to her head, so I could deep stroke the pussy.

"Don't do it like that! I'ma scream if you do it like that. A-a-a-ar-r-rg-g-gh-h-h-h! Boo-o—oo, stop it!" she moaned.

"You know my grandmother is downstairs, so you can't scream. Then again, hold on for a minute." I reached down beside the bed and felt around for Sanaa's thong I had just removed. I found them and picked them up. "This is my pussy, right? That's what you just said, right?"

"Yeah, it's yours."

"Well, let me put my mark on it then. Here, put these in your mouth and bite down on 'em, but just don't scream."

I put Sanaa's feet on my shoulders and stood up in the pussy. I heard her cries a minute later, but didn't understand a word of it. I saw the face that she made and knew she was in pain. On the hard, my dick is about ten and a half inches, so I knew I was digging in too deep. "That's right, girl. Take that dick. Take that dick!"

Sanaa spit the thong out of her mouth and said, "Put my legs down some, Boo. You too deep in me. I feel it in my stomach!" She panted. "B-o-o-o-o-o-o, wait a minute! Wait—a—minute!"

"Wait for what? Take all this dick, baby. Don't be scared of it. Take that dick."

"I'm taking it! Damn—I'm—taking it. I love it. O-oo-o-o-oh. I love this shit!"

"Well, cum for me then. Cum on my dick for me. Cum for me, Sanaa!"

"I'ma cumming! It's about to cum, Boo. I feel it. Boo, I'm cu-m-m-m-ming!"

"You still talking? You ain't cum, yet?"

"I'm cumming right now, baby! I'm c-c-c-c-u-u-um-m-ming!"

I felt Sanaa's pussy contract a few times, then tighten up. The muscles in her pussy grabbed my dick and held it. Her arms wrapped around my neck and squeezed the wind out of me.

"Boo, I wanna suck your dick! Let me suck your dick, baby."

I wanted badly to see what Sanaa's head was hitting on, but my dick had a mind of its own. I kept giving her the dick.

"Boo, let me suck your dick so you can cum in my mouth. I wanna suck the cum outta your dick! I wanna swallow your cum, baby. Please cum in my mouth, Boo!"

To myself I said, "*Shorty gone off the dick.*" I still didn't stop. I poked my chest out a little further and kept drilling. "You wanna suck this dick, huh? You want me to cum in your mouth?"

"Yes! I wanna suck your dick and swallow your cum."

I decided to try my hand. "You gon' let me fuck you in the ass?"

"Your dick too big, Boo. It's gonna hurt too much."

"All right then, no deal. I'ma keep hitting this pussy and cum in you. I'ma get you preg—"

"Okay, baby. You can do it, but you gotta go slow and be gentle, okay?"

"I got you, baby. You wanna suck this dick, huh?"

"I wanna suck your dick, baby!"

How could I deny her what she really wanted? I pulled my dick out of her and turned over onto my back. Sanaa grabbed my dick and sucked it like a porn star. Watching her give me head had me rock hard and ready to blow. When I did blow a few minutes later, Sanaa swallowed every drop of my seed. After taking a brief intermission, I made Sanaa keep her word to me. I found a bottle of baby oil on the dresser. We fought and wrestled around on the bed for a while, but eventually I left my seed in every orifice on Sanaa's body.

For the next week or so, I didn't hear a word from Khadafi. I chilled with Sanaa, my daughter, and my grandmother. Just when I was starting to worry about him, Khadafi called.

"Cuz, I had to lay back for a minute. You know, put my feet up and relax for a while. I was a little stressed out, but I'm good now. That's why I haven't called you. I needed that rest. I been putting in work since I came home. What's up with you and the fam?"

"We good, slim. Everybody is kosher."

"That's good news, cuz. But the vacation is over. You tryna get this money the ski mask way or are you good with the fifty I gave you?"

It took me all of fifteen seconds to make a decision. I knew Khadafi needed me and I wasn't going to let him down. The fifty grand I had wasn't going to last forever. "C'mon slim, you know how I ride. You my muthafuckin' man. How am I not going to roll with you? You lunching good as a muthafucka, but I'm with you."

"That's exactly what I wanted to hear, I'ma scoop you in the morning and put you down with the get down, so be ready to roll about eleven. I'ma call you in the a.m., cuz, a'ight?"

"A'ight, slim."

"A'ight, cuz. In the a.m. Death before dishonor."

.CHAPTER TWELVE.
MONEY

The handcuffs she put on me were kinda tight, but I didn't complain. Sometimes a little pain can be pleasurable in a freaked out sorta way.

"I had to handcuff you until somebody cums," she said.

"It doesn't matter to me. When you do bad shit, bad shit happens." I shrugged, tryna mask my nervousness. I was sitting in a metal chair, handcuffed from the back, with my parole officer standing directly in front of me. She dropped to her knees. Thomasina Jones unzipped my Red Monkey jeans and pulled my dick out. Then I was in her mouth. Slowly, lovingly, she stroked my dick with one hand and sucked me deep. My toes inside my Prada boots curled up instantly. I wanted to reach out and grab her head to guide her further onto my dick, but my hands were cuffed.

All I could do was plant my feet, arch my back and thrust my hips up at her face. I watched as Mrs. Jones' head bobbed up and down on my dick and tried to hold my composure.

Mrs. Jones was a dime piece straight off the covers of the *Straight Stuntin'* magazine. Standing at around five nine in heels, the statuesque beauty reminded me of Vivica Fox. She was married to a doctor whom she rarely saw and no longer loved. She was a part-time mom to two children who drove her crazy. I was her release.

"I'm about to cum!" I announced.

As I started to erupt, her hand and mouth moved in perfect sync with a renewed sense of purpose. My cum shout out in gushes and Mrs. Jones caught it all and swallowed. Suddenly, she looked up and said, "Damn, that was good. I've been waiting to do that to you all day."

I smiled. "So does it taste like my urine was dirty?"

"Not unless you been snorting pure honey because you tasted too sweet. You been doing drugs?"

"You know I can't tell you that, Mrs. Jones."

"And why is that?"

"Because then you'd have to violate me and I ain't tryna get violated."

She smiled. "I would never violate you Diamonte. Your dick is too good for prison. I just hope you stay out of trouble and maybe violate me every now and then."

"Violate you how?" I asked confused.

Mrs. Jones stood up and wiggled out of her skirt. She stepped out of a pair of Ferragamo heels and unbuttoned her blouse to reveal a black lace bra. After unhooking the bra, her breasts fell free. I stared at those pretty brown nipples and my dick got rock hard in seconds. Mrs. Jones walked over and uncuffed me. Then she grabbed me by my hand and led me to her desk. With a swipe of her hand, she knocked everything off. Standing only in her black laced panties and a Nina Ricci blouse, she opened a desk drawer and extracted a small bottle. She opened it and squirted a gel onto her fingers. Then she tossed the bottle to me. It was a bottle of KY jelly. I watched as she wiggled out of her panties. Mrs. Jones reached behind her and rubbed the gel in between her ass cheeks. Then she turned back to me and bent over the desk. She looked at me over her shoulder and said, "Put a lot of lube on your dick. My husband doesn't believe in anal sex. I do. I want you to violate my ass."

I undressed in a flash and did exactly as I was told.

An hour later, I was exhausted and I was hungry as shit. Leaving Mrs. Jones' office, I knew that I had to make a move at 10 p.m. But I needed to eat first. I decided in the elevator that I would hit the Sporty's on Benning Road before making my next move.

I walked outside and noticed that the sun had gone down. I tried to remember just how long I had been at my P.O.'s office. My Cadillac EXT was parked across Connecticut Avenue on the corner of 18th street. As soon as I reached it, I detected movement out of the corner of my eye. Before I could react, I felt cold steel at the side of my head.

"Don't move, cuz. Try and run and I'ma blow your whole head into the middle of next week," a voice whispered in my ear.

I knew that I was being robbed, because if it was a hit I'd be dead already. "I ain't tryna move, homie. What you want? The truck? Go ahead and take it." I heard the man beside me laughing. That caught me off guard.

"The truck? I ain't no muthafuckin' carjacker, cuz. I jack dollars and lives. Fuck your truck and the big bamma-ass rims it's sittin' on. I want the loot, cuz. A lot of drugs wouldn't hurt either. I know you hustling, so where that shit at?"

I always knew that one day this day would come, so I prepared for it. I had purchased a house out in Maryland and semi-furnished it to look inhabited. I put a safe in the house and made sure to keep some money in it and a few keys of dope. The person bringing me the move would believe that he had hit for the whole stash and probably let me live. But the real answer to the question of would they let me live could never be known. There was no way to plan for that. I had to shoot my shot. "At my house. But how do I know that once you get it, you won't kill me anyway?"

"I guess you gonna have to trust me, huh, cuz? Let's go to my car—" I cut him off.

"I ain't gettin' in no cars, homes. At least not alive. You might as well go 'head and kill me right here. If you want my life, you can go ahead and take it. It ain't nothing that I can do about that. But, if you want money and drugs, I can direct you to it. All you have to do is send somebody to get it. I'ma either live or die, right here. I don't know what you look like. You don't have to kill me. I'll just eat the loss. That's it. If you kill me right here, you get nothing. My family can get that half of mil—"

"You know what, cuz? You right. I'ma send my man to your house to get that shit. If everything goes well and we get that money and shit, I'ma let you live. I ain't geeking to kill you, cuz. If something goes wrong, I'ma nail your ass to that pavement. Aye cuz, come here."

Out of the shadows stepped a second man dressed in all black. The mask that he wore didn't cover the fact that he had long dreads.

"This is what's up. You gon' go to his house to get the money and drugs. He gon' tell you where to go and exactly how to get the stuff. When you get everything, call me and let me know you have it. Then, I'ma let this nigga go. If anything goes wrong, I'ma fuck cuz around, right here. A'ight?"

"That's a bet. I'm ready when he ready."

"He gon' stay here with me, cuz. Here, take my cell phone. When you get to the address that he's about to give you, call me."

The first gunman looked at me and said, "Give me your keys, your cell phone, alarm codes, if any, and the address to the spot. Move slow. I get a little nervous when people move too fast around me. My trigger finger think on its own when I get nervous."

I gave the gunman all the info he requested and silently prayed that he was a man of his word. When I handed him my keys and cell phone, I noticed he had light brown skin.

.CHAPTER THIRTEEN.
BOO

The address I had written down was one that I wasn't too familiar with. I knew how to get to Landover, but that was it. I hit the highway and came off on the 202 exit. I was familiar with the Apple Grove Elementary School and I figured that Apple Grove Court had to be somewhere in the vicinity.

Hitting the change CD button in Khadafi's Cadillac, I switched from the Backyard CD to the Carter 3. I immersed myself in sound as I struggled to follow the directions I had been given. Lil' Wayne rapped and calmed my nerves as I drove. Here I was driving to a house owned by a dude being held at gunpoint. I had no idea what awaited me there. Whose idea was this anyway? The original plan was to snatch the dude and just make him take us to the money. Why deviate from that? What if somebody in the house got the drop on me and then made me call and say that I had the money? Then what? The dude Money would die, that I was sure of, but so would I, right? I repressed my trepidation and said, "Fuck that shit. It is what it is."

The ski mask way is better than the shirt and tie way all day every day. The rewards are greater and they pay off quicker.

Twenty minutes later, I pulled in front of 1320 Apple Grove Court. I circled the block a few times to scope out the surroundings. I looked for any signs of activity inside the residence. I saw none. I dialed Khadafi on the cell. "Aye, slim, ask dude if anybody is in the house." I heard Khadafi asking the question. "No? It don't look like anybody is in there. I just wanted to make sure. I'm about to go in the joint now. I'ma call you back in a few minutes."

I parked the car on the side of the house to not arouse any suspicion. I walked up to the front door, rung the doorbell, and then waited for a response. There was none. I used the keys I had been shown and opened the front door. Immediately the alarm sounded. Quickly, I turned to the left as instructed and saw a numbered key pad. I pushed 1227 and the alarm quieted. So far; so good. I pulled out the .40-caliber handgun that Khadafi had given me and moved through the house. After I was satisfied that I was alone, I pulled the cell out and called Khadafi on the dude's cell phone.

"Cuz, what's up? Khadafi said when he answered the phone.

"Ask the dude where the safe is again. I think I wrote it down wrong."

"Are you still on the floor that you came in on?"

"Yeah."

"Good. Go to the hallway to your left. There's a bathroom at the end of the hall. You see it?"

I followed the directions and ended up at the bathroom. "Yeah, I see the bathroom."

"Inside the bathroom, there's a medicine cabinet attached to the wall. It's a prop. Go to the right of the cabinet and insert your finger into the groove at the back of it. Pull hard and the cabinet gonna swing outward, revealing the safe. Do that."

When the cabinet swung out, I was expecting to be shot by a hidden gun, but that never happened. "I see the safe, slim."

"Okay, the combination is....3 right—7 left—22 right—5 left. Put that in there."

I put the digits in the safe and turned the dial. I pulled the handle slow and held my breath. I heard a click and then the safe opened. I saw stacks of money and packaged keys of something.

"Cuz, you still there?"

It took a minute for me to regain my composure. "Yeah, slim, I'm here."

"Is the money and shit in there? What's up?"

"Everything looks proper from where I stand. It's a rack of money in here and some keys."

"A'ight. Find something to put everything in, but don't leave prints on anything. Snatch up all that shit and meet me back at the park."

Khadafi disconnected our call. I wondered if he was really gonna let the dude live. Knowing Khadafi like I do, the dude was probably being shot at that exact moment that I walked through the house in search of something to put the contents of the safe. The last thing Khadafi said to me was, "Meet me back at the park." I knew that meant he wanted me to go directly to his house in Takoma Park.

I found some trash bags in the kitchen. As I put all the money in the bag, I smiled.

.CHAPTER FOURTEEN.
MONEY

"**S**natch up all that shit and meet me back at the park."
When I heard that last sentence, I figured it was judgment time. They had the stuff, so there was really no need to kill me. I waited to find out my fate. From my sitting position on the curb, I saw that the gunman was rummaging through my truck. I weighed my options and decided that trying to run was probably not in my best interest. So I stayed put. Suddenly, he was back in front of me. My heart rate was off the charts. Thoughts of my family crossed my mind. I thought about the money I had hidden in their homes. I thought about my life and what it had all come down to.

"Well, cuz, this is where I say goodbye. I told you that I would let you go after we got the money, but I can't bring myself to do that. Lay your—"

What the fuck was I being so naïve about? Hadn't the muthafucka just said that he was gonna kill me? I made a mad dash toward him in an attempt to save my own life. The gun went off before I could get my hands all the way on him. I felt a burn in my side, but kept going. We wrestled around for a second before the gun went off again. Before I knew it, I was laid out on the ground. I heard sirens in the distance. I heard another explosion and then I faded to black...

.....I heard voices around me. I wondered if I was dead. Was I having an out-of-body experience? I felt the pain in my head as I was being lifted. Someone was pumping my chest, while someone else wiped my face. I heard the sirens again and then I heard nothing.

.CHAPTER FIFTEEN.

KHADAFI

The crap game was full of niggas from the hood and I was breaking them all. I was about $18,000 richer by the time I threw the dice on the roof. I walked over to where my uncle was standing. "What's up, Unc?"

"That muthafuckin' dope you gave me the other day. That shit was the atom bomb. I know that nigga had way more than that in the house."

"We didn't shake the whole house down. We just went for the safe. It probably was some more shit in there, but we didn't stick around to find out. I figured that that was all of it because it was in the safe. Why put five bricks in the safe and leave ten of 'em in the bedroom?"

"I feel you, nephew. But I know that nigga had more shit than that. Fuck it. Ain't no sense in crying over spilt milk. What I wanna know is, why ain't nobody talking about slim being dead? You say you killed him, right?"

"You know how I get down. I don't leave no breathing potential witnesses. I hit that nigga in the head twice. Unless his head was bulletproof, that nigga dead."

"Fuck that nigga, nephew. Walk with me. I got something for you."

I followed my uncle to his car. He popped the trunk and said, "Voila!"

"What the fuck is that?" I said as I openly ogled the machine gun with the large drum attached to it.

"It's a bad muthafucka, that's what it is. It's called a Calico. A Calico 9 m.m. The drum holds one hundred 9 m.m. bullets.

My man gave me this joint about a year ago. I never used it. I figured that you'd want it, so here, it's yours."

I picked the Calico up out of the trunk and inspected it. I was in love. A hundred shots? I couldn't believe it.

"Here, take this, too. You gon' need this one day." The bulletproof vest that Marquette handed me was black, lightweight and thin. "It's the latest in synthetic fabric—polymer or something like that. It'll look like you ain't got nothing on. Go and put that shit in your trunk and come back. I need to holla at you."

I felt like a kid at Christmas as I darted around the corner to my Range Rover. The Calico and the vest went in my stash spot. I ran back around the corner and jumped in the Benz with Marquette.

"Let's ride and talk. I need to get something to eat. Let's hit Ruby's on Georgia Avenue. I got a taste for some jerk chicken."

"That's a bet," I said and leaned my seat back in anticipation of what my uncle had to say to me.

After we copped our food, my uncle and I sat in the parking lot.

"These niggas I keep telling you about, nephew, got that real money. They got it like they printing the shit. Big E's real name is Eric Miller. Does that ring a bell?"

I tossed the name around in my head, but came up blank. "Naw. Why should it?"

Marquette frowned. "Don't you watch TV, nigga? Anyway, Eric R. Miller is the nigga that owns Escape Records. His big fat ass be in all his artists' videos. He on some real live Suge Knight shit. He got that rap group called "Da Southside Mob" and that other young nigga out of the city named "O.G." Their videos be all over MTV, VH1, and BET." He glanced over at me to see if anything was ringing a bell but it wasn't. His hands reach all the way back to the hood on some drug shit. Him and his men come from Northeast, over Trinidad. I know everything about them niggas. The advantage we hold over them is that they think everybody scared to get at 'em. We can catch 'em slipping. From here on out, you gotta make sure that you kill these niggas. We can't bullshit with them. Feel me?"

I nodded my head but kept quiet.

"I got a list as long as my arm of niggas that we gon' get. But the next man on my list is a dude named Walter Henry. The funny part about that is his nickname." Marquette started laughing.

I wanted to laugh, too, so I said, "What's his nickname?"

"Money. They call him Money."

I failed to see what was so funny about another potential victim having the same name as the last one.

"Then we get Andy Daniels and George Foreman."

"George Foreman? The nigga that make the grill?" I asked.

"I wish. But naw, not that one. This George Foreman is a regular old street nigga. A regular old caked up street nigga. We gon' get this money, but we always gotta remember the golden rule, nephew."

"The golden rule?"

"Yeah. The golden rule. And that is…he who has the gold makes the rules. So we always gotta keep the gold, nephew. By any means necessary."

What my uncle said made a lot of sense. I nodded my head again to show that I comprehended and agreed with what he said. As I dug into my food, my cell phone vibrated in my lap. The call came up on my screen as unavailable, so I knew it was a long distance call. And only three people out of town had my number—Ameen, Umar and Mouscy. I flipped open the phone, listened to the recording, smiled and then pressed 5.

"Mousey, what's up, cuz?"

"You, slim. It's good to finally hear your voice."

"I feel you. I see you got the letter from Kemie. Did the money hit?"

"Aye, slim, I checked that joint and thought somebody was playing games with me. I ain't never had that much money on the books at one time. I got the letter the next day. I appreciate it, slim. On all levels, you feel me?"

Mousey had just told me in code that he appreciated what I'd done for him in Beaumont. "I feel you, cuz. Real dudes do real things. I know you would've done it for me."

"No doubt. I heard about that last year and said to myself, "'Allah is the Greatest' "and I ain't even no Muslim."

Laughing, I said, "Go 'head with that bullshit, cuz."

"Man, I'm serious as shit. I went to church, the mosque and sat in the hut with the Indians. We was in there naked smoking the peace pipe."

I cracked up laughing. I pictured Mousey in the sweat lodge with all the Indians naked and laughed even harder.

"That was a good look. No bullshit. What's the big homie name that's riding the beef out?"

"Ameen. Cuz is a gangsta for real. You'd love him," I replied, instantly getting serious.

"I already love him. How Kemie doing?"

"She good, cuz. That's my bitch. You know how I feel about her. We good. Everything is good.

"I'm glad to hear that. How it feel to be free?"

"Cuz, I can't even put it in words. A lot out here done changed, but I love it. Get down or get laid down. You know how I do. I'm eating. My family eating and all my men eating, so it's lovely out here."

"I heard that. You heard about Rosco?"

"What Rosco?"

"Vincent Smith, Rosco," Mousey replied.

"Naw, what's up with Rosco?"

"Slim got killed in Big Sandy a few days ago."

"Man, stop it, cuz!"

"You know I'd never bullshit about nothing like that. Slim gone."

I thought about what Mousey said and got an instant headache. Rosco was another one of our men in our circle. I couldn't believe he was dead.

"They say," Mousey continued. "he was fighting a homie and the nigga stabbed Sco'. We still fucked up about that."

My phone showed that I had another call waiting. "Aye, cuz, let me get off this jack, on that note. That's crazy as shit, though. Call me back tomorrow, early, and we'll rap, a'ight?"

"A'ight, slim. I love you, man."

"Love you, too, cuz."

"Death before dishonor," Mousey said and hung up.

I clicked over to the waiting line and hit the talk button.

"This is a prepaid call. You will not ---," Beep.

"Hello?"

"Khadafi?" It was Ameen.

"I was just talking about you, cuz."

.CHAPTER SIXTEEN.

AMEEN

Ever since the day I copped to the murder, I've been on a three-man hold. That means I can't go anywhere in the institution without two officers and a lieutenant present. So a lot of times I miss rec because the Seg. Lieutenant be busy or out of the S.H.U. I told the other cops on duty that I ain't going for the bullshit today. I need my outside rec. Since these cops think I killed a muthafucka and chopped up his body, they fear me. I use that fear to my advantage. I hooked it up with one of the cops for Umar to be brought outside with me to rec. I needed to see the young boy before he left.

"Felder, you ready to go rec?"

Speak of the devil. I knew instantly without looking that the voice belonged to the Seg. Lieutenant.

"Yeah, I'm ready," I shouted and grabbed my orange jumpsuit off the bed. I stripped down to my boxers and let the cops see that I wasn't hiding anything. Then I got dressed.

"After you cuff, Felder, face the back of the cell and back out," the lieutenant said.

"What the hell—"

"It's the new policy, Felder. Nothing personal."

"Yeah, a'ight."

I cuffed up and backed out of the cell. I was escorted to a one-man cage and told to strip. "Y'all muthafuckas is trippin'. Didn't I just strip in the cell for y'all?"

"Like I said, Felder, there's a new policy in effect. It's straight from the director of the Bureau. If you don't strip again, I can't let you go outside. Plain and simple."

I went into the cage and stripped naked. I truly believe that a rack of the officers be on some gay shit. The S.H.U. holds at least 300 dudes. They rec everybody five days a week. That's 300 different dicks that they look at five days a week for ninety days straight.

That's 1,500 looks at a dick every week. They have to remember at least one of 'em. And that makes them gay as a muthafucka.

They put me in the rec cage at the far end of the rec yard. Ten minutes later, they put Umar in the cage next to me.

"Assalaamu Alaikum," he greeted me in Arabic.

"Wa' laikum as Salaam, young boy. What's up with you?"

"Nothing at all. I'm just getting too anxious. My turn is taking too long to come."

"I feel you, ock. Just be cool and it'll be you sooner than you think. I talked to Khadafi last night."

"I can't catch him when I call. They keep bringing the phone to my range early as shit. What he talking about?"

"The same stuff. He making it happen out there. Niggas out there is anything...him and Boo out there chilling...Kemie be on some bullshit....you know how slim is."

"Did he get at your peoples yet?"

"Not yet. But he says that he's gonna go through in a few days and drop something nice off. He said that he's going past your mother's house, too."

"That would be a blessing. I need all the help I can get. I ain't tryna go out there and stand on nobody's corner scrambling for no loot. My flat foot hustling days are over with, ock. I done gave these people too much of my youth as it is. I'm tryna find me a Muslim woman and get married. Have a coupla kids, ya know?"

I felt everything that Umar said. I'd be lying if I didn't admit that I was a little jealous. I was jealous of all of them— Khadafi, Boo and Umar. They represented what I'd never have again— my freedom. I would have no wife, no more children, no house, no car, no job, no life. The life that Umar looked forward to was over for me. Even if by some miraculous and divine intervention, I beat the murder beef, I still have thirty-five years before I can see the parole board. I'm still in bad shape. I'd be seventy years old by then. What the fuck would I do on the streets at seventy? My chances of living that long wasn't even all that great. All I have left is my daughters and my men. I'd have to be satisfied with living vicariously through them.

"That's definitely what's up. You gotta stay out there once you get there. You know you can never get this time back, so cherish the time you have left. Being in here is the next worse thing to being dead. Remember that. When you leave here, don't ever come back."

"I'm not. Ock, Insha'Allah. Let me ask you this. Do you think Khadafi's gonna make it out there? We both know how wild he is."

The question Umar asked me kinda caught me off guard. I had never really given that a lot of thought. "Allah knows best, ock. Dudes like Khadafi only know one way to live and that's by the gun. He ain't gon' work no job every day and live no regular life. It's not in him. You can be a friend to him and even love him and remain loyal, but you can't make Khadafi's life-style your own. Boo will do the right thing, but not as long as Khadafi is whispering in his ear. So again, I say that Allah knows best."

"Have you heard anything from the courts?"

"Naw, they haven't even indicted me yet. I'ma play it by ear and see what happens. You know how I do."

"When I go home, can't you flip the script and say you didn't do it and that the confession was forced or something?"

"I'll think about that once you done left here. How long do you have left?"

"Sixteen days. I can't wait, ock. I'm fed up with this jail shit. This shit is for wild animals, not people."

"I feel you, young boy. This shit is wild, but it ain't nothing. This is the price we pay for the life we live. I'm a survivor. No matter what happens, these people will never break me. You'll never count me amongst the broken men. Live your life out there. Don't worry about me. Do what you gotta do to build your life up first, but after you do that, get at me. All I need is an occasional kite and a rack of pictures. Stay on top of Boo and don't let Khadafi take him down. And make sure that y'all keep y'all word to me, especially Khadafi. Don't ever let Boo and Khadafi forget about what I did for y'all. I sacrificed myself for everybody. Don't you forget that either, ock. Y'all gotta hold me down."

.CHAPTER SEVENTEEN.
MONEY

"You are a very lucky man, Mr. Smith. When you were admitted you gave us quite a scare. You lost a lot of blood, but we took good care of that problem. You were shot four times. You were shot once in the side, two inches more and you would've had a perforated lung and kidney. The second bullet entered your abdomen. It did a little internal damage, but nothing major. Your stomach muscles will heal and the scarred tissue will repair itself. The bullet then exited you here," my doctor, an older white man with gray hair said. "The miraculous part comes in with the two gunshot wounds to your head. You were shot twice at close range. Both bullets entered your head at a 45 degree angle and literally ricocheted off of the skull and exited above your ear. Both bullets followed the same path in and out of you. All you have now is eight stitches to close the entry and exit wounds. In all my years here at Howard University Hospital, I have never seen anything like it."

The officer I was told to ask for wasn't inside the precinct when I got there. I looked down at the card in my hand and remembered the morning that the detectives from the 3rd District Department came and saw me at the hospital. It had been right after the doctor told me how lucky I was to be alive. The detective who asked me all the questions was Todd Oliver. The questions he asked me came to mind.

"Mr. Smith, do you know who shot you?"

"No. He was wearing a mask."

"Well, do you know of any reason why someone would want to shoot you?"

"Jealousy, maybe. I don't know."

"Tell me how everything happened again."

He probably knew I was lying, but fuck him. I don't do no squealing. That's for rats and I ain't never, nor will I ever be one of them. I live the street life. That means that I agree to live and die by the rules that govern the street. So this situation calls for street justice, not police justice. The dude who tried to kill me will never make it to jail, if I could help it. I just needed to find out who he was.

My truck was released to me thirty minutes after arriving at the police station. By the time I jumped in the truck, I was a little light headed. The pain medicine the doctor gave me was making me feel fucked up. I probably needed to lay down for a while, but I couldn't. My curiosity, pain and anger kept me moving on raw emotion alone. I needed answers to a rack of questions. But first I needed to get rid of my truck.

"All the paperwork is in order, Mr. Smith. You can just have your father come by sometime next week to sign off on everything. I hope you enjoy your new Hummer experience."

"I'm sure I will."

I walked outside to the Caddy truck and started taking all my stuff out of it. If the sun hadn't been beaming through the windshield, I probably would have missed what I saw next. Under the back seat on the left side of the truck was a metallic object that kept the glare of the sun hitting my eyes. I looked under the seat and to my surprise, there was my cell phone. As I reached to grab it, a thought came to mind. The dude who shot me was the last person to use the phone. At least he had it when I saw it last and he wasn't wearing gloves. I remembered that vividly. Either he had dropped the phone in the truck in haste as he made his getaway or he mistakenly left it. All I know is the phone is here and I might've just caught a good break.

I instantly thought about my cousin Cassandra who works for a D.C. police department. If anybody could help me get the answers I needed, it would be her. I grabbed a plastic Athlete's Foot shoe bag out of the back of the truck and wrapped the phone in it.

Then I called my cousin from my new cell phone. She picked up on the third ring.

"Hello?"

"Cass. It's me. I need –"

"Who the hell is me?" she asked with a hint of attitude in her voice.

I laughed out loud. Then I said, "Your cousin."

"Which one? I got a lot of cousins."

"Damn, girl. That's fucked up. You don't know my voice?"

"Your ass should call me more often. What do you want, Money? I ain't heard from your ass in months and don't tell me you in jail."

"Naw, I ain't in jail. But I am in kind of a bind. I need your help, but I don't wanna talk about it over the phone. Can I come up there and see you."

"Come on. You know the way. I'll see you when?"

"I'm on my way right now."

When I walked into Cassandra's office a few minutes later, she saw the bandage on my head and the first thing she said was, "What the hell happened to you?"

Three days had passed since I went to see Cassandra and she just called and told me to come and see her. I hope it's good news. Over the last couple of days, I emptied the house out in Landover and removed the other two safes I had in there. I called my real estate agent and had her put the house up for sale. I trashed everything that reminded me of that night, even the jewelry I was wearing. To me it was bad luck to keep any of that stuff.

Parking the brand-new Hummer H2 by the curb at the Gallery Place subway station, I made the short trek to the Municipal Center. Then I decided to get some exercise by walking up the stairs to the third floor.

"How're you doing?" I asked the receptionist. "I'm back to see Officer Cassandra Smith."

Ten minutes passed before Cassandra appeared. She grabbed me by my arm and led me out of the office. We walked to the basement of the building where the cafeteria was located. Cassandra ordered pizza and I just got a soda. Her silence was killing me. What had she found out?

"Boy, you know I can lose my good government job over this, right?" she finally said as she sat down and bit into her pizza. "You better be glad you my cousin." She handed me a black and white photo.

I stared at it. It was an old mug shot of the person whose hand had last touched my phone. The fingerprints that were pulled from the phone had to belong to the dude who tried to kill me. My blood started to boil as I realized that the skin complexion matched the skin on the gunman's hand that I saw. The photo was ten years old.

"You couldn't get a more up to date picture than this? This is a kid right here," I said.

"Listen, you ungrateful-ass nigga. I had to damn near turn a trick with the nigga that works in that office. Ain't nobody processing no prints that fast. I had to promise that nigga some ass to get him to do that and you gon' sit here complaining about how updated the picture is." She rolled her eyes at me. "That kid did a bid. A ten-year bid. According to our computers, he just came home three months ago."

"Damn, and somebody put him straight on me?" I said as I scanned the single sheet of paper attached to the photo. It contained vital statistics, but very little info. Luther Fuller Jr. had been arrested for murder in 1997 at the age of sixteen. *Why does the name Luther Fuller ring a bell in my head? Who the hell is he?*

"I'd sure like to meet the chick that got your nose this wide open. She must be a bad bitch. You going through all this to find out who she fucking. And the crazy part is that my stupid ass is helping you."

Cassandra is my blood cousin and I trust her with my life. But the fact remains— she's a cop—so I had to lie to her. "Naw, the crazy part is that she ugly as shit, but she got the best pussy I ever had. I love her, Cass."

"Y'all niggas are some anything-ass creatures. You chasing behind a monster with good pussy?"

"Cass, be nice. Only God can judge me," I said and smiled. "I appreciate what you did for me. I owe you one."

"You sure do, boy. Bye. Be safe out there and don't let none of them niggas out there kill your pussy-whipped ass."

I gave Cassandra a hug and left her at the table eating pizza.

When I turned onto Birney Place, I spotted the man I had come to see, stooping down beside a forest green '96 Chevy Impala SS. Cochise Shakur was a known killer for hire. One that I used often in the past and the perfect man for the murders I now had in mind. I pulled behind the Impala and jumped out the truck.

"What's up, Money?" Cochise said as I approached. "I haven't seen you in a minute."

"CoCo, I need you, baby. Let's take a walk and let me fill you in on what's what."

Cochise stood up and wiped his car down. Then he threw the rag in the back seat and followed me down the street.

"So, how do you know it was him?" Cochise asked as soon as I finished my spiel.

I continued to pace back and forth in the alley as I got my thoughts together. "It took me a while to figure it out, but I cracked the case. Remember when I last saw you, I told you I had a man down Capers who moved a rack of dope for me?"

Cochise looked confused. "Refresh my memory."

"I told you that I had to cut off his water a little because I found out he was using the shit. He was cutting the dope and making my name look bad in the street."

"Oh, yeah. I remember now. The dude's name is Mark or something like that, right?"

"Marquette. Right. Anyway, me and slim go back some years, but we never got close until we were down Lorton, over Occoquan. He went home before me and we lost contact. When I came home last year, I saw him at the parole office building. We ended up with the same P.O. You remember my P.O. I told you about?"

"Yeah, the freak bitch, Mrs. Johnson."

"It's Jones. But anyway, come to find out, Quette was fucking her before me. I don't know if she was fucking us both at the same time or what, but I could sense that slim was a little fucked up about me fucking her. Marquette's last name is Henderson. His sister Margaret Henderson got killed when we were young. I remember him telling me that his sister left a son behind, his nephew. I saw him before I went to jail. He told me that his nephew had just went in on a body. He was real messed up about it. "Shorty was only sixteen years old," he said. Then I remember he said that his sister was fucking with Mr. Fuller that owned the barbershop on 8th Street. I did my homework and found out that Mr. Fuller's whole name is —?"

"Let me guess, Luther Fuller?" Cochise asked and grabbed the photo off of the hood of the car he leaned on. He stared at the photo.

"You looking at his son, Luther Fuller Jr., Marquette's nephew."

"But, all that still doesn't mean that Marquette sent him."

"Oh, he sent him. I'm sure of that. The day I got shot, I went against my better judgment and made a move with Quette about three hours before I went to see Mrs. Jones. I slipped up and mentioned to him that I was going to see her later that day. He was the only person who knew I'd be there. He's guilty."

"So what do you want to do?"

"I wanna snatch this nigga Quette, take him somewhere, and force him to tell me where I can find his nephew and his man with the dreads. I wanna murder all them muthafuckers. I'ma need your help, though, Co, I got a hundred cash for your time. You tryna get your hands dirty for a little paper?"

"For a hundred cash, I'ma get more than my hands dirty. Where do I find old Marquette?"

"Where else? Down in the Capers Projects."

.CHAPTER EIGHTEEN.
KHADAFI

I counted the money out and recounted it. I put one hundred thousand dollars into each box and then bagged the two boxes up. It was time for me to fulfill my obligations to Ameen and Umar. I had to break bread while the getting was good. But before I could drop the money off, I had to get my wig tightened up. I stopped by This Is It beauty salon and let my homegirl Rah-Rah wash, condition and blow dry my hair. Then she greased my scalp and put my customary eight cornrow braids in my hair. When she was done, I tipped her and headed for the door. I heard somebody call my name

"Dirty Redds!"

The woman calling me by my nickname was Marnie. She was one of Kemie's friends. I hadn't seen her in years. "What's up, Marnie?"

She stared me up and down. "Damn, boy, you look good as shit. I heard you was home. I was hoping that I ran into you."

"Is that right?" I said and turned to walk out of the salon. Marnie followed me to my truck. The sight of the Rover had her in full groupie mode.

"I see you doing the muthafucka already. Is this your truck?"

"What can I say? I'm a duffel bag boy."

"Okay then, Mr. Duffel Bag Boy. I'm tryna see what's good with you."

I knew good and damn well that Marnie wasn't standing there trying to come on to me. She knew that if I told Kemie, my girl would beat that ass. Maybe I was misunderstanding her. "You tryna see what's good with me. How's Marnie?"

"Being in jail didn't make you stupid, did it? Don't play with me. You know I was on your red ass back in the day. I'm tryna see what that just-came-home dick hitting on. Then we can go from there."

My next thought was that Kemie was somewhere nearby and her and Marnie were playing games with me. I looked around the parking lot as if there were cameras lurking. I felt like I was on an episode of *Punk'd*. "C'mon, shorty, you know I'm still with Kemie. I can't fuck her friends. That's foul."

"Ex-friend, boo. Ex-friend."

"Whatever, ex-friend, used to be my friend, gonna be a friend again. All that shit is off limits."

"Off limits to who? You? 'Cause ain't nobody off limits to Kemie. You talking about foul shit? I can really tell you some foul shit."

At that point something inside me said, "Leave," but I couldn't. I had to stay and find out what Marnie was talking about. "What you mean by that, Marnie? What foul shit can you tell me?"

"Look, you were too far away to see the writing on the wall."

Now I was really confused. "What writing? What wall?"

"When you went to jail back in the day it crushed Kemie for a while. I was there for her in every way. She was determined to hold you down. She did what she had to do to make sure that you had what you needed. I respected her for that. But as time went on, it became more about her. Girlfriend got really cruddy with hers. She was fuckin' with a nigga named Phil then, and he had her ass turnt out. All he fed her was dick and money. She always bragged about how freaky he was and how good and big Phils's dick was. The nigga got back with his baby's mother and dropped Kemie like a bad habit. She never really got over what Phil did to her. Her whole demeanor changed after that. She started chasing money and fucking niggas and didn't care who she crossed. Remember our girlfriend Tecola?"

"Yeah, I remember her."

"Tecola was fucking with a dude from Uptown named Derek Pendleton. Kemie took him from her. I was messing with a dude named Black Junior from over Lincoln Heights. I caught them coming out of a motel on Allentown Road. To add insult to injury, Kemie started fucking your friend Omar, Devon's brother. When Black Bean came home and started gettin' money, Kemie hooked up with him. Who you think paid for that brand-new Altima she pushing? Boy, I can stand here and tell you all kinds of cruddy shit about your girl. That's why I stopped fucking with her. That bitch was my heart, but she crossed me and you only get one chance to cross Ms.Tawana's daughter."

I ain't gonna lie. I was fucked up in the head. My face was long as shit as I struggled to digest everything I had just been told. I knew that Kemie did her thing while I was gone, but to fuck my friends and her girl's men, that was unfathomable. At that exact moment, I believe that I went through a slight metamorphosis. The blinders in my eyes fell out and I could see clearer.

I looked at Marnie again as if I was seeing her for the first time. The Coach tennis shoes that she wore matched her belt and purse. The blue jean Rock and Republic pants hugged her every curve. The beige Coach baby tee was a size too small and made her breasts look like small melons. The jacket she wore was a khaki Dolce & Gabanna blazer. Her hair was cut low in layers and reminded me of the hairdo that Keisha Cole wore in that Game video. And on top of all that, she was drop dead gorgeous.

"You tryna see what this dick do, huh?" I asked her.

"That's what I said. Ain't no shame in my game," she said as she licked her lips.

I decided to call this one a revenge fuck. Kemie fucked my friends, so I had to fuck a couple of her friends or in this case, a used-to-be friend.

"Come and go with me. I'll bring you back in a few hours."

I fucked Marnie in the back seat of the Range. I fucked her in the passenger seat. On the floor. I fucked her standing up outside the truck. I popped the back door and bent her over it. I performed like a porno star.

If we hadn't been parked in the garage of Phillip's Restaurant, I swear somebody would've probably called the police. I had Marnie hollering like she was being raped. For the grand finale, she put her palms flat on my lap and deep throated my whole dick. After I came in her throat, I gave her $500, my cell phone number and a standing ovation for a job well done. I dropped her off at her car and promised to hook up with her at a later date.

It was after 7 p.m. when I finally reached Umar's mother's house. His mother answered the door when I knocked on it. I introduced myself and gave her the box with the money in it. Then I left.

I pulled the paper with both addresses on it out of my pocket and looked at it. The second address was on 56th Street in Southeast. I was familiar with the area, so the house was easy to find. Ameen told me that his baby mother drove a black 2006 Honda Accord. I saw it parked outside of the house. "Take care of my family. Take care of my family." Ameen's last words to me replayed themselves in my head over and over again as I climbed the stairs to the front door of 2712. I knocked and a little girl, the spitting image of her father, answered the door.

"Who are you?" she asked me with more curiosity than attitude.

I stared into the little girl's face and smiled. I remembered Ameen telling me her name was Asia and that she had a birthday before I left Texas. "Can I speak to your Mommy?"

"M-o-m-m-m-m-y!" she hollered. "Ma, there's a… a man at the door!" Seconds later, I heard noise behind the door and then she appeared. I had seen a couple of pictures of Ameen's baby mother, but none of them did her justice. Shawnay Dickerson was more breathtaking in person. I openly stared at the butter pecan ice cream complexioned dime piece now standing directly behind her daughter. I sized her up quickly. She was about five-four and around 135 pounds with wide hips, a small waist and large breasts.

"Can I help you?" she asked.

"Uh...yeah. Damn. My bad. I'm Khadafi. Ameen told me to—"

"Oh! Okay. He told me that you would come by. Come in."

When Shawnay turned around, it was hard for me to keep my eyes off her heart-shaped ass stuffed into a pair of linen pants. I followed her into an upstairs living room.

"Have a seat," she said to me. To her daughter she said, "Asia, go upstairs with Kenya and finish your homework." Shawnay waited until her daughter left the room before she finished talking. "How long have you been home, Ka...? Is Khadafi your real name?"

"I've been home about three months now. And naw, Khadafi is not my real name, at least not yet it ain't. My name is Luther, but I changed it to Khadafi after I became a Muslim."

"You became a Muslim in jail too? Like Antonio? I mean Ameen."

"Uh huh. That's where I became a man and Ameen taught me a lot."

"Is that right? Tell me, Khadafi, how is Ameen doing? I mean, how is he really doing? When we talk it always seems like he's holding something back. How was he when you left him three months ago? I have hundreds of pictures, but we all know that pictures only show what you want people to see."

I wasn't about to get caught up in no deep conversation about Ameen with his folks. If he wanted her to know his heart, he'd tell her. I ascertained that what Shawnay spoke of Ameen holding back was probably about the murder. Ameen hadn't told her his current situation. Well, neither was I.

"Listen, boo, no offense, but I didn't come here to discuss Ameen. You need to ask him those questions the next time he calls. I just came to drop this box off." I handed her the box. "It's from him. He said it's for you and his daughters. If you should need anything at all, just call me." I wrote down my cell number and gave it to her.

The look on Shawnay's face as she opened the box of money spoke for itself. "Whoa. How much—"

As bad as I wanted to stay and talk to Shawnay, I knew that it was time for me to go before I said or did something stupid. Everything about Shawnay captivated me. When I glanced down at her stocking feet and saw how pretty her toes were, I almost melted. I turned around and left.

Shawnay never said a word to me as I left the house. A $100,000 in cash seemed to have that effect on people. Inside my truck, I saw that Kemie had called my cell phone twenty-seven times in the last hour. As I was about to check my voicemail, the phone vibrated. It was Kemie.

"Muthafucka, why was that bitch Marnie in your truck?" she yelled.

I laughed and hung the phone up on her ass. I knew for a fact that I was in for a fight when I got home, but fuck it all. I still had all that shit Marnie told me fresh on my mind. I hadn't decided whether or not I wanted to confront Kemie with what I heard. What I did know for sure was I wanted her to show me some more of that freaky shit she learned from Phil.

.CHAPTER NINETEEN.
MARQUETTE

Y ou know I don't like fucking with niggas I don't know. But you say that's your man, so I gotta fuck with him. I trust you, nephew, and if you fuck with a nigga, then he gotta be gangsta."

"That nigga right there is my heart, Unc," Khadafi said and pointed at the dark-skinned dude with dreads who leaned on the car across the street. "He came home a month after me and he been rockin' and rollin' ever since. I trust him with my life."

"You gon' have to trust him with both of our lives then. 'Cause these niggas we about to go at are the real deal, baby boy. He can't breathe a word of this to anybody."

"He straight, Unc. I got him."

"A'ight." I popped the trunk of the hoopty, a Buick Rivera. "Call him over here."

"Aye, cuz. C'mere for a minute," Khadafi called out to his man.

I waited until the young dude got into the trunk before I proceeded with the plan. "This right here is called a noise reduction device. It's a muffler, not a silencer. The good thing about this lick is that these niggas are cocky. They been around the world a few times and they think they gangsta. They don't think niggas will come for that ass. They built this studio all the way back here in the warehouse district to avoid people coming through unannounced. That works in our favor because when we let these guns go, it'll be hard to hear what little noise that'll be made." I handed Khadafi and Boo a suppression device. "These screw right into the barrel of the Mach 11.

Both of y'all grab a Mach. The clips got fifty bullets in 'em. They're equipped with a cooling system to prevent jamming. I know somebody that knows somebody and what I've been told is this. The CEO nigga, Big E, gotta safe inside his office in that studio. My man tells me that the nigga got maybe a mil or better in that joint. I was out here when them niggas went in there. It's seven of them altogether, including Big E. All of them niggas are probably strapped, four of them are for sure. They're the bodyguard niggas. The other two are executive/street niggas from Trinidad Projects that put all that music shit together with Big E. One of 'em I know. That's the nigga Cliff. Him and his team made a rack of noise in the '80s and '90s, until his brother Roy got killed in 1998. Cliff is a real live street nigga, so he might be strapped. He might not. It don't really make no difference because if we surprise 'em the right way, they ain't gonna get the chance to pull no guns. The other nigga is a toss up. I don't know much about him, other than his name is Big Head. Big E, Cliff and one of the security niggas is rolling in that black Maybach back over there. Big Head and his security got out of that Escalade and the last two niggas riding in the Navigator. We gon' lay on 'em. Boo, you lay on the side of the building and crush anybody that we miss, but don't hit Big E."

"How do I know which one is Big E?"

"He'll be the biggest muthafucka in the crowd. He's like six-four and 350 pounds. He got his hair pulled back into a ponytail and he rockin' a beard like Suge Knight. I saw him go in the studio. He got on a blue velour sweat suit, white tennis shoes and a whole lot of ice." I pulled out two Glock .45's with extended clips and mufflers. Me and Khadafi gon' post up on the blind side of both trucks. The mission is to crush everybody around Big E. Then we grab him and take him back inside the studio, make him open the safe and we get the money. Then we leave. It's that simple. We meet up at the car and we go from there. Is that clear to both of y'all?"

Khadafi and Boo both nodded.

"A'ight. Let's rock. Aye, nephew, on second thought, we gon' have to slide up under the trucks until they come out. We ain't gon' be able to just lean on the other side because we might be spotted."

"A'ight, Unc. Let's go."

I walked over to the Navigator and slid underneath it. Khadafi did the same with the Cadillac. I was uncomfortable as hell, but I laid still and kept my eyes on the entrance of the studio.

My legs and arms were starting to cramp up and I had to piss like a race horse, but I laid still and willed myself to block out everything but the move we needed to hit tonight. As if on cue, the door to the studio opened and I heard voices. I rolled from under the truck and rose up slowly. Out of the corner of my eye I saw my nephew do the same thing. I saw the entourage spilling out of the door, headed our way. I glanced at Khadafi and nodded my head. He nodded back. Big E was in the middle of the crowd. I waited until the posse began to split up before I made my move. Big E, a dude named Cliff and the bodyguard nigga were about eight feet from the Maybach when I ran around the truck and surprised them with both Glocks drawn. Muffled gunshots rang out as I gunned Cliff down first, then the bodyguard. Big E dove on the ground and covered his head. I quickly surveyed the scene around me and saw that Khadafi and Boo had both done their jobs well. Big Head and the three other security niggas were all down and leaking. "Make sure nobody is still breathing, nephew. I got Big E." I stood over Big E and said, "You better not move fat boy."

I heard more gunshots and then Boo and Khadafi were at my side. "Let's get this nigga up."

Khadafi reached down and grabbed Big E's ponytail. He pulled on his hair until Big E's face could be seen. They were all shocked to see the big 350 pound man with tears in his eyes.

"P-p-l-l-l-e-e-e- a-s-e don't kill me," he begged.

"Get your big bitch ass up off the ground. Slow and easy, big boy. And don't think about trying shit," Khadafi said. "We gon' walk in this studio and get the money you got in there. Then we gon' let you go. If you wanna live, give us that bread. If you wanna die, bullshit with me and I'ma crush your ass. Now, c'mon."

I let Khadafi take over the show. After all, this was his expertise. I followed everybody into the studio. "My office is upstairs. T-t-h-hat's where the safe is." Big E stammered as we headed for the elevator.

I looked at the elevator and didn't see an up or down button. "How the fuck do you summon the elevator?"

"You have to use the key."

"Where is the muthafuckin' key?" Khadafi exploded.

"Cliff, my man, has it. I left mine at home."

"I'll be right back," I said and ran outside. I ran up to Cliff and rifled through his pockets. I found the keys, but I also came across a fat wad of money. I took that, too. Inside the studio, I handed the keys to Big E. "Make it happen, fat boy."

Seconds later, we were inside Big E's office. There were gold and platinum plaques all over the walls. I stopped to look at photos on the wall as Khadafi ordered Big E to open the safe. When I turned around, the safe was open and Boo was pulling out a box of trash bags.

"Jackpot!" I heard him say as Khadafi ordered Big E to his knees.

"You said you were gonna let me go, man. You got the money. Don't kill me over no paper. I got kids—"

"Shut the fuck up. Get your big ass up and strip, nigga. You heard me right. I said strip!" Khadafi shouted. My eyes went from Boo putting stacks of money in the bags to my nephew holding the gun on Big E as he stood up and shed all of his clothes.

"I see you tatted up, big fella. Unc, come and get this nigga's clothes."

I wondered what the fuck my nephew was doing.

"Nephew, we gotta get outta here," I said as I picked up Big E's 5X dark blue shirt and jeans. "We ain't got time for all of this. We gotta stick—"

"Aye, Boo, this nigga is a Crip. He got a whole rack of Crip shit tattooed on him. He got the same kind of tattoos that Jack Rabbit, Mouse -Loc and Nutso had on them. They got Crips in DC? You a Crip, cuz?"

My nephew was losing his mind. What the fuck did any of that shit have to do with the price of tea in China? "Nephew, we need—"

"Chill out, Unc. We getting ready to bounce. You a Crip, huh, cuz? That's why you got on all this blue shit, huh? That why all the furniture in this office has a blue scheme to it. Gimme that watch. Just like I thought, blue diamonds. You ain't gon' be needing that chain, either. Let me get that."

When Khadafi pocketed the jewelry and then threw Boo his Mach11. I was puzzled. Why was he giving his weapon away? Why didn't he just shoot Big E and come on? I was about to ask the questions on my mind, but my nephew's next act quieted me. He put Big E on his knees. Then he pulled out a big ass Rambo knife and plunged it into the man's throat. I saw Big E struggling to remove the knife, but his attempt was futile. Blood poured into his throat and choked him. The sounds of his gurgling and gasping would probably stay with me forever. We stood there and watched the big man die. He fell out on the floor and became still. Khadafi grabbed at the knife and pulled it out of Big E's throat. Then he unscrewed something at the base of the knife. Khadafi struck a match and doused the dead man with whatever he pulled from the base of the knife. He set Big E's body on fire. As the dead man burned, we all ran to the getaway car. We threw the bags of money in the trunk, got in the car and got ghost.

"Aye, cuz?" Khadafi said to Boo as he drove the Buick up Mt. Olivet Road.

"What's up, slim?"

"Did you smell that shit, cuz?"

"Smell what?" Boo asked.

"That fat pig-ass nigga. When that nigga started burning, his fat ass smelled like bacon."

"You a wild nigga," Boo said. "But, let me ask you this. Why did you strip slim in the first place?"

"Cuz, that sweat suit that nigga had on was a bad muthafucka. I didn't wanna ruin it. I knew I had that new knife on me and I wanted to test that joint out. It came with some flammable shit that was supposed to start campfires. I just lunched out and barbecued that nigga."

From my seat in the back, I laughed. I didn't laugh because of what Khadafi said. Burning a man after you killed him wasn't funny. It was excessive and cocky. I laughed because it was the first time that I really realized my nephew was insane.

I pushed the gas pedal and floored the Benz to 110 miles per hour. I stopped at the light at the intersection of Firth Sterling and Suitland Parkway. I grabbed my straw, stuck it into the bag of dope and sniffed a generous portion into both of my nostrils. Fireworks shot straight to my brain as I held my nostrils and threw my head back. I heard the car behind me blow the horn. I ignored the horns as I drunk fruit juice from a cup. Fruit juice lessened the acidic taste as the dope drained and coated my throat.

I pulled off and zoomed up the Parkway. I was driving an $89,000 car, blowing dope and not giving a fuck. I'm rich again; why should I? Ever since we went on that lick a few days ago at the studio, shit been popping big time. The streets and the nation were fucked up about Big E and his entourage's deaths. The cops were scrambling to find out who committed the heinous murder of seven people. The money that we got from the safe turned out to be $875,000 . I took 500 grand off the muscle and gave my nephew the rest to break down with his man. I immediately put in an order with the nigga Manny Stone for ten keys of coke and three bricks of some new dope he put out called *Ghostface Killa*. That shit been moving like hotcakes. I don't know what the fuck that shit is, but the dope fiends love it. In the last two days, I done made so much money, it's scary.

I felt like the king of D.C. I got a house out on the lake that sits next to a golf course. I got a driveway full of expensive whips and money all over the place. I'm fucking the baddest bitches in the city and moving drugs like it's legal. And I got a certified young assassin on my team. So what I snort dope? I'm the muthafuckin' man. Fuck Carlos Trinidad and all them of niggas. Me and Khadafi is gonna have all this shit on smash real soon.

My cell phone belting out the tune of Scarface's song, *Girl U Know*, let me know that my baby mother was calling. "Hello?" I answered.

"Quette?"

"Yeah. Who else gon' be answering my phone?"

"It didn't sound like you. Smart-ass nig—."

Knowing that Tosca only called when she wanted something, I was ready to cut to the chase. "What do you want, Tosca?"

Sounding offended, she responded. "Why you gotta say it like that? Like I'm some kind a groupie or something?"

"You ain't no groupie Tosca. They at least get paid for stalking a nigga. You more like a hoodrat," I said.

"Yeah, what the fuck ever, nigga. I got your hoodrat. You wasn't talking that hoodrat shit when I kept this ass and pussy in your mouth. I wasn't a hoodrat when I was bringing you that shit down Lorton. You getting a little money again and now I'm not good enough for you? Now, I'ma buncha hoodrats and shit, huh?"

"I'ma ask you one more time before I hang up on you. What do you want, Tosca?"

Defeated, Tosca smacked her lips. "Your son needs some shoes, a new bookbag and a jacket for school. And I need some money for food, laundry soap and quarters to wash clothes."

"I'ma pick my son up and take him to get what he needs. But that other shit, you can miss me with all that."

"What do you mean by that? Miss you with what?"

"Don't you got a nigga living there, Tosca?" I asked, knowing that she did.

"W-w-h-a-t does that have to do with anything?" she stammered.

"Let me tell you what that has to do with this. You moved that nigga in there, knowing how I feel about you having niggas around my son. You tried to hide it, but your hoodrat buddies tell me everything you do. All of them wanna fuck me. You got a nigga living with you, eating all your food and fucking your stupid ass whenever he feels like it, but you ain't got laundry money. You hustling backwards. And you wanna know why I call you a hoodrat?"

"Quette, fuck you!" she screamed. "Who the fuck are you? Like you better than a muthafucka or something."

"Bitch, I am better than you. I'm definitely smarter than you. You wish you could fuck with me again, but you can't. Who am I? I'ma gangsta. I'm the muthafuckin' Don..... The king of D.C.... I'm the muthafucka with laundry money, broke ass!"

Tosca had hung up.

Fuck her, I thought to myself and kept pushing. I almost missed my turn onto Stanton Road. I was headed to Congress Park to see my man Squirt. Squirt was moving all of the Ghostface Killa dope for me. I pulled my car to a stop in front of 3320 14th place and double parked. I ran upstairs to the apartment that Squirt shared with his girlfriend Taishia and knocked on the door. Squirt answered the door.

"Come on in, moe. I'll be right back." Squirt said and disappeared into a back room. Minutes later, he returned with a black bookbag.

"It's all there, moe. When am I gonna get some more of that?"

"Call Bowlegged Deon and tell him I said to give you the rest of that work. You call me when you ready to go back."

"That's a bet, moe. Be safe."

"All the time," I mumbled as I walked out of the building. Something crashed hard into my head as soon as I hit the front porch. I don't know what it was. The next thing I knew I was on the ground looking up. There was a dude standing over me who I didn't recognize. He pointed a large handgun at me and said, "Get your faggot ass up before I punish you right here. Try to run or reach and I'ma dog you."

I slowly made my way to my feet. I was still a little dizzy from the blow I took to the head. Silently, I cursed myself for leaving both of my hammers in the car. I never was supposed to move without them. Hadn't the events of the last three months taught me that? Was I being robbed? The bookbag was still on my arm. The dude with the gun on me walked me to a black caravan. I looked around for any visible means of escape. I found none. The building was fenced off down the walkway. If I tried to run, the dude would have a clear shot to down me. I decided to just be cool and see how things panned out. Who was the man behind me? Who sent him?

Disgusted and somewhat afraid, I promised myself that I'd kill Squirt the first chance I got, if I survived. In the street, parked directly behind my Benz was a silver Hummer H2. When I saw the face behind the wheel of the Hummer, the color drained from my face. The driver of the Hummer shouted to the man behind me.

"Leave the Benz, here. We'll come back for it later." Then he hopped out of the Hummer and followed us to the van. When I was hit over the head again and forced into the van, I became very afraid. I glanced at my old friend Money and knew that I was in deep shit.

.CHAPTER TWENTY.
MONEY

"See this spot right here, slim?" Cochise asked while pointing to a bloodstained gathering of leaves behind the recreation center on Ainger Place in Woodland Terrace. "That's where my man Gary Freeman--you don't remember Gary from up the Lane?"

I shook my head and watched as Cochise duct taped Marquette's arms together and then his legs.

"Well anyway, G-Money, that's Gary's nickname, caught this nigga named Fila Frank and brought him back here a few days ago. That's how I got hip to the spot. G-Money whips out this big ass 454 revolver and blows Frank's brains all over that tree right there."

Cochise methodically ran a length of rope over a large tree branch and then made a noose. He put the noose around Marquette's neck and stood him up. Marquette was semiconscious and bleeding profusely from the scalp due to all the blows he took from Cochise's gun on the way to Woodland. Even though Quette was in bad shape, I wanted to talk to him.

"Coco, you go back and get the Benz before it draws too much attention. Drive it somewhere nearby and park it. Then come back here."

I watched Cochise run back the way we had entered the woods and disappear. I turned and faced Marquette. His bloody chin rested in his chest and his speech was incoherent. "Quette, can you hear me?"

He looked up at me and nodded.

"I got a few questions for you, homes. If you give me the answers that I need, maybe you and I can work something out. I'm not tryna kill you. I just need to know a few things."

"What you wanna know?"

"Why did you do it, homes? What did I do to you to deserve to die? I put you on your feet when nobody wasn't fuckin with you. Why bite my hand? Was it the P.O. bitch?"

Marquette laughed a deep maniacal laugh. "Slim, you done kidnapped a nigga, had your man beat the shit outta me and got me hung from a tree and now you wanna talk? You could've asked me all that before you did all this shit."

"True dat, true dat. But what's done is done. I can't change the past, but I can dictate the future. Answer them questions for me and I'ma cut you down."

Quette licked at the blood that was now running into his mouth. With a blood-toothed grin he said, "I don't know what you talking about. Next question."

The grin he gave me with the wrong answer stirred up hate inside of me. "You don't know what I'm talking about, huh?" I pulled my gun and shot him in both feet.

"A-a-a-r-r-r-g-g-g-h! You bitch nigga!"

"Where can I find your nephew Luther?" I asked him.

"What nephew? My sisters were all dykes."

I laughed despite my anger. I had to respect the way Quette was carrying it. I shot him in both knee caps. His body buckled. But the noose stopped him from falling. "Who was the dude with your nephew?"

"I don't know what you talking about, slim."

I shot Quette in the stomach twice. His screams were guttural. "Where is my money at, Quette? Fuck the dope. Where's my money?"

"What money?"

"The money your nephew sent his man to get outta my safe. I want it back, Quette."

"The Bureau of Engraving makes that shit. Go get it from there," Marquette said and laughed.

"You a funny muthafucka. That's why I always fucked with you. I respect your gangsta. I always looked out for you and you crossed me. You put your nephew on me and told him to kill me. That's some snake-ass shit, homes. Your nephew shot me in the head, Quette. Right here. Look. See that? That's where both bullets went in at. The doctors said I was a lucky muthafucka. And I guess I am. I wanted to know why you did it, but fuck it. You can carry that to your grave. But do know this. I'm going to find your nephew and his man and I'm going to kill 'em. Fuck the money. I don't even want it back."

I was startled by a noise. I looked up to see Cochise coming back through the woods.

"Go ahead and do what you do and then kill him. Call my phone when you finish."

As I walked through the woods leading to the main street where I'd catch a cab back to my truck, I could hear Marquette's screams and cries. I loved it.

.CHAPTER TWENTY-ONE.
COCHISE

Marquette was in bad shape by the time I got back to the spot. Money had shot him so many times, which made my job a little easier. It was my job to torture the nigga enough to make him talk. I put that knife game on him and that was all it took to make him see things my way. He tried to be strong at first, but when I sliced off his ear and showed it to him, Marquette begged for a quick death. He told me that his nephew had converted to Islam in prison and now went by the name Khadafi. He told me that Khadafi's buddy with the dreads that went to Money's house was named Boo. He didn't know exactly where his nephew lived. He just knew that he lived somewhere in Takoma Park. Boo, he didn't know anything about.

According to Marquette, Khadafi drove a smoke gray Range Rover. He told me that after they robbed Money and Khadafi shot him, they met up and split everything. He also told me that Khadafi still hung out in Capers Projects. That was all I needed to know. When I was satisfied that Marquette had suffered enough, I killed him. I stabbed him in the neck and then shot him in the head twice. By that time it was dark outside and it was easier for me to drag his body to the Benz without being spotted. I drove the Benz to the Blue Plains sewage dump and abandoned the car.

That was all done yesterday. Today, I sit on I Street patiently waiting to see if I can catch Khadafi or Boo. The van has tinted windows, so nobody can see inside and notice me just sitting here. I reclined my seat and rolled me a big ass jay of weed. Weed always made me more relaxed and that's what I needed, relaxation.

I thought about back when I met Money. I was rolling with my man Marvin Sanders. Marvin was beefing with niggas from down Sursum Cordas. They had come through Florida Park, where Marvin lived and shot the block up. The only person injured that day was Marvin's little brother, who was only twelve years old. The bullets to his back confined him to a wheelchair. Marvin wanted blood. Having grown up in the juvenile joints with me, Marvin knew I loved to bust my gun and he needed a fresh face to get up on the dudes he wanted to crush. So he called me and I came running.

Marvin was getting major dope from Money then, but he shut shop down to go to war. After we killed about ten of his enemies, Marvin got knocked off and went to jail. I wanted to help him pay for his legal fees, but I was broke at the time. From D.C. Jail, Marvin hooked me up with Money. I met Money at the Wendy's on Florida Avenue. We discussed some problems he was having with dudes that weren't trying to pay his money. I went to work for Money and crushed everybody that opposed him. That's how I came to know him. He respected my loyalty to Marvin and how I put my murder game down. So he continued to seek out my services when needed.

When I first spotted the Range Rover hours later, I thought my eyes were deceiving me. It rode right past me and stopped in front of a house on the corner of 7th and I street. I watched the dude with the long cornrow braids get out of the truck. He fit the description and resembled the photo I had. It was definitely him. A smile crossed my face as I watched Khadafi interact with other dudes congregating in the front of the house. "I got him," I said to no one at all and wondered where his man Boo was.

I picked up the SKS assault rifle off the floor and put it in my lap. I slammed a fresh clip into it and sat there and stroked it like a cat. Soon, I would hear it purr. When the Range pulled off about thirty minutes later, I let it reach the corner and turn before I pulled off after it. I followed the Range safely from four cars away.

Khadafi headed east on M Street and made a right by the Washington Navy Yard. Weaving in and out of traffic, we both crossed the 11th Street Bridge. At the third traffic light on Martin Luther King Avenue, the traffic stalled because of a red light. Instead of waiting to turn in the left turn only lane, the Range jumped lanes and sped up M.L.K. I maneuvered the same way and stayed behind it. At the intersection of M.L.K. and Talbert Street, the Range had to sit still for the red light because there was no way to jump lanes due to construction on the other side of the street.

The Range was stuck, sandwiched between two cars with no escape. It was time to make my move. I hopped out of the van with the SKS concealed under a towel. I covered the ground of three car lengths in seconds. I crept up on the driver's side of the Range and opened fire. I zoned out and sprayed the SUV until the thirty round clip was empty.

.CHAPTER TWENTY-TWO.
KHADAFI

Still crouched down on the floor of the truck, I removed my arms from over my head and laughed. I was able to move and laugh so that proved that I was still alive. I quickly did a body search for holes to see if I was hit and where. I felt blood on my neck and cheek. And my upper body was in pain. *How many times had I been hit?* I had to get out of the truck and find out. If I laid there, I'd die, that I was sure of.

What the fuck was he shooting? I asked myself. It seemed like he was busting that joint forever. I thank Allah for my paranoid ways. Paranoia and fear have saved many a life on the streets and they just saved mines. Stuck in traffic, I always paid attention to my surroundings. I'm a killer, so I know how to trap a man off. That's how I was able to see the dude approaching with the machine gun under the towel. He tried to creep up on me in broad daylight, bare faced. By the time he reached my truck, I had dove to the passenger side floorboard. I anticipated the barrage of bullets and balled up under the dash. The tinted windows had come in handy, too. My would–be killer couldn't see that I was on the floor covered up. The majority of his bullets whizzed right by me.

Some found their mark, though. The pain in my back told me that. I was thankful again. This time for the bulletproof vest that my Uncle gave me. It was the real life saver.

I quickly inspected the inside of the truck and saw the extent of the damages. They all looked superficial. I got off the floor and got behind the wheel. When the Range started, I exhaled deeply. I put the gear in drive and pulled off. I can't say that I wasn't surprised that the truck was still operational, but after all it was a Range Rover. I pulled the bullet-riddled truck into the first housing complex I saw.

At the top of a hill and in the back of the complex, I got out of the truck and stood up to inspect myself. I was relieved to see and feel that my wounds were not life threatening. That was a blessing. My thoughts were racing a mile a minute. Who was the dude that came at me? And why did he come? He spit a whole clip at me, so that tells me he meant business. Had somebody found out about the Escape Records move? Whoever it was that tried to kill me would think I was dead, at least for a day or so. And that would be enough time for me to regroup and find out exactly who he was.

Looking at my totaled Range Rover, I wanted to cry for it. I knew that I'd have to leave it and fast before somebody told the police where I went. And that wouldn't be a good look at the present. That's why I had to roll out from the scene and avoid medical attention. The vest strapped to my upper body, the gun in my waist and the extra clips in my pocket would send me back to jail forever. And going back to jail wasn't even an option for me.

I noticed my cell phone had also survived the attack. I called my uncle several times and got no answer. I called his house and talked to Lijah. "I haven't heard a word from him since early yesterday. He didn't come home and he's not answering his phone," she said.

I hung up the phone, praying that my uncle was somewhere laid up with a bitch. Bad bitches were his Achilles' heel.

The next number I dialed was Boo's. He didn't answer his cell or his house phone. What the fuck is going on? Who else could I call to scoop me? As the pains in my body threatened to take over and sit me down, the answer came to me out of nowhere....

She was a registered nurse before she gave up her scrubs to take an administration position at the hospital.

I scrolled through my phone for the numbers that she'd given me the last time I dropped some money off. I could get her to look at my wounds and dress 'em. But most of all, I'd get to see her again. I called the number in my phone. Shawnay answered on the first ring. "Hello?"

"Shawnay, I need your help. I just got shot."

"Khadafi?"

"Yeah, it's me. Listen, I need you to come get me before the police get here. P-l-e-a-s-"

"I'm on my way. Where are you?"

.CHAPTER TWENTY-THREE.
SHAWNAY

I dipped the towel into the hot water. "This may sting a little bit, but you'll be okay. You need to thank God that you're not dead."

The dark blue and black bruises on Khadafi's body would heal, but he'd definitely be in a lot of pain for a while. He showed me the bulletproof vest that had absorbed most of the direct hits. I had never seen or touched one, so I was obviously astonished. We counted at least thirteen hits to the vest that would've been inside his body had he not worn the protective armor.

After receiving his call, I left work to go and pick Khadafi up. He needed me and I couldn't say no. How could I say no to the man who had just given me almost $200,000 cash in the last ten days? That money instantly made life a lot easier for me and my girls in a lot of ways. My job at Washington Hospital Center only pays me 40 grand a year. Once the mortgage, my car note and my car insurance get paid, then the health insurance is due. Add that with food, toiletries, household supplies, and school tuition, and that's both of my checks for the month. And I ain't even about to mention the high gas prices. I don't know where that money came from. I don't know who had to die for me to get it. And guess what? I don't care. That's not my concern. But taking care of my babies is. Struggling every month to make it is one of the reasons that I always resent Antonio for being in prison. I wasn't supposed to be a single parent with two daughters struggling to get by. That wasn't the way we planned it. He was supposed to be out here.

I don't know if it's right or wrong for me to blame Antonio for all the trials and tribulations that threaten to overcome me sometimes. I may be partially at fault too. Hadn't I stood back and watched his moral decline and constant progression deeper and deeper into the streets, and never said a word? Then there was always the maybe. *Maybe* if I had expressed my fears and warned him more, he would have stopped. *Maybe* if I had threatened to leave or gave him an ultimatum, he could've been saved. Hadn't I known what lied ahead at the end of the road he was traveling? Hadn't I known that drug dealers were all headed to jail or an early grave? But there was a small percentage of hustlers that defied those statistics, weren't there? I now believe that I blinded myself into thinking that Antonio was a part of that privileged few.

The night he called me from the police station brought reality crashing down on me. The weight of the world felt like it was on my shoulders. For some strange reason, when he told me that they had him locked up for murder, I knew that he wasn't coming back. Up until then, Antonio had been the strength and source of wealth that held the family together. His absence forced me to survive and adapt. I had to go out into the world and become independent instead of dependent. I decided to go to school for nursing. With a one-year-old daughter at home, finding a day care was easy. Finding a way to pay that day care was not. In the beginning it was rough, but over time things become more stable. Every time I looked into my youngest daughter's face, I saw her father. And I silently cursed him for abandoning us. I cried every time my children cried for their father. What eventually got me through the rough periods was my faith in God. I leaned on the Lord more. The Bible said that God didn't place burdens on people that they couldn't bear, so I let go and let God.

Over the years, my relationship with Antonio got rocky due to frayed nerves, distance, miscommunications and my inability to understand his struggle. But in the end, our love for one another maintained our bond. Recently, with two growing girls at home and the world constantly changing, the rough period between Antonio and I was rearing its ugly head again, but then came the man laying on my couch. I felt a lot of gratitude toward him even though Antonio sent him. They had saved me at a crucial time when the economy was bad for everybody in the country. Antonio was in Texas. I couldn't show him how much I appreciated him, could I? But Khadafi was here in the flesh and there was no harm in patching him up. Was there? After all, he had just been shot and almost killed.

I gently rubbed the water filled with iodine and Epsom salt on Khadafi's back. My emotions stirred inside of me. Being so close to a man after all these years, it was creating feelings in me that I couldn't control. The copper complexion of his skin and the muscles that strained in his back for relief; the combination had me wet. The tingling sensation in my panties made me think of a young girl discovering her S-E-X for the first time. I thought about the new Plies song that Jamie Foxx sung on. On the chorus, Jamie sang, "Please excuse my hands, they just wanna touch/They just wanna feel/They don't mean no harm..." That's what I wanted to say to Khadafi as I gently massaged the discolorations in his skin. I wanted to run my hands down the small of his back and feel what was in the back and then the front of his jeans... *"Please excuse my hand..."*

I was suddenly grateful for bulletproof vests and whoever invented them. The vest had definitely saved Khadafi. Gunshot wound victims were an all day everyday occurrence at the hospital. I thought about all the countless men and women who I watched die every day and silently thanked God that the man on my couch didn't meet the same fate. I tried and tried, but I couldn't deny the sexual energy I felt growing between us. But that couldn't happen, could it? Antonio was his man. But I needed a man's touch, a man's warmth, strength and love. I needed some....dick. There. I said it. But wasn't there rules to be followed? Wasn't it against the code to sleep with your man's baby mother? Maybe it was. Right then I decided to tread lightly when dealing with Khadafi. He had to have a woman at home or several chickenheads vying for his attention. I didn't need to be added to either of those lists. Maybe

I'm just lonely... and horny. "Yeah, that's what it is." I mumbled to myself.

"What did you say?" Khadafi asked me.

"Uh... nothing." I cursed myself for speaking out loud. "The wounds on your cheeks and neck ain't as bad as they look. They just bled like hell. I'ma put a gauze bandage and some antibiotic ointment on both of them, but your ass need to go somewhere and chill out. You got people shooting at you in broad day light. If one of them bullets would've hit your head, you wouldn't be here right now."

That's the life I live. It comes with the territory. I'ma find out who that wa....."

"And kill him, right?" I asked. "Then you gon' be back in jail, in a cell next door to Anto-, Ameen. Forget I even said anything. Y'all do what y'all wanna do anyway. Can't nobody tell y'all shit. But let me ask you this."

"Go ahead and ask me."

"Is the street life that important to you, that you would rather lose all the people you love and ultimately your life? Wait, no, let me ask you this. Why do niggas gamble their freedom, life and loved ones, all in the name of the streets and as you say, 'The life you live?'"

Khadafi looked to be at a loss for words. Then he finally said, "I guess it's the way we were raised. We are only products of our environment. I didn't ask to live like this. I didn't ask to grow up in Arthur Capers Housing Projects. This life was thrust upon me. The street life is all I know."

I couldn't believe the stupid shit that Khadafi had just said. What really made me mad was that Antonio had said some similar shit to me about a year ago. I threw my hand on my hip. "So you telling me, that you don't have any choices? Is that what you're saying? You telling me that you were born destined to fail?"

"All I'm saying is there ain't no whole lot of muthafuckas that come up like I did, where I did, that made it. What choices do we have? Everybody in the hood grow up learning to rob, kill, steal, sell drugs, carry guns, and fuck at an early age. That's our education. Who gives a damn about us? Nobody cares about what happens to kids in the ghetto. Ain't no jobs out here for nobody. A few, huh? Wendy's and McDonald's."

"That's not true—"

"That is true. They working niggas to death for five dollars an hour, minimum wage. Who can live off that? The cost of living is sky high in the nation's capital. But them muthafuckas downtown ain't sending no money this way. How can you look a starving kid in the eyes and tell him not to hustle to eat? This is the life he was given. He didn't choose to be poor, broke, or born to drug-addicted parents. This life was thrust upon us. That's why I say, 'it's the life we live.'"

I couldn't accept what he was saying, even though I knew it was partly true. "That's a cop out. Excuses, excuses. What about the dudes that don't hustle, stay in school, get jobs and become good people?"

"Very few, small numbers."

"So beefing over streets that don't belong to nobody, neighborhoods that are gonna be here after all of us are gone, killing over drugs and a little bit of money— that's the way life is supposed to be? That's the life you live?" As I waited for him to answer the question, I felt like such a hypocrite. This was the man who had given me almost two hundred thousand in dirty, blood street money. And here I was debating with him about the ways of the streets and I was his co-defendant in theory. I think Khadafi knew he couldn't win the argument with me, so he just gave up.

"Thanks for everything, boo," he said. "I really appreciate you. My man is on the way to get me, so I'ma walk around the corner and meet him. I don't want anybody to see me leaving your house and knowing where you live. I'ma call you later on, a'ight?"

"You do that," I responded and hoped that he would. As I watched him leave my house, I silently prayed that I didn't run him away.

.CHAPTER TWENTY-FOUR.
BOO

"Now, what the fuck happened again?" I asked Khadafi as he got into my car. "You sounded like you couldn't really talk earlier and what the fuck are you doing all the way on this side of Southeast?"

"I got a broad over here that I mess with. She's the one that came and got me. When I was talking to you on the phone, I knew she was ear hustling, so I had to censor my conversation. I don't want shorty in my business this early in the game."

"Okay. So what happened earlier?"

"I went down Capers to holler at a few of my men. When I pulled off, at first I didn't notice the black van that followed me. I mean, I saw it, but paid it no mind. I got stuck in traffic on M.L.K. You know me, cuz. I be on point like a muthafucka. The nigga tried to creep me, but I saw him. He had a big ass machine gun under a towel like he was tryna hide it. It took me all of two seconds to figure out that I was the intended target. Cuz, I couldn't move the truck. I was stuck. He was too close up on me for me to try and get out. So I got on the floor and just covered my head up."

"Man, you should have got out and ran. Where was your heat at? At least barked back at the nigga."

"Cuz, that's all I could think to do. This nigga runs up and fills my shit up. I'm talking thirty or forty shots. I thought he wasn't gonna ever stop shootin'. I thought I was gone, cuz. No bullshit. I jumped in the driver's seat and got outta there. I couldn't let the cops investigate that one. I had the hammer on me and the vest. Later for going back to jail 'cause a nigga tried to cancel my subscription. I pulled into the first complex I saw and gave myself an examination. Then I called your ass."

"Slim, I was in some pussy and wasn't tryna get up. I was ducking Sanaa, anyway. That's why I didn't check the caller ID. That's my bad, slim. I met this lil' young bitch that was phat as shit and all over me. She started out twisting my dreads, then she ended up riding my dick."

"It's all good. I know how it is. I called my uncle about four times and he didn't answer either."

"Does Kemie know that you almost got killed today?" I asked Khadafi.

"You know, cuz, real talk, I haven't really been communicating with Kemie like that. I go home and we fuck and all that, but shit done changed with us. Well, not her part, but mine. She know me, cuz. She knows that something is up with me, she doesn't know what. We haven't talked about anything."

"You still tripping off that shit Marnie told you?"

"Wouldn't you be? That shit really fucked me up. Every time I fuck her, I visualize Bean and Omar fucking her. I can't get that shit outta my mind. I keep seeing a faceless dude getting the head from her, all night until he bust in her mouth. Don't get me wrong, cuz. I love shorty to death. I gotta figure out a way to deal with what I know. Until then, I'ma do me. I came straight home to Kemie. I need to do me. Kemie did her while I was in."

"Nigga, you sound like the rap nigga on the radio. What's his name? Rocko or some shit like that!"

"Yeah, that's his name. That's how I feel though, cuz."

"But shorty held you down, though, slim. What about that? Fuck what she did while you was in. You wouldn't have stopped fucking if she went to jail," I said as I turned onto Sheridan Road.

"Make the right up here, cuz, on Bowen Road. Then make the first right into Oxford Manor. The truck is parked at the top of the hill. Like I was saying, I'ma hold her down, she still my Boo and all that. She got the house, the Land Rover, walk-in closets full of clothes and shoes, handbags and all that good shit. I just gotta go out into the wild and howl at the moon for a little while. Feel me?"

"Yeah, I feel you, slim." We both got out of the car and inspected the Range. I whistled at the damages. "Got damn, slim. That nigga tried to Swiss cheese your shit. You lucky you saw him coming."

"I don't believe in luck. It was preordained for me to survive that hit. It was written in the stars for me."

"You say you didn't recognize the dude, huh?"

"It was broad daylight and that nigga was barefaced. I don't know him from nowhere. If I did, cuz, you know I'd be on his ass right now. Word gon' get back, especially when he find out that he missed. He'll try his hand again, but next time I'll be ready. I'm still tryna figure out why he came at me and who sent him."

"If you would've got—"

"I already know, cuz. Let me get all my shit out of the Range," he said. Then I watched as he made a couple of calls.

"Something ain't right, cuz," Khadafi said and closed his flip phone. "My uncle hasn't answered his phone yet. I know he ain't laying up in no pussy for this long."

"When was the last time you talked to him?"

"About two days ago. He was on the move, so we didn't talk long. I been leaving him messages and he hasn't got back yet."

"Don't even trip. You know slim somewhere chillin'. He probably in some good pussy like I was. You know I talked to Umar this morning?"

"Oh yeah? What he say?"

"He said he'll be home next Friday. The clothes I sent him got there. He said Ameen sends his love and that they still haven't told him anything about the murder beef."

"I wonder why they haven't called me."

"Maybe they can't reach you. I can barely reach you. Umar caught me over Sanaa's house."

"You been playing shorty real close since you got home. Shorty done bunned you up. You sweet," Khadafi said and laughed.

"Look who's talking? You gone off Kemie, otherwise you wouldn't still be fuckin' her," I said and laughed. "On the real, Shorty cool, but she a switch-up artist. In the bed, she put on like that cute new porn bitch Pinky, wanting a nigga to bust in her nose and shit. But as soon as the lights come on, she an ordained preacher or one of the twelve disciples."

Khadafi cracked up laughing at that. "Cuz, cut that shit out!"

"Slim, I'm dead serious. No bullshit."

Khadafi stopped laughing enough to say, "Shorty gon' fuck around and convert your ass. You gon' be calling me talking about, praise the Lord and all that geeking ass shit. And guess what I'ma do?"

"What?"

"I'ma hang up on your ass."

"Man, whatever. Ain't no pussy worth going to the hellfire for."

"Speaking of the hellfire, I know I messed up. I'ma bust hell wide open for all the shit I'm out here doing. I just hope that one day Allah changes my heart and put me back on the right path. I don't wanna die outside the fold of Islam."

"When was the last time you offered the salat?"

"Right before I got on the plane in Texas. I been bullshittin'."

"We both have. I tell you what, when we scoop Umar next Friday, all of us can go to Jum'ah. We got to hold on to the rope of Allah a little bit, at least."

"That's a bet, cuz. I'm overdue for a prayer or two."

We both got back into my Cadillac. We can hit Masjid Al-Islam on Benning Road. I heard Imam Musa be giving it up in the khutbahs."

"Say no more, I'm there. In the meantime, I'ma go and cop me a new truck. I like that new Infiniti joint, the QX65."

"Nissan makes them joints. You might as well cop the Nissan Armada and save some money."

"I'm out this muthafucka living like an outlaw, cuz. Robbing stage coaches and taking no prisoners. Do it really look like I'm out here tryna save money? I'ma get it right back. You know how I do. Ain't no shortage of niggas in the drug game that don't mind contributing to a real nigga's get-rich program. The Infiniti is gonna be on them. Aye, cuz, on some real live shit, my body hurts like shit. Every time I think about the nigga that tried to crush me and the pain I feel, I get mad. That nigga better pray to Allah that I never catch him."

.CHAPTER TWENTY-FIVE.
KHADAFI

"**A**lex, cut that bullshit out, cuz. I'm tryna cop that "08" Infiniti truck out there, right now," I told the owner of Auto Source. "I got cash up front, right now."

"Luther, my man—" Alex started.

I quickly cut him off. "My name is Khadafi, nigga. I told your ass that once before."

"My bad, Khadafi. But I can't do that. I just let you drop 120 grand on the Rovers. I can't cover up another fifty for the Infiniti. The Feds are already all over me. This, I cannot do."

"Well, what if I found a co-signer and just paid on it monthly? Can you do that?" I asked.

Alex sat down at his desk and typed on his computer. "I tell you what, Khadafi. You bring me somebody with a beacon score of 700 or better and I'll let you drop half, twenty-five thousand, and let you pay me in twenty-five monthly payments of a thousand a month. Plus title, taxes and tags. Can you do that?"

I thought about what Alex said. "Give me about two hours and I'll be back."

I walked out of that office mad as shit. But the sight of the midnight blue Infiniti truck calmed me down. I had to cop that joint. But who could I get to co-sign with good credit? Just as I made it back to my caddy, the answer came to me. Picking up my cell phone, I dialed Allied Mutual Mortgage Company.

"Hello? Can I speak to Mary Henderson?"

As I waited for my aunt to come to the phone, I rehearsed my spiel that I was gonna run down to her. I knew that she'd do it. After all, I am her favorite nephew.

Once I pulled off the lot in my new truck, I called Marnie. The things she did to me in the Rover had to be repeated in the Infiniti. I drove to James Creek dwellings and scooped her.

"What happened to the Rover?" she asked as she climbed in the truck.

"I had to get rid of it. Yesterday, a nigga tried to flip my shit."

"For real? Damn, boy, you ain't even been home that long to have enemies already. Am I safe riding with you?"

I laughed at her question. "Have you ever busted a gun, Marnie?"

"What?"

"You heard what the fuck I just said. Have you ever busted a gun before?"

"Yeah. I had a little deuce-deuce before. I busted that."

I reached under my seat and pulled out the Calico. "This is what I carry now for niggas that wanna come for my head. I'ma hold this." I reached into my waistband and pulled out a Ruger 9 millimeter. "You take this. Put it in your purse. If anything should happen to me, you can bust back and save me."

Once Marnie put the gun in her purse, I said, "Does that make you feel safer?"

"Fuck yeah. As a matter of fact, that shit made me horny. Find somewhere to pull over because I wanna be the first bitch to cum all over your seats."

I tried to keep my eyes on the road, but it was hard not to watch Marnie wiggle out of her tight jeans. The girl was sexy as shit and she knew it. Marnie pulled her thong off and hung it on the rearview mirror, right next to my apple tree air fresheners. My dick got as hard as granite stone. I hurried up and pulled into a parking lot behind the Wingate high rise apartments. Once I parked the truck, it was on and popping.

"Does Kemie suck that dick real good for you?" Marnie asked.

"Of course," I responded. I couldn't lie to her.

"I guess that means I gotta do it better then, huh?"

I unzipped my jeans and pulled my dick out. "Can you?"

"Watch me," Marnie said as she took the gum she was chewing out of her mouth.

And man, did I watch her. I watched as she gently kissed the head of my dick. Then she slowly licked the length of it. She went down further and licked my nuts. I watched Marnie kiss and lick her way back up my dick. I watched her jerk precum out of me and then lick it off. It took a lot of restraint not to cum all over myself too soon. I gasped out loud as Marnie put my dick in her mouth and engulfed more than half of it. She adjusted her position, came back up, spit a glob of spit all over me and then went back to work. I watched amazed as Marnie swallowed my dick whole. Her tongue licked my nuts as she slowly moved up and down on me. I couldn't hold back no longer. I came deep in her throat. Marnie kept sucking me until I literally begged her to stop.

"Listen to your ass. Nigga, you sound like a bitch. Be easy and let me make this gun go off again."

At first, I was messed up in the head about Marnie saying I sounded like a bitch, but I let it go. She was right. I smiled at the thought of it. I was moaning and groaning like a bitch. I sat back in my seat and watched Marnie tease my dick until it rose again. Then she deep throated me again. By the time I came again, I was tired and drained. I thought we were finished, but Marnie had other plans.

"You didn't think that was it, did you? I proved that Kemie's head can't fuck with mine, but now I gotta put this pussy on you again. I told you I'm tryna be the first to cum on these fresh leather seats. And besides, I didn't wiggle out of these five-hundred-dollar jeans for nothing."

I didn't say a word as Marnie straddled me. She rubbed her soaking wet pussy on my limp dick until it rose again. It was wet as shit. It felt like she had pissed in my lap. "Damn, boo, your pussy got that wet from sucking that dick?"

"Uh huh. That's crazy, ain't it?"

"Damn."

Marnie put both feet on the seat I was sitting on and lifted herself in the air. She put one hand on my shoulder and used the other to guide my dick into her. Then she hugged my neck and kissed me softly as she rode me like a cowgirl. I grabbed her waist and pulled her all the way down on my dick. It was her turn to holler out.

"Don't get up there and bullshit with that dick. Sit on all of it like a big girl. You sound like a bitch right now, hollering and shit."

Marnie bit one of my ears gently and then said, "Fuck you, Dirty Redds!"

"My name ain't Dirty Redds no more. It's Khadafi. Say it! I pulled Marnie down on the dick and thrust upward at the same time. She yelped out in pain. "Say it! Say my name!"

"Khadafi! Khadafi! Khadafi! K-K-H-A-A-D-A-F-F-F-I-I!"

It was kinda late by the time I pulled up to my house. After I dropped Marnie off, I drove to the IHOP on Riverdale Road and washed up in their restroom before driving home. I silently hoped that Kemie was in the bed asleep and not in the mood for sex. My dick was sore as shit after Marnie got off of it. So I wasn't in no shape to put in a repeat performance. When I got out the truck, I made sure to check out the surroundings before putting my key in the door. I walked into our bedroom a few minutes later and saw that my prayer hadn't been answered. Kemie was up, sitting on the bed, watching television. When she turned around, I saw that she had tears in her eyes. I automatically assumed that she knew about me being with Marnie and shit was about to get ugly for real. I wasn't in the mood to fight with Kemie, so I fake got mad and said, "What the fuck is wrong with you? Why are you crying?"

I waited for Kemie to explode, but she never did. Instead, she said, "Baby, I'm sorry."

Baffled, I just stared at her like she was crazy. What was she sorry about? "Sorry about what?"

Kemie grabbed the remote and turned up the volume on the TV. Then she turned her attention back to the TV and so did I.

"Those who have just tuned in, the big story of the day is the number of homicides in the District. The city is on course to record over five hundred murders this year. One hundred more murders than last year. The discovery of the four bodies today, brings the total to 305 and there are five months left in the year. D.C. Police today, were called to the scene of a gruesome double homicide. Two men identified as Freddy "Lee Lee" Bailey and Mecca Lee-Bey were both found behind a dumpster on the 1200 block of North Capital Street, Northwest. Both men were found nude with the words "Rat Bitch" carved into their chests and shot repeatedly in the face. Sources close to City Under Siege Fox News say that Freddy Bailey testified recently in the case of the alleged notorious killer, George Foreman III. And Mecca Lee-Bey was instrumental in assisting authorities in arresting and charging several D.C. Jail correctional officers and inmates with smuggling contraband into the jail. Authorities were also called to the 1700 block of Independence Avenue in Southeast, where they found a man identified as thirty-five-year-old Terrell Hargrave who suffered from multiple gunshot wounds to the upper body in front of a residence in that block. Medical workers attempted to talk to Hargrave and discovered that his tongue had been cut out. Hargrave was rushed to nearby D.C. General Hospital, where he died minutes after arriving. A man on his way to work at the Blue Plains Sewage Dump, discovered a body inside of a car. According to a forensic specialist, the body has been identified as thirty-four-year-old Marquette Henderson. The dead body had been inside the Mercedes S600 for several days. The cause of death was multiple gunshot wounds to the head and body and lacerations to the neck."

Kemie turned around and locked eyes with me. I didn't realize that I was crying until tears fell and dampened my shirt. My pain was visible in my face and Kemie read it perfectly.

"Baby, I know that you're hurting, right now, but—"

I turned on my heels and walked out of the room.

"Khadafi? Khadafi, wait! Where are you going? Khadafi!"

I heard hurried footsteps and then felt Kemie's hand on my shoulder as I reached the front door.

"Baby, please don't leave! Please let me help you," Kemie said and tried to comfort me.

I had to leave or I'd suffocate in there. I had to get out. "Don't touch me!" I said, as I reached for the door.

I walked outside to the Cadillac and got in. Then I remembered that the Calico was in the truck. I went to the Infiniti and retrieved it. As I drove through the city, the Calico and my 9 millimeter were both in my lap. I wanted to, no, I had to, release my rage on somebody. The tears in my eyes blurred my vision as I drove to an unknown destination.

Who could've killed my uncle? And why? Although I knew that getting killed came with the life that we lived in the streets, I still couldn't accept that somebody took my uncle away from me. Had somebody found out that me and Marquette were the ones who've been leaving bodies everywhere for the last three months? Whoever killed my uncle, were they the same ones who tried to kill me yesterday? They had to be. It was too much of a coincidence not to be connected.

The first person who came to mind was the dude Poo that I had let live after I killed his woman and robbed him out Maryland. Was he the guilty person? I bucked a U-turn in the middle of the street and headed toward Branch Avenue. I remembered my uncle telling me that Poo's mother lived in the building, too. If I happened to come across him, his ass was mine.

.CHAPTER TWENTY-SIX.
KEMIE

All hell is about to break loose and there's nothing I can do to stop it. What am I supposed to say to Khadafi, when his uncle has just been killed in the streets? I tried my best to keep him home, but he wasn't tryna hear it. I know that man like the back of my hand and chances are, somebody is gonna get killed tonight. As I sat on the steps and listened to his car start up, I wondered who'd be the unlucky person that would meet their end in a few hours or less. I could see the pain that was etched in stone on his face. I knew the bond that Khadafi shared with Marquette. It was the same bond that he shared with Damien Lucas several years ago. When that bond was severed by an anonymous gun, Khadafi killed the next best person who was rumored to be involved. Time sometimes served to change people, but in Khadafi's case, time only created a more sinister and more heartless individual. I cried for my man. I cried for the person that he would kill tonight. I cried for the world that shaped us both into the people that we are.

As the tears fell from my eyes, I tried to figure out what our future would be. If Khadafi did return in the morning, would he be the same caring man with the undercurrent of a beast lurking? Or would his uncle's death push him all the way over the edge to the point of no return? I slowly picked myself up off the steps and went to the kitchen. It was definitely time for a cup of herbal tea. I learned a lot from Erykah Badu. A cup of tea and a cigarette would calm me right down. And calmness is what I need right now.

Suddenly, a sense of deja'vu came over me. I felt like I had done this before. Then it came to me. I had done this before. About thirty days ago, I was at work when one of my friends called and told me that Khadafi and my old friend Marnie had gotten into his truck in the parking lot of the beauty salon where she worked. I had called Khadafi repeatedly and he didn't answer the phone. I was livid. I wasn't mad because he wasn't answering the phone. I was messed up about what I knew Marnie would tell him. I ended up leaving work early that day and going home. I knew that Marnie's big mouth ass hated me and would tell Khadafi the things I did while he was locked up, just to get back at me for what I did to her. I had apologized several times for giving Black Junior the pussy. I apologized for what I did to Tecola. Derek's dick was trash anyway. But neither Tecola nor Marnie would forgive me. Couldn't they understand that I was emotionally fucked up behind what Phil had done to me? I wasn't myself when I did those things. Why couldn't they accept that?

Later that day I confronted Khadafi about Marnie and he played me off by saying that he gave her a ride to pick up something for her car. I didn't believe that for one minute. But I was forced to leave it alone because if I pushed, I was afraid I'd pique his curiosity as to why I was trippin' so hard.

The beeping of the microwave broke my reverie. I got my hot tea and then walked back upstairs. In my dresser drawer was my cigarettes. I tapped one from the pack and lit it. When I inhaled the smoke, I sipped the tea. The combination of the tea and cigarette smoke calmed my nerves. I finished them both off, and then laid down to await my man's return home.

.CHAPTER TWENTY-SEVEN.
BOO

At first I thought I was dreaming when I heard the phone vibrating on the nightstand next to the bed. Once I opened my eyes and realized that it wasn't a dream, I reached out for the phone, even though I had to move Sanaa to do it. In my mind, I knew who the caller was before I even answered the phone. If there had been an emergency with Grandma or my daughter, my family would've called Sanaa's house phone.

"Aye?" I said into the phone.

"Aye, cuz. I need to holla at you." It was Khadafi.

I couldn't put my finger on it, but he sounded a little spaced out. I looked at the digital clock on the dresser. It read 1:39 a.m. "Slim, it's 1:40 in the morning. You a'ight?"

"Yeah, I'm a'ight."

"Well, holla at me tomorrow, then."

"Cuz, this can't wait til then. I need to see you, now."

"I'm getting up now, slim," I answered trying to disguise the anger that was building in me.

"Good. Aye, cuz, come down to Anacostia Park."

"Anacostia Park?"

"Yeah, cuz. Drive all the way to the back of the park, past the skating rink and picnic area. I'm at the end of the road where the bridge is overhead."

"I'll be there in twenty minutes." I hit the END button on my phone and laid back down for a minute. What the fuck did Khadafi want to say to me down Anacostia Park at 2 a.m.?

THE ULTIMATE SACRIFICE

I saw Khadafi's Cadillac DTS parked beside the shoreline of the Anacostia River. The area was dimly lit and deserted, except for Khadafi, me and another man. I strained my eyes to focus as I walked up on the scene. There was a person lying on the ground. The closer I got, the better I could see. The man was bound and gagged with duct tape. He was wiggling around the ground like a fish. I saw several empty Remy bottles on the ground by the car. Khadafi sat on the riverbank with his feet over the side of the wall. He never even looked back as I approached.

"Cuz, is that you?" Khadafi called out.

"It's me, slim. What the fuck is going on?"

Khadafi stood up and turned around. He walked over to me and I could see that he was drunk. The whole scene kind of caught me off guard because I had never seen Khadafi drink anything stronger than a soda.

"My uncle got killed."

I wasn't sure that I had heard right. His words were a little slurred. "What did you say, slim? I couldn't hear you."

"Somebody killed Marquette, cuz."

I didn't know what to say to my partner. I couldn't say that I felt his pain because nobody I loved had ever been killed. "I'm sorry to hear that, slim. I—"

"I been looking all over for this nigga named Poo, but I couldn't find him. He was the dude that I told you about, the one from out Maryland. I smoked his bitch and let him live. I was supposed to have killed them both, but I didn't and now my uncle is dead."

"Khadafi, if you couldn't find Poo, who the fuck is this?" I asked and pointed at the bound and gagged man.

Khadafi's eyes followed my finger. "Oh, him? That's m-my man B-e-e-an."

"Your man from down Capers?"

"Yeah, cuz. That's him."

"He killed your uncle?" I asked, trying to understand what the fuck was going on.

"I don't think so. He knows better than that."

"Khadafi, I know you fucked up about your uncle, but, slim, I'm not understanding you right now. You got your man down here taped up and you ain't told me why yet. Why did you tell me to come down here?"

"You my man, cuz. I need your support right now. I'm losing my mind and I need you to talk to me. I don't have anybody else, cuz," Khadafi said and started crying.

I couldn't believe what I was seeing. Khadafi was crying like a baby and I didn't know how to help him. But what I did know was that the liquor was the reason for his tears. I walked up to him and embraced him. I hugged Khadafi and tried my best to comfort him. Then all of a sudden, he broke our embrace and pushed me back real hard. I had to struggle to maintain my footing on the gravel.

"Cuz, this nigga right here was supposed to be my man. But as soon as I went to jail, he went at my bitch. Ain't that some wicked shit?"

Before I could even say a word, Khadafi went on a tirade.

"This bitch-ass nigga was fucking Kemie while I was in and he knew she was my bun. He was sending me money and pictures of other bitches while he was fucking my bitch. Snake-ass nigga." Khadafi ripped his shirt off. "See this tattoo, nigga?"

I watched as Khadafi got down on his knees and made the bound man look at the tattoo on his chest.

"Read it, Bean. What does it say? Read it, cuz. Do you see it? Let me tell you what it says. It says, 'God please protect me from my friends. I can handle my enemies'." That's what it says. But you already know that, don't you, Bean?" Khadafi looked up at me. "Cuz, he knew that shit. You know how I know that? Because this bitch nigga was with me when I went and got the tat. He was with me when I went in my father's barbershop and killed Theodore. When I got arrested, I saw him standing across the street. This nigga was my man, cuz.

But he betrayed me. I hate to be betrayed. Aye, cuz, how long does it take for a man to die by suffocation?"

"I don't know, slim," I replied, knowing what was next.

Khadafi went to his trunk and pulled out the box of trash bags that we used in the Escape Records caper. He pulled one bag from the box. I stood transfixed to my spot as I watched Khadafi snatch the tape off of Bean's mouth.

"Redds, don't do this, moe!" he pleaded. "I didn't have shit to do with Quette getting killed. You know I wouldn't be with no shit like that. And I never fucked Kemie. I swear to God on my mother I didn't. You dead wrong for this, moe. But we can make it right. We can find out who hit Quette and crush 'em. Don't kill me about no bitch, moe! Don't do it!"

"You didn't fuck Kemie, cuz?"

"Fuck no! I knew Kemie was your girl, moe. I would never do that to you. I love you, Redds! I love you. Don't kill me!"

I stood there and tried to decide if I should speak up for Bean. Maybe he was telling the truth. "Slim, what if he tellin' the truth? What if—"

"He lying, cuz. I been knowing this nigga since I was five years old. And he ain't never told me that he love me, even while I was in. He's a lying muthafucka."

With that said, Khadafi put the open trash bag over Bean's head. Then he taped the bag up around his neck.

I couldn't believe what I was seeing. Bean wiggled and fought to free himself and get some air, but his attempts were in vain. The duct tape on his hands and feet made that virtually impossible. Khadafi smiled that same wicked smile he had on his face when he dismembered Keith Barnett. He glanced at his watch, then back at Bean. I watched as the struggling man stopped moving and became completely still. Khadafi walked over to Bean and felt for a pulse. Then he listened for any sounds coming from the bag. Once he was satisfied that Bean was dead, Khadafi stood up and checked his watch again.

"Two minutes and twelve seconds. That's how long it takes for a man to die with no air to breathe. But maybe that was because Bean smoked cigarettes, huh, cuz? Maybe a muthafucka that be deep sea diving and swimming can hold their breath a little longer. What you think, cuz?"

I didn't feel like idle conversation at two in the morning. I was tired and ready to go. "I'm gone, slim," I said and turned around to walk back to my car. I heard Khadafi laughing behind me.

.CHAPTER TWENTY-EIGHT.
KHADAFI

I didn't want to go home. I couldn't go to my aunt's house because she would be grieving over her younger brother's death, just like me. My father's house was also out of the question. I hadn't said more than five words to Fuller since I been home. When I went to jail, he moved to Virginia, remarried and had another son. All throughout my bid, I barely heard from him. I decided halfway through doing my time to close the door on whatever relationship we had. I still feel the same way now.

Killing my childhood best friend had a sobering effect on me that I never experienced before. I actually felt remorse, but not regret. There's a difference, you know. As I drove around the streets of D.C., I thought about how I had tricked Bean into going down Anacostia with me and getting drunk. Then I turned my gun on him, duct taped him up and then called Boo. I had no luck finding Poo, so Bean would have to suffice as the victim of my frustrations.

His days had been numbered ever since I found out that he had fucked Kemie while I was in jail. I needed to lash out at somebody and unfortunately Bean's number got called. I thought about the pain now in my back as well as in my heart. The pain in my back came from me dragging Bean's body over to the wall at the riverbank. I had to lift the body a little at a time to get it over the railing. I still remember the splash the body made as it hit the water, sunk and then reappeared. I didn't stick around to see the body float away.

The question of who killed my uncle still lingered in my head as I pulled to a complete stop in front of the house. The house had red brick and blue wood shutters. It was a house I'd been to a lot in the last few weeks. I pulled into a parking space and killed the engine. A bunch of different questions rushed to my mind as I sat and stared at the house. I quieted the voice in my head and got out of the truck. I looked at my watch. It was now 2:28 a.m. Even though it was the wee hours of the morning, it was the only place I wanted to be.

I walked up to the front door and steadied my nerves. I pulled out my cell phone and dialed her number. On the fourth ring, she picked up.

"Hello?" Shawnay said groggily.

"Shawnay, it's me, Khadafi."

There was a pause. "Khadafi, do you know what time it is?"

"It's 2:30 a.m. on the nose."

"Are you hurt or something? In jail? What?"

"None of the above, Shawnay. I just found out that somebody killed my uncle and I need somebody to talk to."

"Come on over, Khadafi. I gotta get up in a few hours anyway," she said.

"I'm already here. I'm standing outside. I been here for awhile tryna decide if I wanted to wake you up."

"I guess I know what you decided, huh? Give me a few minutes to get myself together and then I'll come to the door. Bye, Khadafi."

Ten minutes later, the door opened and Shawnay stood there dressed in a t-shirt and shorts. I looked down at her bare feet.

"Why are you staring at my feet?"

"Because they're beautiful. Can I come in?"

"Come on." Shawnay opened the door and let me in.

We walked into the kitchen on the first level of the house. Shawnay grabbed two mugs out of the cabinet and emptied a powder into both. Then she added water and placed both cups in the microwave. The microwave beeped a minute later and she retrieved the two cups.

"You smell like alcohol, so I assume you've been drinking. In light of the circumstances, I can understand why. Have a seat on the barstool by the counter and drink this coffee. It's a blend of hazelnut and chocolate. It's good. Drink it. Then we'll talk."

My eyes focused on the beautiful woman who leaned on the counter. I never looked away as I sipped the funny-tasting liquid. The silence that enveloped us was too loud for me. I finished off the coffee and said, "That was good. I needed that."

Shawnay simply smiled and responded, "I'm glad you liked it. Now, tell me about your uncle."

I did just that for the better part of an hour. I never knew that I had so much to say. I guess what they say about liquor loosening the tongue was true. By the time I finished venting about my life, Shawnay was next to me on a stool at the counter. Being so close to me summoned all kinds of thoughts and feelings and I wondered if she felt the vibe.

Then she looked at me.

When our gaze held each other hostage, I knew that she did feel it.

At that moment I did what felt natural to me. I moved in close and kissed her. To my surprise, she kissed me back. I broke the kiss. I rose from my stool and stood behind her. I wrapped my arms around Shawnay's waist and kissed the back of her neck and then the sides. I heard a soft moan escape her mouth as I pulled her up from the stool. I turned Shawnay around to face me and kissed her.

This time Shawnay broke our kiss and said, "I have never—"

I cut her sentence short by kissing her again. My hands had a mind of their own as they felt all over Shawnay as we kissed. The next thing I knew, she pulled me into the basement. There was a sofa, a bar and a television. Shawnay opened my jacket revealing my torn shirt. She never said a word as she removed them both from my body. I felt her hands and her tongue on me. I heard the sound of my zipper being unzipped, and then my dick was free. Before I closed my eyes and surrendered myself to the moment, the last thing I saw was Shawnay drop to her knees. I heard her say, "Please excuse my hands." Then I was in her mouth. I closed my eyes and gave in to the pleasure I felt.

131

.CHAPTER TWENTY-NINE.
UMAR

"**I**f for any reason you are stopped by law enforcement, just show them this," the C.O. in R-n-D said. "This is your identification."

I was handed a piece of paper that said I had just been released from the United States Penitentiary Beaumont. A computer generated photo of me was on the paper as well. I folded it up and put it in my pocket.

"And here's the money that you had in your account." The officer handed me an envelope. "That's a lot of money, Howard. Don't get robbed on your first day home."

The C.O. laughed, but I didn't find that shit funny. I paid the redneck no mind as I pulled the money from the envelope and counted it. There were forty-eight big face hundred-dollar bills in my palm. Folding the bankroll, I put it in my sock. Old habits were hard to break.

"Let's go, Howard. Your plane leaves at 7:50 a.m," my case manager Mr. Zito said to me.

The van ride to George Bush International Airport was about an hour away. I laid back in my seat and daydreamed about what freedom would feel like after six years. I fell asleep. The van coming to a complete stop woke me up. I was ushered through the security check points as if I was a major celebrity. A few minutes later, I was boarding the airplane. As the plane ascended into the heavens and then leveled off at 30,000 feet, I knew that it was real. I was free.

The flight was scheduled to take two hours and some change. After snacking on some peanuts that the stewardess gave me, I sat back and thought about a friend of mine named

Curtis Martin. He wasn't as fortunate as me. I had made it out of prison, but he hadn't. Curtis left me and went to a penitentiary in Florence, Colorado. He was killed there six months later. I thought about Tyrone Johnson who got killed in Pollock. People lost their lives in prison every day. I thought about Marvin "Funk" Moseley, who people say the police in Oklahoma killed. And I wondered did Funk kill himself to escape his reality of doing life in prison. I was so caught up in my thoughts that the plane ride was over in no time. When I got off the plane, I went in search of a pay phone. I found one, called Boo and told him that I was waiting for him.

After I hung up, I walked over to the subway station.

"Slim, your beard big as shit," Boo said as I got into the sleek, gold Cadillac STS. "You look like you just came back from Mecca."

I laughed at what Boo said. "At least I got one. You need to stop bullshittin' and let yours grow back. You out here looking like Screwface on *Marked for Death*. All you wanna do is keep faking like you Jamaican. You Ja-faking."

"You tryna jone, huh, Gonzo?"

"Naw, you got it, ock." I stared out the window at all the major construction going on as we reached the city. "What's that right there, ock?"

Boo's eyes followed my finger. "That's that new Washington Nationals' Stadium. All the surrounding construction is the hotels and shit they building around it. All up and down M Street they building big ass buildings. But that ain't shit. Wait until you see the new Southside."

"The new Southside?" I was confused. "What new Southside?"

"Wait until we cross the bridge and you'll see it. Everything has changed. Southeast look like Northern Virginia now. They tearing down all the projects and putting townhouses in their places. My aunt said they gotta be out of Barry Farms before January 2009."

"I read that in the *Washington Post* a while back. I wonder what they doing all that for?"

"It's obvious, slim. The white people tryna run all the blacks out of the city. They want the Chocolate City to be vanilla again. By building houses that the blacks can't afford, you in essence send them in search of new shelter. That's why P.G. County and all the surrounding counties now have more blacks than ever before.

I thought about the words Boo had just said. They had a ring of truth to them.

"Slim, they got an IHOP on Alabama Avenue."

"Alabama Avenue? Where at?" I inquired.

"Right across from where 15th Place used to be. Around the corner from Congress Park."

"Get the fuck outta here with that shit."

"You think I'm bullshittin'? Wait until you see this shit. They got Miegos living on Branywine Street in condominiums. I'm telling you, shit is wild out here."

I saw the infamous Big Chair once we crossed the 11th Street Bridge. It was good to see that joint. That's when a real Southeast nigga knew he was home for real. "I see the Big Chair is still the same."

"You almost didn't see that. They took that joint for a minute, my girl told me. She said after a strong outcry by the longtime residents on this side, they put it back. They tried to say that they only took it to do repairs on it."

"I can't imagine Southeast without the Big Chair."

"Get over it, slim. They do what they wanna do out this muthafucka. I couldn't imagine D.C. without the Awakening Statue down Haynes Point, but they took that."

"They took that joint?" I asked genuinely shocked.

"That joint been gone. It was gone when I got home. They moved that joint out to Maryland somewhere. Haynes Point is all grass and gravel now."

"That's crazy."

As we cruised up Good Hope Road, I noticed how much everything had changed.

"You think that's crazy. Wait until you see how niggas dressing in the hood."

"Oh yeah?" I replied.

"The city is some shit now, slim. We used to have our own identity. You used to be able to spot a real D.C. nigga in a crowd. These bamma-ass niggas done fucked the game up for real. The bitches dress in anything. All these lunchin' ass colors and wild shoes and shit. They wearing these big geeking ass high heels. All the niggas out here were wannabe Dipset affiliates. No bullshit, slim. Niggas think they Kanye West, Lil Wayne and Jim Jones out this joint. These niggas wearing tight jeans and little ass T-shirts. I ain't never seen no wild shit like this before in my life. Everything is Black Label this and Black Label that. That hip hop shit has driven these muthafuckas mad out here. Niggas wearing blue Timberland boots."

I cracked up laughing. I couldn't believe what Boo was saying, but it was true. As we turned up 16th Street, I saw everything that he had just pointed out. We both became silent. I looked out the window in amazement. Things really were different. The cars, rims, clothes, the music that blared from passing speakers. The whole attitude of Washington, D.C. had changed. I couldn't believe it. I glanced at my watch. It read 11:36 a.m. "Where Khadafi at?"

"He down Capers, tryna find out who killed his uncle."

Ten minutes later, we pulled onto Southern Avenue and parked in front of the HOBO shop. It was just as I remembered.

"This was your favorite spot back in the day, you said. So I figured that you'd want to check out the new HOBO' 08, shit. C'mon."

I followed Boo into the store and I was surprised to see that my man Moochie that owned the store was still in it. We embraced. "Moochie, what's up, slim?"

"Ain't shit, soldier. Hold on for a minute." He walked into the back of the store and shouted. "Angie! Come out here and see who's out here."

Angie was Moochie's wife. She and I used to bet on all the William Joppy fights since HOBO was the sportswear that sponsored him. Angie still looked good.

"I know that ain't Lil' Harold?" she said.

I smiled. "It's me. How you doing, Angie?"

"Boy, look at you with all that hair on your face. When did you come home?"

"Today. About forty minutes ago, actually."

"Well, it's definitely good to see you. Go ahead and pick you out some stuff. On me."

"You ain't gotta do that, Angie. My men got me. I'm straight," I protested.

"Boy, if you don't let me get my blessings. I ain't tryna hear that I'm a'ight shit. You need some HOBO gear. We run the city. You ain't heard?"

I glanced around at all the mannequins and noticed that all the outfits looked different. The jeans and shit looked smaller, tighter. I heard Boo snicker behind me. I wanted to laugh, too. But I didn't wanna disrespect Angie and Moochie, so I picked out a couple of 'fits. I thanked them for their hospitality and promised to come back soon.

In the car, Boo joned my ass out. All I could do was laugh all the way to Capers.

I saw the midnight blue Infiniti truck before I saw Khadafi. I had to admit, the truck was a bad joint. The tinted window came down and Khadafi's head appeared. I jumped out the car and I walked toward the truck. Khadafi met me in the street. I threw my hands up with my fists balled up. Khadafi immediately did the same. I threw a few jabs and side stepped a few that Khadafi countered. Khadafi weaved a lightning quick combination that I threw at him. He threw a few back. One landed flush on my chin, the others I caught easily.

I stepped back, grabbed my chin and smiled. "You still hit like a broad," I teased.

"And you are still too slow to outbox me."

Breathing a little heavy, we embraced in the street. It was good to be home and to be with my men.

"It's good to see you, cuz, especially out here in the real world. Breathe the fresh air. Remember the times when we never thought we'd see the streets again?" Khadafi said.

"Hell yeah, especially when that body dropped in Beaumont, ock. I ain't gon' lie. I was scared as hell," I added.

I wanted to shed a tear. One solitary tear for all the struggles that we had to overcome together.

"We dreamed about this, cuz. All of us out here together. Three the hard way. How they gon' stop three of us, when one of us is too much? We about to eat good for real, cuz. I'ma see to that. On my dead uncle's grave, I'ma see to that."

I listened to Khadafi without saying a word. I felt what he said and all that, but I was feeling something else, too. Never once did Khadafi mention Ameen or acknowledge the fact that Ameen was a part of the dream, too. Our dream was the four of us, not three. It was supposed to have eventually been four the hard way. Leaving Ameen out didn't sit well with me. Was it just a slip of the tongue? Or had Khadafi already forgotten Ameen and the selfless act he committed to save us? Was I reading too much into what he didn't say as opposed to what he did said? Was I overreacting?

I thought of Ameen still in Beaumont, in a cell, probably working out and felt disturbed. Khadafi and Boo had never even asked me about Ameen and his well being. That crushed me the most as I stood there in the street with them. I tried my best to disguise my discomfort and hurt. It was time for me to pray to Allah. I looked at my watch. It was time for Jum'ah.

.CHAPTER THIRTY.
MONEY

The gunshot wound to the side of my head had healed nicely. My hair grew back and covered that area completely. I was starting to look like I did before that fateful night. Why couldn't a man be left alone to get money in the streets without thirsty niggas coming for his head? That was the question for the ages. I remembered something that my father told me a long time ago: "All birds fly. Some fly higher than others, but they all have one thing in common. They all come to the ground to eat."

I gave that saying a lot of thought and then pronounced it a true bill. No matter how high I was able to fly in the drug game, I still had to come back to the ground to eat. And coming to the ground to eat made me prey just like everybody else. I put the windows in my truck up and turned on the AC. The heat of the early afternoon was becoming unbearable. At the intersection of East Capital Street and Benning Road, I made a right turn and headed toward C Street. I spotted Cochise's black van parked on the opposite side of the street as I drove by. I rode to the corner and quickly made a U-turn. A minute later, I was parked behind Cochise.

I blew my horn once and motioned for him to come get in the truck.

"What's up, Co? What's so important?" I asked.

"Khadafi and the dude with the dreads are in that building," he said casually and then nodded at a building across the street.

I looked across the street and saw the building he spoke of. I read the sign that hung on the building's façade. "Masjid Al-Islam."

"How do you know they in there?"

"'Cause I know. I saw them go in there about thirty minutes ago."

"And that's when you called me?"

"Yea. I figured you'd want to watch me crush them, so I called you."

"And how did you come to see them here?"

Cochise gave me this look I can't describe. Then he said, "Let me do me. I got this."

"I know you got it. I just asked—"

"If you must know, when I was following Khadafi that day, I noticed that he had a couple of Islamic bumper stickers on the back of his Range Rover. One had Arabic script on it that I couldn't read. The other sticker read "Support Masjid Al-Islam." At the time I didn't think anything of it. Later, I remembered that he became Muslim in prison and changed his name to Khadafi. I know a little about Islam because my man Buck is Muslim. I know that they go to service on Fridays, so I decided to post up out here every Friday to see if Khadafi showed up and worshipped. I don't know how he survived the last hit. Man, I flip—"

"You didn't do shit, slim," I said, cutting Cochise off. I saw the smug look on his face and vented. "You tried to flip him, but instead, all you did was kill his truck."

"Shit happens, moe. What can I say? That nigga had a guardian angel or some shit. It is what it is, though. I missed once, but I won't miss again."

"I sure hope not."

"I also found out a little info on his buddy with the dreads. They call him Boo. He's from over Northeast somewhere. I can get his whole hookup if you want me to, to try and recover some of the money. Either way, it don't even matter because I'm about to smash both of these niggas today."

"Go take care of that business, then."

I kept my eyes glued to Cochise as he got out my truck and walked back up to the van. I was ready to leave. I didn't need to stick around to see the outcome. But just as I started the Hummer and was about to pull away from the curb, I thought back to the night I was robbed and shot, then left for dead. I remembered how helpless I felt, how vulnerable I was. I remembered how I was commanded to sit on the curb with my head in my lap. I thought about what I had lost. I thought about the brief struggle between me and my captor. I remembered being shot and blacking out. I thought about the four shell casings that the detective said were found at the scene of the crime. He tried to put two in my head. He tried to kill me, despite having the money already. Khadafi had tried to take my life. The longer I sat and thought, the angrier I became. I killed the truck's engine and decided to stay awhile. I wanted to stick around after all. I wanted to watch Khadafi and his man feel the same things I felt that night. I wanted to watch them die. All of a sudden, my head started pounding. The migraine headaches that I had been experiencing off and on since being shot had returned. I reached into the compartment on the Hummer's dash console for a pain reliever. Then suddenly, I decided against taking one. I sat back and endured the pain. I welcomed it. The only thing that would make me truly feel better was Khadafi's death.

.CHAPTER THIRTY-ONE.
KHADAFI

"**A**nd verily the best speech is the book of Allah. And the best guidance is the guidance of the Rasoolalah, Muhammad Ibn Abdullah. The worst affairs are the newly invented matters. And all newly invented matters are an innovation. Every innovation is going astray. And everything going astray leads to the hellfire..." the Imam said and finished his khutbah by saying, "If I have said anything wrong here today, it comes from me. If I have said anything right and good, then it comes from Allah. I ask Allah to send blessings upon Muhammad and the family of Muhammad as he sent blessings upon Ibrahim and the family of Ibrahim, Yaa ay you hal-lathee na amanuwt, taqul-laha haqqa tuqa te hee wa laa, ta-muw tuna illa wa antum muslimun, lqamati-salat..."

It felt good being in the presence of the Muslims. I sat and listened to the muezzin call the lqamah before rising.

"...Allahu Akbar. Allahu Akbar, Ash hadu anal ilaha illalah, Ash hadu anna Muhammadan Rasoolalah...

I stepped up to the second rank and stood in between Umar and Boo. We stood heel to heel and shoulder to shoulder as did all the Muslims. Then the Imam led the Jum'ah prayer.

"I heard a lot about Imam Musa from the Chaplain in Cumberland." Umar stated. "We listened to him on some CDs. Everything he just said about apostates had me thinking he was talking directly to me. The khutbah had me on my jihad-al nafs type stuff."

I smiled at Umar. I felt the same way. Even though I believed wholeheartedly in Islam and the Creator, there was a dark side to me that I couldn't get rid of. "I know how you feel, cuz. I feel like the biggest hypocrite in the world. I'm out here twelve feet deep in the dunyah. Insha Allah, one day, I'ma get back. I just pray to Allah that I don't die in a state of kufr. I wanna change, but right now, I'm in too deep. I'm still tryna catch the dudes that shot at me and killed my uncle."

"You might've done that already, slim. How many niggas have you crushed already, tryna find out who got at your uncle?" Boo asked as he grabbed his shoes off the shelf and put them on.

There were people that I slumped that I hadn't shared with my men. Not out of mistrust, but the fact that I didn't want them to know that I used Marquette's death to get at the dudes who fucked Kemie while I was in prison. I didn't want them to see my weakness for a woman who was a whore. "I only got at a few dudes. I still need something concrete. So, I'ma press the issue until I know what happened for sure on both fronts. Cuz, this a personal mission of mine. Don't feel compelled to roll if you don't want to. I can—"

"You saying anything right now?" Boo said, cutting me off. "I done came this far. What I look like abandoning you now? Come on, slim, you be on your anything too much. But I got a question for you. After we get the dudes that brought both moves, then what?"

"I'ma lay back." I said with no conviction at all. When I was done tying the laces of my Prada tennis shoes. I led the way to the basement of the Masjid where the food was.

"Who you think you telling that bulljive to, slim? It's impossible for you to lay back. The ski mask is all you know. That and bodying sh—. My bad. We still in the Masjid," Boo continued.

"Maybe you right." I said. "Let's get this food and bounce. We gave Allah his. Now it's time for my man Umar to get his."

When we stepped out of the Masjid, I noticed that the ground was a little wet. I concluded that it must've drizzled a little while we were inside the Masjid. Umar and Boo were debating about something Islamic as we walked down the step in front of the Masjid with throngs of other Muslims. I ignored my comrades as my paranoia kicked in and caused me to scan the street for any enemy faces. My love for trucks is what would later save our lives. A metallic silver Hummer H2 sitting on 24s caught my attention. It was one just like the one I had looked at before deciding on copping an Infiniti. That's when I noticed the black caravan that sat in front of the Hummer. It took my mind mere seconds to flashback to the day I was shot. I vividly saw the man who approached the Range and opened fire. I saw the black caravan that he drove. That black caravan and the one I now stared at were one and the same.

Time moved in slow motion as I reacted. I reached for my hammer and pushed Umar at the same time.

"Boo, it's a hit, cuz!" I shouted as I saw the dude who had tried to kill me another day, attempting to do the same today.

The dude carried a tennis racket case. As we locked eyes, he raised the case and fired. People on every side of me screamed and scrambled to get out of the gunman's aim. I saw people hit by bullets fall in my path as I rushed to take cover behind the closest car. I heard shots of a different caliber and knew that Boo was returning fire. I looked around the car I crouched behind and saw the man with the case. I rose to my full height and sent several shots his way. I tried to take his head off. The sound of an empty gun brought me out of my haze and my mind said, "Get away from here."

I saw Boo retreating and running up the block in the opposite direction of my truck. When I turned back around, something else caught my attention. The driver's side window of the Hummer was now down. A face stared at me. We locked eyes. Then the person smiled. With that face and smile etched in my mind, I turned and ran in the same direction that Boo had just run.

THE ULTIMATE SACRIFICE

"This is Maria Wilson of City Under Siege Fox News, reporting to you live from the corner of Benning Road and C Street. Behind me here, medical technicians are still scrambling to attend to all the victims of a broad daylight attack on a local mosque. D.C. Police are on the scene and investigating this crime scene as we speak. I've been told that the death toll here has reached double figures."

Witnesses say that as Muslim worshippers exited the mosque behind me, a lone gunman opened fire on the crowd. Witnesses also report that someone in the crowd may have returned fire on the gunman. The gunman then fled the scene in a dark colored van. The make and model of that van are unknown. D.C. Police are asking that anyone who may have witnessed this brutal attack or has any information that may lead to the arrest of the gunman, to please call D.C. Crime Stoppers at the number on your screen. Authorities are also looking at this horrific crime as a possible hate crime or terrorist attack. Homeland Security agents and the F.B.I. are also on the scene. More on this story as details become available. Aniyah, back to you."

I hit the off button on the remote and watched the screen go blank. I could feel Umar and Boo staring at me as if they could see through me. As if they could see my pain and turmoil. As if they could see my anger and joy at the same time. I sat in Sanaa's living room and mourned for all the innocent people killed at the Masjid. I silently prayed to Allah to grant them all paradise, but there would be no paradise for me, that I was sure of. I had unintentionally caused the deaths of many.

How had my enemies tracked me to my place of worship? How did they know I'd be there? The silence in the room threatened to grab me and strangle me. My mind kept replaying the events of the afternoon that occurred over two hours ago. I wondered without asking, how had Boo and Umar met up at the same place after running in different directions? I thought about the face from the dead. A face that I thought I'd never see again was back and continued to haunt me hours after trying to kill me for the second time.

Boo and Umar remained silent. They both left me alone with my thoughts, with my pain and my anger. All I saw was the smile. The perfect smile of the man who wanted me dead. I couldn't get Money's smile out of my head. This was my penance, my torture.

I was thankful to be among the living and also thankful that neither of my men were hurt. But I was still in pain. As the realization that Money was behind the two attempts on my life, it also dawned on me that he was the person responsible for my uncle's death. How do I know? It was all in the smile. All of the conversations me and my uncle had that pertained to Money came to mind. I knew that I had to kill Money, but the how part eluded me. I engaged myself in a mental battle of tug-of-war. I pulled and tugged until finally the answer came to me.

Umar finally broke the silence. "What the fuck was that all about? Who was that tryna knock our heads off at the Masjid?"

I locked eyes with Boo momentarily and then turned away. "We—me and Boo went on a move and robbed a dude named Money. I had the dude hemmed up while Boo went to his house and got the money and the drugs. I told the dude that if he cooperated, I'd let him go. He did. I didn't. I shot the nigga in the head twice. I rolled out and left him leaking on the sidewalk. I thought he was dead, but he's not. He's alive and he wants blood."

"How did he know you'd be at the Masjid today?"

I thought again about what Umar had just asked. "Cuz, that shit been eating at me the whole time I been sitting here. But your guess is as good as mine. All I know is that the dude that brought the move today is the same dude that tried to hit me the last time."

"That was Money?" Umar asked.

"Naw, Money was sitting in the silver Hummer parked behind the black van."

"Didn't you tell me that the dude who tried to get you that day was in a black van?" Boo interjected.

"Yeah, cuz. That's what saved our lives. I spotted the van as soon as we came out of the Masjid. I saw the dude coming toward us. That's when I pushed Umar and called out to you that it was a hit. I saw it coming. The nigga had a black tennis racket case in his hand. It ain't no tennis courts nowhere in the area."

"The dude that brought the move wasn't concerned about nothing but killing. He wasn't even masked up," Umar added.

"I'm hip. And that's the second time he did that. It works in my favor, though. His indiscretions are gonna help me find out who he is. And when I find out, it's curtains for his ass. His show is over. But what fucks me up the most is the nigga, Money. He smiled at me right before I ran off. That smirk on his face still haunts me."

"I feel you, slim," Boo said and stood up. He paced around the living room. "But why would the dude Money show himself like that? You wasn't hip to him. I damn sure wasn't hip to him and for all he knew, we thought he was dead. Why would he do that? And my next question is the most important one. Do you think Money is behind Marquette's death?"

"For sure. Cuz, I been in this murder game for almost fourteen years. I know the killing field. Can't nobody tell me shit about the mind of a killer. You have to be a killer to understand another killer. What motivates him or her to kill, etcetera. The dude Money has the mind of a killer. He couldn't resist not showing me his face. Him showing himself to me was his way of saying, 'Fuck you. I'ma kill you and, by the way, I killed your uncle.'" It was the smile, cuz. The arrogance. The cockiness. The smile said it all to me."

"How does the smile tell you that Money killed Marquette?" Umar asked.

"It was all in the reason why he rolled the window down and showed me his face. He figured it out. Some kinda way, he figured out that my uncle was behind what happened to him. He survived the hit. He's fucked up about the money and the shit that we took. He put two and two together and came up with four. Either him or the dude he put on me, killed my uncle or now he's after me."

Boo stopped pacing the floor suddenly. "Then, that would mean that Marquette-"

I nodded. "Told Money about me," I said, finishing his sentence. "I already figured that out, cuz. The news report and my family said that my uncle was beaten, stabbed and shot. They tortured the info out of him. I can't be fucked up about that. The day after we made the move, my uncle questioned me about Money being dead and why we hadn't heard about it or seen it on the news. Me being me, I explained it away and said that I was sure that he was dead. My arrogance came back to get me. Money tried to have me killed... twice. There won't be a third time."

"I can't believe this shit. I ain't even been home a full day and I almost got killed. I haven't even seen my mother, my family, nothing. I ain't even got no pussy yet. This is crazy." Umar said as he rubbed his temples. "Aye, Boo, get me something to drink." To me, he said, "You still haven't explained how the dudes knew to come to the Masjid. They didn't follow us there. How did they know we were gon' be there?"

"I don't know the answer to that question, cuz. But I plan to find out."

Here I was again. Right back in the same place I was the night this all started. I sat in the Infiniti and stared at the building across the street. The sign on the door read: U.S. Parole Office.

I rubbed my eyes and tried to erase the images of my uncle being tortured from my mind. For days, I had called my uncle and he never answered. That was unheard of. As greedy as Marquette was, he would've been all over me to go on the next lick. When it came to that cheddar, there wasn't no such thing as a vacation with Marquette. Greed was what propelled my uncle forward and caused him to cross all his men. He was loyal only to the money. It was always about the money. Money was the root of all evil. Hadn't I fell victim to the same thing, the money? With the exception of the dudes I killed for my mother, Damien and Kemie, the rest were killed for money. It was also the reason my uncle was now dead.

When my uncle first put the move together to get Money, he suggested that it would be best to catch Money at the P.O.'s office. It was then that Marquette had explained to me that the P.O. was a woman named Thomasina Jones. The same Mrs. Jones, who was his P.O. as well. According to my uncle, Mrs. Jones was married to a doctor, had two children and a picture-perfect life. "But everything that glitters ain't gold," he said. Mrs. Jones loved criminals. She was turned on by bad boys and thugs—young thugs. Marquette told me that he had been fucking Mrs. Jones for about a year when she suddenly ended the relationship.

My uncle said he later learned that she was fucking a friend of his who also was his drug connect, Money. When the opportunity arose, he wanted to hit Money. That opportunity eventually arose and the rest was a wrap, as they say. Now, here I sit waiting for the sun to go down so that I can pay Mrs. Jones a visit.

The fact that Mrs. Jones loved to work late was a blessing in disguise. I knocked on her office door, and then let myself in.

"May I help you?" The lady behind the desk asked.

"I was told to come and see you. Are you Thomasina Jones?"

"I'm Mrs. Jones. And you are?" she said and she stood up.

I couldn't believe how sexy she was. Mrs. Jones was wearing gray pinstriped slacks that hugged her every curve and a black blouse. The material of the blouse was sheer and you could easily see the contours of her breasts. Her hair was pulled up and around into a bun. The wire rimmed glasses that she wore gave her a scholarly, yet lustful flair.

I walked across the room and pulled my gun. "You can call me Mr. Ruger. Don't do anything stupid and you might live through this. Do you understand?" I watched Mrs. Jones nod her head. "Good. I'ma make this real simple. I came here for some information. If I get it, I'll leave and you can act like you've never ever seen me. Do you understand that?"

She nodded again. I knew that she was afraid and that was a good sign. "I need to see your file on one of your clients. I don't know his real name. All I have is his nickname. I'm gonna describe him and hope that you can help me. If you bullshit me, I'm gonna kill you. I know that you have a family. Your husband is a doctor and you have two children. Do you wanna make it home to your family?"

"Yes." Mrs. Jones said clearly.

"About a month ago, one of your clients came to see you here. It was late. Around 6 or 7 o'clock in the evening. He was driving a black four-door Cadillac Escalade. He was wearing black jeans, black Prada boots, and a black Hugo Boss sweatshirt with the drawstring in the collar. He's about six feet and weighs about 180 pounds. Do you know who I'm talking about?"

"I-I-I-I don't—"

I pulled the hammer back on the single action Ruger .45. "Don't lie now. I know he came here and I also know that you two had sex in this office." I threw that lie out there to see what response it would get. "I followed him here and I was outside when he left you. I don't want to kill—"

"His name is Diamonte Smith."

"Do you have a picture of him in his file? Something on the computer?" I asked.

Mrs. Jones dropped into her seat and pulled the computer keyboard in front of her. I went and stood beside her to make sure she wasn't trying to do anything slick. Her fingers moved across the keyboard in a blur. A minute later, the screen came alive with information. I was suddenly looking into the face of my newest enemy.

"I need whatever addresses you have for him and phone numbers. Print that out for me, please. And make sure I get a printout of his face. Blow it up for me. Thank you."

Mrs. Jones did everything I requested. The thought of me killing her crossed my mind, but I shook it off. I had another idea. Once the printer beeped and spit out the papers I needed, I used the gun to trace the outline of Mrs. Jones pretty face. "You did your part and now I'ma keep my word and leave. But I have to tell you one thing. My beef is with this dude, not you. Don't make this a personal beef between you and me. Why? Because you are at a disadvantage. I know you, but you don't know me. I also know your husband." I paused to let that lie sink in. "I also know where you live. And most of all, I know where your children go to school. If you breathe a word about this visit to anybody, I'ma kill everybody that you love. Do you understand me?"

"Yes. I understand you perfectly."

"Good. Before I leave, let me just say that you are the prettiest parole officer I have ever seen."

A small smile crossed the lady's face as I made my exit.

Our Alaskan crab legs arrived at the table steaming. I grabbed a cluster and broke a leg off, then dipped the crabmeat into a small bowl of melted butter. Our table fell silent as the three of us tore into the crab legs and ten pounds of spiced shrimp.

"How did you get his address?" Boo asked and wiped his mouth with a napkin.

I purposely took my time downing the last of my lemon-lime PowerAde drink before speaking.

"That's neither here nor there. The fact is that I have it and I'm tryna end all of this tomorrow. I just ran the plan down to y'all. All I need to know is who's with me and who's not."

"Who are you referring to, ock? Me?" Umar asked defensively.

"Cuz, when have you ever known me to bite my tongue? I said what I said and that question was for both of y'all. But check this out, Umar. I respect the fact that you just got home and all that, but we are a team. If you ain't tryna roll on this move, I can understand and respect that. That nigga tried to hit me and Boo, not you. You wasn't home when the beef started. But you definitely profited from it. That hundred grand that you about to tear into, belongs to the dude that's tryna kill us. You can decide to not roll, even though we might need you, and I ain't gonna be mad at you. The choice is yours. The move we about to make is a strong move and it's gonna take strong nig--"

"Are you questioning my manhood, Khadafi?" Umar asked visibly upset.

"Never that, cuz. Never that."

"I'ma go home and see my family and at least see what a hundred thousand looks like before I make my decision. I'll hit y'all in the morning and let y'all know what's up. Boo, I'm ready to bounce. Drop me off."

I was still picking over the leftover shrimp long after Boo and Umar had left. The questions that Umar asked me continued to dog my thoughts. They were questions that I hoped to get answers to. If not, then they'd go unanswered, but either way Money would die.

My eyes fell on the paper in front of me with the addresses on it. One address was for the house that we robbed. I went there after leaving Mrs. Jones' office. That house was deserted and up for sale. The second address was for Money's parents. It was the address that Money lived at when he first came home from jail. It was the address where I planned to go tomorrow. It was time to change the game a little. The hunted was about to become the hunter. And we all know that it ain't no fun when the rabbit got the gun.

.CHAPTER THIRTY-TWO.
KHADAFI

"**I** don't know for sure how many people are in there, but there didn't sound like a lot," I said as I closed the flip phone and put it in my pocket. I had called Money's parents and asked for him to see if he was there. He wasn't, but they were. I looked at Boo and Umar. They were as ready as they would ever be. "Y'all know what to do, right?" They both nodded their heads. "When I call y'all, y'all hurry up and come in. We gotta secure the whole house first, then I'll handle the rest. Y'all got me on that?"

"Got it," Boo said.

"I hear you."

"Aye, cuz?" I said turning toward Umar. "I appreciate you rolling with us."

"Let's get this over with," Umar replied.

We separated and went to our vehicles. I was in a stolen Mazda MPV and Boo was driving his Cadillac. Our destination was four blocks away. We made it there in two minutes flat.

I stepped out of the van that had a sign on top of it that read "Tony Ramono's Pizzeria." Giving myself the once-over, I was ready. I balanced the two pizza boxes in my hand and walked up the path leading to the front door of the house. I rung the doorbell and waited. A few minutes later, a voice on the other side of the door said, "Who's there?"

"Tony Ramono's Pizzeria, sir."

"Uh...hold on for a minute, please."

I could hear the same man who answered the phone and the door moments ago, ask somebody else in the house if they ordered a pizza. I silently hoped that somebody in the house was hungry. I needed somebody to open the door. That was the key to a successful mission. After hearing bits and pieces of a conversation that I couldn't decipher, the man came back to the door.

"Uh...I'm sorry, but nobody at this address ordered a pizza. Wrong address."

My spirits nosedived. Thinking quick on my feet, I improvised. "This is 21810 Summerset Lane, right?"

"Yes," the man answered.

"Well, sir, could you please just sign this waiver form saying that I did come to this address to deliver the pizza?"

"But, if we didn't order a pizza, why would I have to sign—"

"It's the new policy, sir. There were complaints of deliverymen never showing up to deliver pizzas. Signatures are required. I'm just trying to protect my job. Could you please sign the form?"

When I heard the locks click, my adrenaline soared. I was ready to pounce. As soon as I heard the door open, I opened the pizza box and withdrew the Mach II with the noise reduction device on it. I turned around and put the barrel of the Mach in the man's face. "Back your ass into the house and don't say a word. If you do, I'ma kill everybody in there."

"What do you—"

I swung the Mach upward and cracked the man on the jaw. "Didn't I just say, don't say a word?" We both stepped into the house. Once the door was shut, I dropped the pizza boxes and looked around the house. Nobody else was in sight. Hitting the walkie-talkie button on my cell phone, I said, "Come on in."

A minute or so later, Umar and Boo entered the house. "Cuz, both of y'all go through the house and round everybody up." I turned back to the man. "Lay on the floor and don't move." After he complied I asked, "How many people are in here with you? And don't lie to me."

"What do you want from us?" the man asked me. "We don't have any money in here."

"That's not what I asked you. You got five seconds to answer my question or die right now."

"Three," he said in defeat. "Me, my wife and my grandson."

"That's more like it." I turned back to Umar and Boo. "Y'all heard the man. Go get 'em." I figured that the man on the floor had to be Money's father. "Do you have a son named Diamonte?"

"Yes."

"Thanks for being honest. Listen, I'm here for one thing and one thing only. I'm not here to rob you and I don't wanna hurt anybody here, but I will if I have to. I need your help. I want your son, Diamonte. In the streets they call him Money. I want him. If you help me, you, your wife and grandson will survive this. If you don't help me, I'ma kill everybody in here. As simple as that. It's your choice to make. Think about it. One life to save three. It's the ultimate sacrifice. Your son's life for your own. Surely, he'd give his life to save you. But don't sacrifice the lives of your wife and grandson to save his. It doesn't equal out, especially when I'm gonna kill him eventually, anyway.

A noise in the stairwell diverted my attention. It was Boo and Umar coming down the stairs with the wife and kid. I watched the shapely older woman descend the stairs with a look of terror on her face. Her resemblance to Phylicia Rashad was uncanny. "Sit her and shorty over there on the couch."

The woman was openly crying now. The little boy looked to be around seven or eight years old. He was dressed in Power Rangers pajamas. "As a matter of fact, find something to tie everybody up with, cuz." Boo came back moments later with a clothesline and a knife. Once everybody was tied up, I surveyed the scene and said. "Let the games begin."

.CHAPTER THIRTY-THREE.
Boo

Watching Khadafi work the room was like watching a movie. I had to admit, in any situation, he was a natural.

"What's your name, cuz?" Khadafi asked.

"My name is William," the man replied.

"Is Money your only son, William?"

"Yes."

"William, always remember that you can make more sons. Is this Money's child?" Khadafi asked, pointing at the little boy tied up on the couch. The father shook his head no. "Good. The kid won't lose a father, just an uncle. He'll be a'ight. Look at me. I look a'ight, don't I?"

The father never responded. He just stared at Khadafi.

"I just lost my uncle, too. As a matter of fact, that's why I'm here. Your son killed my uncle. That's why I have to take his life. The decision is yours to make. What's it gonna be? You are the protector of this family, William. Don't gamble with their lives. All I need you to do is call Money and get him here. When he gets here, I'll do the rest. You don't even have to see him. You can remember him the way you last saw him. Then we'll be gone. I'm not worried about you going to the cops because if you do, I'll find you and kill you, William. Then I'm gonna kill your wife, this little kid and his parents. Make that call for me, William. Make the call and spare your family."

I thought that at that point Money's father would agree to give his son up. I thought he'd make the call, but he didn't. He never said a word as Khadafi waited for an answer. A lone tear fell from the man's eyes. I knew then that he'd never give his son up.

"I –I-I- ca-a-n-n-'t do it," the man said as several other tears followed the first one.

I secretly admired the man's stubborn resistance, but Khadafi didn't. Khadafi didn't see him as a father protecting his only son.

"Umar, take shorty upstairs. I don't want him to witness this. Stay by his side. When I give the word, kill him."

Without hesitation, Umar picked up the bound kid and carried him upstairs. As soon as the kid was out of the room, Khadafi went off.

"I was tryna be nice, cuz. I can be a mean muthafucka when pushed. And right now, William, you're pushing me. Why the hell would you protect a son that lives the street life and kills people himself? Especially at the risk of losing your own life and the lives of your family. Talk to me, William. Are you gonna make that call or what?"

Tears continued to fall down the man's face as he looked up at Khadafi and said, "If I give up my only son to be killed by you, how could I continue to live with myself knowing that I did that? I would be a walking, breathing dead man. He's my son, my flesh and blood, and no matter what he does in the streets, I can't give him up like that." He shook his head.

"And what about your life?"

"Take it. I'm fifty-one years old. I've lived a blessed life."

"And your wife's life? What about her life, William?"

William Smith glanced to his right at the woman whom he loved. They were both crying. "May God have mercy on our souls. Jesus is our shepherd. We shall not want…"

"You are very stubborn. I don't need to hear Bible verses right now, William. What about shorty upstairs? Does his life mean anything to you?"

At the mention of the little boy, I was sure that the father would break. But again, he didn't. He simply closed his eyes and dropped his head.

"Aye, cuz, gimme that knife that you just had," Khadafi told me.

I didn't know what he planned to do with the knife, but I knew that it wasn't gonna be pretty. I picked up the knife that I had just used to cut pieces of clothesline and handed it to Khadafi.

"William," Khadafi said. "I don't believe that you are that strong. What you said sounded good, valiant and all that, but I think you bullshittin'. I'ma make you suffer for a little while and then we'll talk."

Khadafi walked over to Mrs. Smith and cut the rope that binded her legs together. Then he pulled her to her feet. Khadafi unzipped his zipper and pulled out his dick.

"Please, God, please. Don't you touch her! Don't you touch her!" William Smith shouted.

"I'ma show you I'm not bullshittin', William." Khadafi led Mrs. Smith over to the Lazyboy recliner. In full view of her husband, Khadafi bent the woman over and lifted her night-gown. Then he pulled her panties down until they were around her ankles.

"Don't let me do this, William. Don't make your wife suffer because you wanna be stubborn. This can all end right now. All you gotta do is make the call. Talk to me, William."

William Smith still didn't say a word. I watched as Khadafi calmly turned around and pushed his dick into Mrs. Smith. The screams that tried to escape her mouth got caught in the gag in her mouth. Her animalistic muffled screams could still be heard, especially by her husband. I stood transfixed to my spot and watched Khadafi rape Money's mother. Even as I watched, I couldn't believe that he would do something so foul, just to exact revenge on his enemy. The death of his uncle had robbed Khadafi of what little humanity he had left. Now, he was 100% animal. In and out he pumped himself into a whimpering Mrs. Smith. The woman's moans and muffled cries were no deter-rent to a man possessed.

Khadafi turned and faced her husband. "You can stop this, cuz. I'ma keep fucking your wife until I can't fuck her no more.

Then I'ma pop a Viagra and fuck her some more. I'ma fuck her in her ass, too. I got all night, William. You still ain't got nothing to say?" He shrugged. "Okay."

Khadafi resumed his sexual assault on Mrs. Smith. A few minutes later, he shivered and pulled out of the woman. "William, your wife's pussy is the bomb. As soon as my dick gets back hard, I'm going back. Call your son for me, William."

I had seen enough. Khadafi had just skeeted inside Money's mother. He had just left his DNA at the scene of a crime. I had to try and talk him out of raping the woman further. "Slim, you slippin' bad. You need to ease up. We can just—"

"Cuz, shut the fuck up with that bitch shit," Khadafi vented. "What the fuck is up with you? Talking about I'm slippin' and ease up. Don't tell me to fuckin' ease up. I lost my uncle, not you. Them muthafuckas been tryna hit my head, not yours. If you can't stand the heat, then get the fuck outta the kitchen. I ain't easing up until somebody in this muthafucka calls Money and gets him here. I'm tired of looking for his ass."

Khadafi pulled the gag out of Mrs. Smith's mouth. "Do you wanna call your son for me and end your pain?" She sobbed and cried, but didn't answer the question. "Okay, have it your way."

Khadafi walked past me into the kitchen. Minutes later, he returned with a large bottle of Canola cooking oil. He put the gag back into Mrs. Smith's mouth. "William, we gon' do this all night. Think about your wife." Khadafi squirted a generous amount of oil into his hand and rubbed it into the crack of Mrs. Smith's butt.

"William, I'm about to fuck your wife in her ass. Call your son, William." Khadafi forced his dick into the woman's rectum. I watched her back arch and her knees buckle. The loud muffled scream that she let out gave me goose bumps.

"I'm a young nigga, William. I got plenty of stamina. You know all about that second nut and how long it takes to come. You can put a stop to her pain and suffering. I'll stop right now, William. Call your son for me. Call your son."

William Smith looked at me with pleading eyes. "Please, stop him! Oh God, please stop him!"

"Leave God out of this, William. This is between you, me and her." Khadafi laughed a maniacal laugh. "All you gotta do is pick up that phone and call Money for me."

William Smith dropped his head again and Khadafi continued to pound himself into the man's wife.

.CHAPTER THIRTY-FOUR.
KHADAFI

"I'm getting ready to cum again, William. Your wife's ass is good as shit. Did you ever get some of this? Call your son, William," I said as I continued to long stroke his wife's asshole. Her barely audible screams had stopped and been replaced with wracking sobs. I could smell the feces and blood mixed and it excited me more. It made me more determined to violate Money's mother. I pounded her from the back relentlessly. "She can't take too much more of this, William. What kinda monster are you? Stop your wife's pain. Stop her pain, William."

I heard the man on the floor mumble something. I thought that maybe his spirits were broken and he was ready to call Money for me. "What was that, William?" I stopped my assault on his wife's anal cavity. "Did I hear you say something? Are you ready to call your son? Speak up, cuz."

William Smith defiantly looked into my eyes and what I saw was hatred, rage, and despair. He spoke clearly when he said, "I pray that God kills you soon and that you die a slow and painful death."

I couldn't believe what I had just heard. "You said you hope that God kills me?"

"Fuck you, muthafucka!" William spat before I could finish my sentence. I laughed at the doomed man's words. I respected his gangsta. He'd rather die a thousand deaths than betray his son. There was honor in that, but it still didn't harness my unbridled fury.

"Fuck me, huh?" I repeated and became more enraged every second. "Die slow, huh? Fuck me and die a slow, painful death, huh?" I pulled my dick out of his wife. I repeated what William had said over and over as I wiped blood and shit off of my dick with his wife's nightgown. I picked up the oil and put some more on my dick. I walked over to William and cut the ropes that bound his feet. I cut the fabric of his pants all the way up to his boxers. Then I split his boxers open. "Fuck me, huh, William? Naw, nigga. I'ma fuck you."

I stuffed a gag into William's mouth. Then we wrestled all around until I forced my dick into him. His muffled screams made me more determined to emasculate him. Black flashes of emptiness clouded my head as I penetrated him further and further. Never in my life had I engaged in a homosexual act, but what I was doing to my enemy's father felt right. I kept humping him until I felt the familiar stirring in my loins. Then I released myself. "I just fucked you, William. Take that to your grave."

I rose quickly and went to the kitchen. I used dishwashing liquid to wash myself in the sink. The dark clouds inside my head dissipated slowly and the stark reality of what I had done dawned on me. I felt no remorse.

Tiring of the whole game, but dedicated to finishing what I had started, I walked back into the living room and picked up the Mach II.

"I wouldn't be here now had I stayed to make sure that your son had died the night I shot him. I'll never make that mistake with you." I aimed the Mach at the back of William Smith's head and fired a volley of bullets that opened his dome like a ripe melon.

Then I walked over to Mrs. Smith and said, "You should've just called your son." I blew her brains all over the chair. "Fuck tryna back track and wipe this place down. We gon' torch this bitch," I said to Boo and went in search of a flammable liquid.

.CHAPTER THIRTY-FIVE.
UMAR

The muffled screams I heard continuously told me exactly what was going on downstairs. Well, actually it was the timing of each scream. They were consistent with sex. Somebody was getting raped. I shook my head and felt stupid as hell. What the fuck was I doing here? Why had I let my love and loyalty put me in a situation that I knew I didn't wanna be in? This was the same situation that I was in in Beaumont and I still hadn't learned my lesson. *Stupid ass me.* The acts that I'm now accessory to are life offenses. I haven't even been home three days yet.

I wondered which of my partners was downstairs committing the atrocious act of rape and then decided it had to be Khadafi. Rape had never been something I could do. I got too many females in my family for that. Too many females and too many kids. That's why there ain't no way in the world I'ma kill this little boy. Allah would punish me forever for that. Khadafi has officially lost his mind, but that doesn't mean I've lost mine.

If he tries to give me the order to kill this kid, I know exactly what to do—ignore him. I turned my head into the direction of the kid, who had to be petrified. But surprisingly, he was tearless.

"You a'ight, little man?" I asked him.

The kid nodded his head and said, "Are you going to kill me?"

"Why would you ask me something like that, shorty? What's your name, anyway?"

"Malcolm," the kid said. "My name is Malcolm."

"Malcolm, huh?" I thought about all the people I knew named Malcolm. I thought about the most famous Malcolm and felt terrible all over again. What we had done tonight would traumatize this little kid forever. I quickly untied his hands and legs. "Naw, little man. I'm not gonna kill you."

"But the other man said—"

"Don't worry about what he said, Malcolm. I got you. No-body is gonna hurt you."

As soon as those words left my mouth, I heard the unmis-takable sounds of muffled gunshots. Sadly, I knew what time it was. The man and the lady downstairs were probably dead.

"Listen, Malcolm, this is a game that we're gonna play. You like games?"

"I like games," Malcolm answered.

"I want you to play hide and seek with me. Get under the bed—"

The crackling of the walkie-talkie on my cell phone stopped me in mid sentence. "Umar?" Khadafi called out.

"Yeah, ock, what's up?"

"Go head and slump shorty. Shit didn't go right down here. We gotta bounce. I'm about to torch the place as soon as I find what I need. Handle that and come on down."

The cavalier way that Khadafi told me to kill the kid left me with a sour taste in my mouth. I shook that off and told myself to act quickly. Reaching under the bed, I grabbed Malcolm's feet. "There's been a change of plans, little man." I walked him over to the window. Opening it, I peered out and judged the distance to the ground. I was sure that the kid could survive the drop.

"Listen to me, Malcolm. Don't be scared. You gotta hang from my hands and drop down to the ground. When you hit the ground, roll over and lay there. Don't move until you hear a car start up. You understand?" Malcolm nodded his head. "Let's go." I held the kid out the window and dangled him as low as I could. "Remember what I said. Lay on the ground and don't move or they are gonna kill you."

Little Malcolm nodded again. I let him go. He hit the ground and did as I said. He was okay. I pulled the gun that Boo had given me at his house and fired three shots into the bed. Then I ran downstairs. Khadafi was pouring something all over the two dead bodies and the furniture. As he lit the match, Boo and I were out the door. We ran all the way to Boo's car and then drove back to make sure Khadafi was outta there. When we pulled around the corner, we saw him pulling off in the van.

"Aye, slim, that nigga Khadafi is fucked up in the head for real. You should've seen what he did to them people," Boo said. "He raped both of 'em, slim. He raped both of 'em. He put Crisco oil on his dick and fucked both of 'em. Then he killed them. That nigga don't be bullshittin' at all." Boo shook his head, still in disbelief and hit the radio button. He turned the dial to WPGC 95.5. The sounds of the new Young Joc and Hot Styles filled the car.

As I zoned out off the crazy song that was playing I thought about what Boo had just said. He was right. Khadafi was fucked up in the head and I knew that I needed to get as far as I could away from him.

.CHAPTER THIRTY-SIX.
SHAWNAY

"This is a prepaid call. You will not be charged for this call. This call is from Ameen. To refuse this call, hang up. To accept this call, dial five now."

I pressed the 5 button on the phone. I had been anticipating a call from Antonio. "Hello?"

"What's up, baby?" Ameen said.

"Nothing much. How you doing?"

"I'm good. How you and my girls doing?"

"Fine. All of us are fine. We miss you."

"I miss y'all, too. Let me speak to the girls. I wanna say hi to 'em."

"They ain't here. Asia is at my grandmother's house. She wanted to spend the weekend with her cousin Rena. And Kenya went over her best friend Marshay's house. Her parents are taking them to Adventure World tomorrow, so she won't be home until then. But Asia will be home later. She has summer Prep school. I'm going to get her in a few hours. Can you call them back tomorrow? I know they wanna hear from you."

"I'll have to see what I can pull off. I only get one call every thirty days in the S.H.U." He paused. "You just said that the kids wanna hear from me. What about you? You don't wanna hear from me?"

"Of course, I do. Why would you ask me something like that?" I asked.

"Because it's all in your actions."

"How you figure that?"

"Easy. You don't write a nigga no more. If I don't call you, we wouldn't even communicate. I send you cards and write you letters and you can't even holla back. I can't get no pictures of you and the kids, nothing. You carrying a nigga like a sucka, for real."

"I work, Antonio. You don't understand how hard it is for me out here. I come home after working eight to ten hours a day and gotta help Asia and Kenya with their homework. I gotta do their hair, cook, clean and get ready to do it all again the next day. I'm not neglecting you on purpose, I'm just a little swamped out here. I am doing it all by myself. Remember that."

"You right, you right. I understand and appreciate all that you do to raise the girls. I was just saying that you can take five minutes out your day to holla at a nigga and let me know what's up with you and the girls. I might not be able to get to a phone all the time. You feel me?"

"Yes, Antonio."

"My man been hitting you off with that loot, right?"

"Yeah. He brung us money about four times."

"Was it a lot of money each time?"

"Yeah. It's over a hundred thousand—"

"Got damn! I knew that slim was gonna look out, but not like that. I respect him for that. When was the last time you seen him?"

"Not since the last time he brought some money over here," I lied.

"I'ma tell slim to buy you one of them digital cameras and the printer to go with it. That way you won't have no excuses not to send me a rack of pictures of you and the kids. Feel me?"

"Yes, Antonio."

"Let me hurry up and say this before the phone cuts off. I need you to go to the Internet and order me a few books. Can you handle that for me?"

"Of course, I can."

"Good. Go to Amazon.com and get...you got a pencil nearby?"

"I can remember them. What do you want?"

"Order the Mike Sanders joint *Thirsty, What's Really Hood?* By Wahida Clark, the *Trust No Man 2* joint by a dude named Cash and *Cheetah* by Missy Jackson. You got that?"

"Yeah, I-*beep* got it."

"The phone is about to hang up. I'ma try and call back if I can get the cops to give me the phone. If not, I'll call back when I can. Give the girls my love. I'ma write you soon. I love you, Shawnay, with all my heart. Don't ever forget that."

"I won't. I love you, too."

"A'ight, boo. I'm gone. I love you."

"Love you, too. Bye."

I put the cordless phone back on the base and lifted the covers to look into the man's face that was between my legs. It took everything inside me to talk normal while Khadafi gently nibbled and sucked on my clit. "Why did you do that?"

"I couldn't resist. You taste so good that I couldn't stop just because that call came in."

"But I told you it was Antonio."

"And I heard you. But like he told me before I left him. He told me to take care of the family. Haven't I done that? I'm just taking care of you in a different way. Didn't you tell me that you haven't been kissed, loved and sexed since Ameen went to jail?"

"Yeah, but—"

"No buts. Stop beating yourself up over this. It will be a long time before Ameen comes home. You need to be loved by somebody. I'm sure he would want it to be me."

"Do you really think so?"

"Definitely. I know so. But you just can't tell him that. He'll be a'ight. Ameen is a warrior. Let Ameen look out for Ameen and I'll look out for you and the girls. As a matter of fact, I need to take care of something right now."

"Oooooh, Khadafi! Don't lick it like that. Don't lick it right there...You gon' make me cum all over your face. Ooooh...ooooooh...Oh my.... Khadafi, don't do it like that. Ooooh. Don't put your tongue in me like that! Aaaaaahhh!"

I felt like I was levitating. The way that man was making me moan and groan, it was amazing. I hadn't cum that much in years. I laid back and gave up the ghost. My tongue spoke in languages not invented yet. I purred, hissed and even barked like a female dog a few times. I knew in my heart that I was wrong for what I kept participating in, but I couldn't help myself. I needed every inch of Khadafi's dick in me, on me and over me. Ever since that first night that we made love, it's no longer just my hands that are out of control. It's my lips, my feet, my body, and most of all my pussy. She has a mind of her own. As much as my heart tells me that I'm wrong for what I'm doing to Antonio, my hands, lips, and pussy tell me that I'm justified. My body calls out for Khadafi. What can I say?

"I want you to get on your knees for me, baby," Khadafi said as he slid up my body and kissed my lips. "I wanna look at that big ass wiggle as I hit it."

"No!" My heart screamed out to me.

But my body was already up and walking to the bottom of the bed. "No!" My heart cried out again. My left leg had already risen to the bed. "Please don't give in to him." I could no longer hear my heart as my right leg went up and over. I drowned out all voices as Khadafi got behind me and rubbed his dick at the entrance to my pussy.

"Don't tease me!" I cried out. "Gimme that dick!" I guess my voice was the only one that Khadafi heard because he pushed that dick in me inch by inch. I surrendered my whole body to the feelings of fullness and ecstasy. As he slammed his dick into me, even my heart cried out for more.

.CHAPTER THIRTY-SEVEN.
MONEY

For some strange reason, listening to Biggie Small's *Ready to Die* CD during rough times always seemed t o hclp me think— that and a game of chess. The fact that the late great rapper was in the middle of an intercoastal b e e f that had turned deadly and he still had the equanimity to be witty and write metaphors that captivated millions, was something that couldn't be taught. You had to be born with that.

"Picture a nigga hiding/my life in that man's hands, while he's just deciding...."

I swiped at another tear welling up in my eyes. In a lot of ways, life was like a game of chess. Every piece wanted to survive and protect the Queen. To lose, it was like one had died. Having already torn up the entire condo where I live, it was time for major thought. I had to think and carefully orchestrate my next move. I had to be able to see the whole board before I moved.

As I moved the chess pieces around the board, I reminded myself to be strong in the face of adversity. I wiped my eyes again. If adversity had a name, it would be Luther "Khadafi" Fuller.

After I was told about my parent's death and by whose hand they had died, my first reaction was to find Cochise and kill him. Had he done a better job of getting close to Khadafi and killing him, I wouldn't be in the position that I'm in now. But killing Cochise wouldn't solve my immediate problems. Finding Khadafi and killing him would. Cochise had a knack for finding people and I needed that skill, so I decided to kill Cochise after we found Khadafi and his friends. I could do nothing but curse myself for underestimating the young dude. How had I allowed my arrogance to cloud my judgment? The words that my distraught sister said to me earlier today kept replaying themselves in my head.

"It's all your fault!" Cherelle had screamed after telling me that our parents were dead. My tears started instantly when she spoke of the house burning to the ground." Mommy and Daddy are dead because of you!"

I was confused, angry and hurt. Why did she blame me? I asked myself over and over as I cried. Then I asked her, *Why am I to blame, Relle? What did I do?*"

She broke down into screams, coughs and moans. "They were looking for you. They were there looking for you."

"Who was there looking for me?" I asked.

"The men. Malcolm heard one of them telling Daddy to get you to the house. 'Call your son,' he kept saying."

"Who kept saying what, Relle? Who did Malcolm see?"

"He saw them. He saw them!" she yelled. "The three men, he saw them. He said that the pizza man kept telling Daddy to call you. He wanted Daddy to get you to the house, but Daddy wouldn't do it. He was protecting you."

My heart was broken into little tiny pieces. What did my nephew mean by the pizza man? What could I say to my sister to heal her broken heart? I needed to know everything that happened at my parent's house. "Relle, I need to speak to Malcolm."

"No! Stay away from us. I don't want you around us ever again."

"Okay, Relle. But I need to know everything. Did Malcolm say what the three men looked like?"

"He said that the pizza man was red like me. One of them was dark skin with long dreads. The one who helped him had a long beard. He was the one that dropped Malcolm out the window. He told Malcolm to lay on the ground and don't move or they were gonna kill him. That's how he got out of the house before they set it on fire. Malcolm said that the pizza man called the one with the beard Umar or something like that."

"Has Malcolm talked to the police, yet?"

"No. He's too shaken up."

"Keep the cops away from him, Relle. They will only fuck his mind up. You know how much I loved Mom and Dad. I would never purposely put them in harm's way. That's why I never went home to live. I don't know how them niggas found the house. But you're right, Relle. It's my fault." I had started crying again by then. "But I'ma take care of everything."

"Momma and Daddy are dead, Money. You can never take care of that." Then she hung up on me.

I stopped swiping at the tears that formed in my eyes and let them fall freely. I moved my Rook to the opposite side of the chessboard. Cherelle had been right to blame me for our parents' deaths. I had allowed the loss of a little blood, a punk-ass half a mil and some drugs to move me aimlessly across the board of life, as easily as the Horse moved.

I knew exactly who had killed my parents. The pizza man was Khadafi. The man with the dreads was Boo. The third man, the one with the long beard who had saved Malcolm, he was a new addition to the game. I flashed back to the day Cochise opened fire on Khadafi and Boo as they left the mosque. I remembered seeing a third man with them. The man that Khadafi had pushed to the ground when the shots rang out. The man had a low haircut and a long beard. He was the man called Umar. But why had he spared my nephew? On the battlefield, killers rarely showed acts of compassion. While I am totally grateful for that compassion, my thirst and desire for revenge knows no such compassion. I will not be so kind.

The dudes who killed my parents will pay. And their children will not be spared. The angrier I became, the harder I cried. The harder I cried, the more my moves became calculated. I checkmated myself in three moves. As I set the board up to play another game, another thought crossed my mind. How had Khadafi gotten my parents' address? I never went to their house, so I know nobody followed me there. My folks had moved into the house on Summerset a little over four years ago and nobody had the address but me and Cherelle. Cherelle hadn't given it to anybody. That I was sure of.

I knew that the Summerset address wasn't written on anything of mine. My driver's license had my cousin's address on it. Then I remembered the one instance when I did use my parents' new address. When I was getting released from Lorton, I had to use their address to get released to. And the only person who had that address was my parole officer.

The realization of what must have happened hit me hard and fast. Thomasina Jones had given Khadafi my parents' address. Either willingly or unwillingly, she was the culprit. And for that, she had unknowingly signed her own death certificate.

I picked up the phone and called Cochise. He answered on the second ring. "What's up?"

"Big boy, did you get that address on Boo yet?" I asked.

"I just got it a few minutes ago from this bitch named Tangie. She knows him real well."

"That's good news. I want you to kill everybody in his house and then kill him. But Khadafi is mine. When you find him this time, I'm gonna kill him myself."

"No problem, moe."

"I also want you to find Khadafi's father, old man Fuller, so I can kill him."

"Again, no problem."

"I'ma get at you tomorrow after I come from seeing my PO. I'll fill you in on everything else then, a'ight?"

"A'ight, moe. Peace."

After disconnecting the call, I finished setting up the chess pieces on the board. I rapped along with Biggie as he said, "Somebody's gotta die."

.CHAPTER THIRTY-EIGHT.
BOO

"**B**oo, he on his way over here right now," Tangie said to me over the phone.

"A'ight, that's good looking out. I'ma holla at you after the show," I replied. Tangie knew that I was referring to the gunshot fireworks show that was about to go on outside her house.

"The show, huh? Is there an after party after the show?"

"Believe that. For you, it's always an after party. V.I.P. all the way."

"Hurry up, boy. Bye."

There was something that I never told anybody, not my men I was locked up with and not anyone on the outside either. But when I was around sixteen, I was messing with this girl named Tamara. I was high off the dippa and lunching like a muthafucka, when she came over my house to chill. I ended up getting her high and tricking her out of the pussy. Her older brother Eric found out that I took advantage of his sister and came to confront me about it. He picked the wrong youngsta on the wrong night. When he stepped out of his car, I could detect that he was on something. He walked up to me and smacked the shit outta me. Without saying a word, I pulled the .380 out of my jacket pocket and wore his ass out. I had tears in my eyes that night as I stood over him and dogged him out.

The episode that Khadafi pulled the other night was a constant reminder of what I did to Tamara and a wake-up call to something else.

When I was in Beaumont, I called Tangie on her cell phone. As we were talking and she was walking through the neighborhood, a dude kept trying to get her attention away from the phone. I sat on the phone and listened to Tangie check the dude about bothering her while she was on the phone. The dude got mad and tried to snatch her phone. I could hear them wrestling over the phone, until Tangie said, "Boo, hold on for a minute."

The next thing I heard was, "Boo? What Boo is that?"

"Is that Boo from 4th Street?" the dude asked Tangie. He succeeded in taking her phone from her because the next thing I heard was, "Is this Lil Boo from 4th and W?"

I thought he was a fan. "Yeah, this him," I replied. "Who dis?"

"Boo, don't you come home next year?" he asked. "As a matter of fact, you come home in July, on the twenty-first, right?"

"Who is this?" I asked, curiosity piqued.

"This is Death, nigga. I'ma smash your bitch ass as soon as you get home."

"Is that right?" I asked and smiled. I still thought that somebody was playing with me. "You gon' smash me, huh?"

"Kill my mother. I'ma be waiting on you, nigga."

"Put Tangie back on the phone, slim," I told the dude.

"Naw, dawg, I can't do that. Me and Tangie about to go and smoke. Then she gon' suck my dick. I'll see you when you shine."

The line went dead and I walked around Texas fucked up in the head for days. I couldn't catch Tangie for the next couple of days after that. When I finally caught her, what she told me gave me the chills. The dude that had threatened me was on the bricks, putting the most work in. According to Tangie, everybody in the neighborhood and beyond was afraid of Steve Tyler. Steve Tyler. I tossed the name around in my head for a moment and then it came to me like a light in the dark. The girl I had forced myself on years ago was named Tamara Tyler. Her older brother was E.T. also known as Eric Tyler, the same Eric Tyler I had killed on 4th Street. Steve Tyler was their younger brother. When I went to jail, Lil Steve had to be twelve years old. At the time he had threatened me, he had to be nineteen or twenty. Today he's maybe twenty-one. I don't know for sure, but I do know that he's a dead man walking. I never saw him when I first got home because he was over at a D.C. Jail fighting a body. A couple of days ago my homegirl Tangie informed me that Steve was home.

The government had failed to indict him on the murder due to a lack of witnesses. I sat on the info and was gonna just avoid shorty. But the one thing I've learned in the last thirty days is that you can't bullshit with your life. And if a mutha-fucka really wants you dead, they gon' do all kinds of shit to get you and make you dead.

I watched what Khadafi did to Money's parents and rea-lized that it's real in the field. You gotta hit first and hit hard. Like the *48 Laws of Power* said, "Never leave an enemy de-feated halfway. Annihilate him totally or else he will recover and seek revenge." And that was exactly what Khadafi and Money were both learning the hard way. I didn't wanna learn that lesson too late, so I called Tangie and enlisted her help in me getting to Lil Steve Tyler. She told him that she was throw-ing him a private welcome home party and like a damn fool he took the bait. I jumped into my Caddy and did the whole I-40 on the dash, getting back to Northeast. It's a thirty-minute drive from Sanaa's apartment to Tangie's, but I covered it in ten.

Tangie had already put me on point about Steve and every-thing there was to know about him. I knew what he looked like as a kid. I just needed a little help in updating him. As I pulled onto Edgewood Terrace, I looked around for the black Chevy Caprice SS that I heard he drove. The car wasn't there so that let me know that I had made it there first. I drove to the other end of the street and parked my car. It wasn't quite dark out-side yet and the street was still filled with children and others outside gathered on fronts and cars. The building that Angie lived in was off to the side and adjacent to the rental office. I quickly surveyed the scene and surmised that Steve had to park in the parking lot across from Angie's building if he planned to stay awhile. Because if he didn't, he'd have to double park in front of one of the cars where people were gathered. Knowing Tangie like I did, her head and pussy was on one thousand, so if she promised Steve some welcome home action, he definitely planned to stay awhile. I got out of the car and walked over to the building where Tangie lived. I laid low on the side of her building. The advantage that I had was that nobody in Edgewood knew what I looked like. I picked up weight and grew my dreads in prison, so they couldn't pick me out of a crowd. I rolled my dreads up and tied them with other dreads. Then I pulled a nylon cap down over them. The .40 I got from Khadafi was ready to spit and I was ready to aim and squeeze.

Fifteen minutes passed before I saw the SS pull up. And just like I figured, he pulled into the parking lot across the street. From my position on the side of the building, I saw him get out of the car and walk across the street. Angie told me that the front door to the building was locked at all times and a visitor had to be buzzed in. So I knew that Steve was a sitting duck in front of the building as he waited for Tangie to let him in. I took my time walking around the corner. I caught Steve on the front loafing, smoking a blunt. He never even turned in my direction when I crept up to him. I hit him up close with that .40 and knocked his ass through the plate-glass window on the door. I had to literally run into the building to finish him off. "That's what you get for running your mouth." *BOK! BOK! BOK!*

All eyes were on me as I ran up the street to where my car was parked. In seconds, I was miles away from the scene.

I listened to my stomach rumble as I put my key in Sanaa's apartment door. Walking into the door, I smiled to myself. The girl had pictures on the wall of The Last Supper. Jesus and everybody was white. Her living room was devoid of any traditional living room furniture. All she had was work out equipment, a big screen TV and DVDs everywhere.

I stopped at the hall closet and put the .40 on the shelf. Sanaa hated guns. They scared her, she said, so I always kept it on the top shelf, out of her sight. Sanaa was in the bedroom when I walked in. She was laid out across the bed dressed in nothing but a peach-colored thong and a wife beater. My dick got hard instantly and I forgot all about my hunger pains.

"I didn't hear you come in," Sanaa said as she turned over. She smiled at me as she watched me undress. My dick was standing tall and she knew that it was about to be on. Sanaa was fine as hell. At five-two she was all hips and ass, weighing in at about 125 pounds. Her short curly hairdo, flawless cara-mel complexion, and soft pouty lips always turned me on.

I wondered what she'd say if I came out and told her that I had just killed a man. I was completely naked as I came toward her, "Girl, I'm hungry as shit."

"I cooked some food for you."

"That's cool. But right now, I'm not hungry for that kind of food."

Sanaa rolled over onto her back and eased out of her thong. Then she pulled the wife beater over her head. She enti-cingly spread her legs revealing her hairless pink pussy that I loved so much. "Well, you know that Sanaa's Pussy Shop is an all-you-can-eat establishment. And for you, it's open twenty-four hours a day."

I stared at her pedicured toes, shapely thighs and perky breasts. I kissed her feet up to her inner thighs and said, "Do I get to eat for free?"

"Only if I get to return the favor."

"You got that," I said and dived head first into my meal.

Spent, exhausted, and famished, I sat up and asked Sanaa, "Didn't you say you cooked something?"

"Uh huh."

I threw my leg over the bed and stood up. "What you cook?" I asked as I headed for the kitchen.

I heard Sanaa say, "Lasagna."

"What did you put in it?"

"Five kinds of cheese, ground turkey and sausages."

In the kitchen, I was about to make me a plate, when I saw the wrapper for the sausage in the trash. It caught my attention. The label read, "Jimmy Dean sausages, made with turkey, chicken and pork."

What the fuck? I said to myself and closed the lasagna back up. I put that back in the refrigerator. I grabbed the turkey deli slices and some cheese and made me two sandwiches.

When I got back in the bedroom, I saw the confused look on Sanaa's face as I sat the two sandwiches on the nightstand.

"Why are you eating sandwiches and not the lasagna?"

I greedily ate half of one of the sandwiches before I spoke. "Because them sausages you put in there had pork in 'em."

"They had pork in 'em? How? They were turkey sausages."

Instead of speaking, I walked into the kitchen and got the sausage package out of the trash. Then I went back into the bedroom and showed it to Sanaa. "You gotta read the fine print."

Sanaa read the label. "Oh, that's right. You don't eat pork because you a Muslim."

She went from zero to sixty in two seconds flat.

"Mr. Fake-Ass Mohammed himself. What? You got tested in prison? That why you decided to join the Muslim nation? I mean, when you left you was a holy roller. 'I pray to God they don't give me twenty years'," she mocked me. "Yeah look at you. I know you remember that. Now you talking about Allah this, Allah that and got the nerve to know Arabic. You can't even spell and write with yo' retarded ass."

This bitch gon' make me slap the fuck out of her. I let her keep going, my silence pushed her on more.

"Oh, you don't hear me now, huh, ock? Ain't that what y'all call one another?"

She pushed my head.

"Aye, don't put your hands on me. For real, chill."

"Whatever Sabor. Oops, I mean Boo. Which is it? You so confused you don't even fucking know. What religion in the world makes you change your name? You are who you are with Christ. He accepts you just like you are VERNON. That is what I am calling your confused ass from now on! VERNON, miss me with that bullshit, talking about some pork. Please."

"You finished, bitch? Huh? You finished!" The tone of my voice must have scared her. I had heard enough. "Shorty, quit while you're ahead. You done said more than enough."

"Nigga, need I remind you that this is my house? Don't tell me when the hell I've said enough. I'm not finished. I want you to answer my questions."

"Shorty, let it go."

"I ain't letting shit go, 'cause you fake as shit. You out there robbing people, shooting and killing muthafuckas, selling drugs, and all kinds of shit. But you a Mooslim. Real Mooslims don't do that shit. Mooslims don't carry guns and rob people. Here I am, tryna love your ass and do what a girlfriend is supposed to do and you gon' give me your ass to kiss. I slaved over that hot stove for hours cooking for you and you gon' turn your nose up at my cooking, talkin' bout, 'It got pork in it.' Your ass was raised on pork. It ain't never killed nobody. You ungrateful as shit, boy."

The rage I now felt culminated in my toes and came upward. "You finished, shorty? Let me tell you something. I'ma grown ass man. I don't have to answer to nobody or defend my actions or beliefs to nobody but Allah. And you ain't him. I do what the fuck I wanna do. Boys do what they're showed; punks do as they're told, and men do what the fuck they wanna do. Don't ever question my manhood as long as you eat, sleep, piss, and shit. Ain't a nigga alive that can press me, in jail or out. Bitch, you better ask somebody about me."

I became Muslim, and it is Muslim, not Mooslim, ignorant ass woman, because I stopped believing in that fake-ass Christianity stuff. You all on your high horse, going off on me. Y'all Christian muthafuckas are some of the worst people on the planet. Look at what the Christians did to the Indians, the Jews and Africans. They are the greatest robbers, murderers and drug dealers.

"You better read your history books before you come at me like that. Your stupid ass running around here giving the church all your money. T.D. Jakes and them got millions, million-dollar homes and cars. You? You living in a muthafuckin' one-room shack. You got all these muthafuckin' pictures on the wall of all white people. Don't your stupid ass know that all them people were really black? Or do you even care?

"Yeah, I do a rack of shit that I ain't supposed to do, but that don't make me no fake Muslim. It just makes me a sinner, just like you. How the fuck you gon' judge me? What makes you better than me? I don't know what possessed you to pop that slick shit to me, anyway. Like I got a skirt on up in this muthafucka. You better recognize who the fuck you playing with."

"Boo, just get out of my house, please," Sanaa hissed.

"You been harboring all this shit in your heart all this time. It took some damn lasagna with pork in it to bring that shit out. You the one that's fake." I stood up and put my sweatpants on. "You gon' call me a fake Muslim, but you in this joint, eating my dick every day and swallowing cum. What type of Christian does that make you?" I put my boots on and tied them up. "Ain't what we been doing premarital sex? What does the Bible say about that?"

"Boo, I'm asking you to leave my house. Now!" Sanaa screamed. Then she came around the bed and pushed me. "Get the fuck outta my house! Right the fuck now, Boo!"

"Sanaa, don't push me no more. I'm leaving your house." I reached up into the closet to get my hammer.

"Don't make me call the police on your ass."

At the mention of the word "police" I snapped. I spinned on my heels and grabbed Sanaa by the throat. I shoved her up against the wall in the hall and I put the barrel of the gun to her forehead.

"Bitch, what did you just say? Say it again." I watched as her tears started to fall real heavy, but they didn't soften me. "If you ever in your muthafuckin' life threaten me with the police again, I'ma blow your muthafuckin' head off. Do you hear me?"

Sanaa nodded, so I let her go. Then I left. As I pulled out of her complex, inwardly I hoped that she'd see the error of her ways and call me so that we could make up and put this night behind us. I realized then that I went a little too far when I put the gun to her head. I promised myself that I'd make it up to her. Why did she have to come at me like that and cause me to lose my temper? Why couldn't she respect my faith and just let me do me? Why couldn't she understand the life I lived in the streets? Why was it important to her to break me, feed me pork and domesticate me? Life for me was one big question mark.

When I pulled in front of my grandmother's house, I noticed that all the lights in the house were out. My grandmother never turned all the lights out. She said a well-lit home kept the burglars away. Even if nobody was home, she left all the lights on. It was only twenty-five minutes after ten. They wouldn't all be gone or in the bed this early. I quickly put my key in the door as an alarm rose inside of me.

"Grandma!" I called out repeatedly, but got no response. The sound of the ringing phone stopped me in my tracks. The voice that exploded from the answering machine filled my ears. "Mrs. Dammons, if you are there, please pick up. Mrs. Dammons, I been calling for the last three hours. Is everything all right? I need to pick up Shakira. She has school tomorrow, Mrs. Dammons? Call me when you get this message, okay? Bye." *Click.*

Shakira was still with my grandmother? If Tangie hadn't picked her up... I ran up the stairs and headed to my grandmother's room. The door was shut, but not locked. I knocked on it and called out to my grandmother. After receiving no reply, I went into the room. It was dark, but the streetlight from outside shined through the window. My heartbeat started to ease up as I saw that my daughter and grandmother were in the bed asleep. The closer I got to the bed, the better I could see the crimson stains that covered the sheets. What the fuck? I reached for the lamp beside the bed and damn near knocked it over trying to turn it on. I finally hit the light and the scream that emanated in my throat never left my lips. I felt like I had asthma and couldn't breathe. My tears fell and my knees buckled. I reached for my child and screamed. It was all I could do. I pulled her close to me and cradled her small body in my arms. She appeared to be sleeping, but the neat little hole in the middle of her forehead told the true story. I laid my daughter on the floor and tried to give her mouth to mouth. With every breath, I willed her to cough, to speak, to breathe. My tears stained her face as I blew into her mouth and pressed down onto her small chest. I gave up the futile battle and sat up. Rocking back and forth on my knees, I cried.

"N-o-o-o-o-o-o-o-o! Please God, n-n-n-o-o-o-o-o-o! Don't take my daughter!"

I shouted at the ceiling in my rage and expected Allah to answer me, but he never did. I couldn't bring myself to get up and check on my grandmother. I knew that she had met the same fate as my daughter. An unbearable pain took over my whole body as I cried and cried.

I looked around the room and saw no signs of a struggle. Everything was normal. Then I saw it. Wiping the tears from my eyes to focus better, I saw that something was written on the mirror that sat atop of the dresser. The letters were a little smeared but legible. The words cut me deep, straight through to my heart.

Just because y'all spared my nephew didn't mean that I was gonna spare your children.

As my tears started again, so did the realization that the gruesome act was premeditated. And I knew exactly who was behind it. There had only been one situation that involved a child and that was the killing of Money's nephew. But the message said y'all spared my nephew.

Hadn't Umar killed the little boy? And if not, why didn't he? How had Money gotten my grandmother's address? The person responsible for the death of my family had to be Money. I was ready to kill everybody moving. At that moment I became a carbon copy of Khadafi. I understood how he could lose his mind after his uncle's death. I could now empathize with that 'cause I knew his pain. I pulled my cell phone from my hip and called Khadafi. I tried several times, but he never answered the phone. Then I dialed Umar's number.

"Assalaamu 'Alaikum," he answered.

I couldn't get the words out.

"Hello?" Umar said.

"They ....dead, slim," I finally whispered.

"Boo? Is that you?"

"They dead, slim. My family, my daughter."

My composure broke again and it took a moment to get myself together. "She...she wasn't even supposed to be here this weekend. She, they... gone, slim. Grandma, Shakira, they gone."

"Stay there, ock. I'm on my way to you."

"It was Money, slim. That bitch nig—"

"How do you know it was him?" Umar asked.

Then I had another thought. "Did you kill that little boy, slim? Don't lie to me, Umar. It's important. Did you kill the kid?"

After a slight pause Umar said, "I couldn't do it. I couldn't do it. I threw shorty out the window."

"It was him, slim. He left me a message."

"What message?"

In my haste, pain and desire for retribution, I never heard the footsteps that crept up behind me. I had made a mistake. I never searched the house for a culprit. I had assumed that whoever killed my family was gone. My mistake would prove to be fatal.

.CHAPTER THIRTY-NINE.
COCHISE

"Hello? Hello? Boo! Boo, what the hell was that? Hello? Boo?"

I reached down and picked up the cell phone. I put it to my ear. "Hello?"

"Boo?"

"Naw, moe, this ain't Boo. Boo can't come back to the phone because he's dead and you and Khadafi are next."

Standing over the fallen man, I put two more bullets in his skull. I did that because I was still upset that he made me wait twenty-three hours to kill him. I pulled my cell and called Money.

"Yeah, Co?"

"One down and two more to go, moe."

"Oh yeah? And what about the loved ones?"

"There was two. One big and one small. I left him the message you told me to."

"Did he understand it?" Money asked.

"Perfectly. I let him call his man and let him know."

"Which one? Khadafi?"

"Naw, he spoke to a dude he called Umar. He asked the dude did he kill your nephew. That's about as far as the conversation got."

"That's good news. I'ma holla back after I come outta this office. Feel me? Ole girl was the one that gave them niggas my people's address."

"No bullshit?"

"I'm about to find out why she did it."

"Let me get at her, moe. That one will be on me." I pleaded.

"Never that, homes. I got her. I'ma holla back."

I put my phone back up and pocketed Boo's phone as well. It was time to leave. I needed some fresh air. Being cooped up in a house with two dead bodies was stifling after a while. My mind flashed back on the events of several hours ago.

I entered the house from the back. The back door had an antiquated lock on it that was easy to pick. As I made my way through the house, I had the twin Glocks out by my side. I checked the whole house for people and then found the old lady and the little girl in the bedroom. They were sleeping peacefully and never knew what hit them. I fired a single round into each of their heads. I hated to kill women and children, but in time of war, casualties were to be expected. I didn't know when Boo was gonna come home, or even if he was, but I decided to stay, wait and see if he did. My luck turned out to be better than I thought. I saw Boo pull up and park outside, so I hid in the closet of the room where I killed the old lady and the girl. I watched Boo lose it about his family and then make the phone call. That's when I opened his muthafuckin' head up. Rest in peace, homes. Like I told Money, one down and two more to go.

.CHAPTER FORTY.

MONEY

"Diamonte, what are you doing here?" Mrs. Jones asked as I walked into her office and shut the door behind me.

I clicked the lock on the door and faced her. "I thought you'd be glad to see me."

I pulled out the chrome .45 that I had in my waist. At the sight of the gun, the color drained from her face.

"Diamonte Smith, what the hell are you doing in my office with a gun?" Mrs. Jones asked.

"Why did you do it, Mrs. Jones?"

"Do what, Diamonte?"

"You gave them niggas my parents' address."

"What niggas are you—"

I chambered a round into the gun for visual effect. "Don't fucking lie to me! You were the only person with that address. You didn't know that, huh?"

"Diamonte, I—"

"Let me tell you what they did. They dressed up like pizza delivery men and gained access to my parents' home. Then they killed them both—my mother and father. One of them helped my nephew to escape and then they burned the house down with my parents still in it. And you are responsible for their deaths. You can sit here all you want and deny it, but I know you did it. Why don't you just tell me the truth and I might spare your life."

With tears in her eyes, Mrs. Jones weighed her options mentally. Then she said, "He came here about four days ago.

Just like you, he had a gun. He threatened to kill me if I didn't help him. I was afraid, just as I am now. He knew so much about me. He knew that my husband was a doctor. He said he knew where we lived, where my husband worked and where my kids went to school. He made me give him a picture of you and the addresses in your file. I had no choice, Diamonte! What was I supposed to do? I wanted to tell you, to warn you. But he said if I did, he'd kill my whole family and I believed him. I didn't mean for anyone to die—" Thomasina broke down crying at that point. Between sobs she said, "I'm sorry, Diamonte."

Her tears had no effect on me. I had come there to right a wrong perpetrated against me and my family and that's what I intended to do. "You were like a pawn in a chess game. I understand your position on the board of life. But just like the pawn sacrifices itself for the Queen, so must you."

I walked over to the desk and fired the gun repeatedly into Mrs. Jones' face. The force of the hollow point bullets knocked her out of the chair. I walked around the desk and emptied the clip in her. Then I left through the same door in which I came.

.CHAPTER FORTY-ONE.
UMAR

By the time I reached Boo's house, the yellow tape was up and the house had been cordoned off. The small street was filled with cops. I pulled up just in time to see the people from the Coroner's Office load a body bag into an all-white van. I wondered if the person in the bag was Boo.

I still couldn't believe what had just happened. It seemed like a bad dream that I wanted to wake up from badly. Boo had called me and questioned me about the little boy. I came clean and told him that I couldn't bring myself to kill that kid. Then *Boom! Boom!* Just like that, Boo became quiet after I heard what sounded like gunshots. In my heart I hoped I was wrong. But when I called out to him and he didn't answer, I knew that something was very wrong. Then the voice came on the line and told me that Boo was dead and that me and Khadafi were next. The realization of what happened, the voice and the threat, chilled me to the bone. I thought maybe it was all a hoax, a trick being played on me by Khadafi and Boo. So I drove here to see if indeed things were as they sounded over the phone. They were.

I picked up my cell phone and called Khadafi. I got no answer. I programmed the phone to dial Khadafi's cell every five minutes. I called his house out in Maryland, no answer. Where the hell was he? I cupped my hands in front of my face and said a prayer for Boo and his family. I was starting to worry about Khadafi's well being. Had the dude on the phone gotten to Khadafi, too? I hit Rhode Island Avenue and headed for the beltway. Takoma Park was about thirty minutes away.

The house that Khadafi lived in was a beige brick Colonial-style house. I saw that Kemie's Land Rover and Khadafi's Cadillac were parked in the driveway. So why isn't anybody answering the door? I got out of the brand new 2008 Chevy Tahoe and walked up to the front door.

I rang the doorbell again and waited for someone to answer. When no one did, I knocked loudly and looked around for a way to get in the house to inspect it. For all I knew, Kemie could've been inside the house dead. I looked around for a brick or a large rock to break the window, but that wouldn't be necessary. The door opened suddenly and Kemie stepped out onto the front.

From Kemie's appearance I could decipher that something was wrong. Her clothes were tattered and her hair was unkempt. The few times I had seen her with Khadafi, her appearance was always impeccable. Now Kemie stood before me with large black circles under her eyes like she hadn't slept a wink in days.

"What do you want, Umar?" Kemie said. "Can't you take the hint that a person doesn't want to be bothered? I didn't answer the phone when you called a hundred times and I didn't answer the door when you rang the bell. And now you out here knocking on my shit like you the police. What do you want?"

I couldn't help but wonder if Kemie was really a crackhead. "Uh, I was tryna talk to Khadafi. I need to speak to him. Is he here? I know how he gets in his moods sometimes, but it's important that I holla at him. He hasn't been answering his—"

"Phone. I know. I been calling his ass, too. He knows it's me and he still ain't answering." Kemie started to cry. "I know that bitch told him about my past. I know it. He's been acting real funny toward me ever since the day he was with her. I never told him that I didn't fuck with other niggas on the side while he was locked up. So what the fuck is the big deal? Was I supposed to stop living because his life had been put on hold? Was I supposed to not fuck until he came home? I took care of him, Umar, and you know that. I did what I had to do to take care of both of us. I held his ass down for ten years and this is the thanks I get? This muthafucka won't even come home and check on me. He won't answer my calls or nothing."

"Look, Kemie. Maybe it's not you. The brother been going through a lot of shit lately, especially after his uncle got killed. Then his man Bean got killed. That shit is real traumatic. And now I gotta tell him that Boo got killed."

Kemie looked at me with genuine concern in her face. Her tears were flowing like the storm that flooded New Orleans. "Oh my God. No! What the fuck is going on with y'all, Umar? Why is everybody around y'all dying? When did Boo get killed?"

"About an hour ago, I was on the phone with him when he got shot. That's what I came to tell Khadafi, Kemie. I don't know what's going on," I lied. "All I know is that I need to find Khadafi, and fast."

"Yesterday he came home to get some clothes, I think. I wasn't here when he came, but I was bending the corner down the street when he left. I followed him to a house in Southeast. I think that's where he's been staying."

"What house in Southeast? Who lives there?"

"Your guess is as good as mine. I have the address in here somewhere. Come on in and I'll find it for you."

I followed Kemie into the house and sat in the living room. A couple of minutes later, she came in the room and handed me a small piece of paper with an address on it.

"If he's there, give him a message for me," Kemie said and lit a cigarette. "Tell him I said that he doesn't live here anymore and to stay his ass where he been for the last three days. Tell him I said fuck him and the plane that brought his ass home. And tell him I hope the bitch he's with makes him happy."

I looked at the address on the paper as I left the house and something seemed vaguely familiar about it. I couldn't put my finger on it, though. I jumped back into the Tahoe and headed to the address on the paper.

When I got there, I checked the paper again. The address on the house and the one on the paper were one and the same,

2172 56th Street, Southeast. I looked across the street and saw a midnight blue Infiniti truck with 'Honk if you love Islam' bumper sticker. I was positive that the truck belonged to Khadafi.

Looking at the house and the address brought back memories of my days in Texas. Since me and Ameen were in the same unit, I often spent a lot of time in his cell and I always got his mail for him. I now knew why the address looked familiar to me. I had seen it a thousand times before. The address belonged to Shawnay, Ameen's baby mother. The more I stared at the house I remembered it from the photos I saw in Ameen's photo album.

What the hell was Khadafi doing staying at Ameen's baby mother's house? I picked up my phone and hit the program button. The phone dialed Khadafi's number. Again, he didn't answer. I couldn't for the life of me come up with a good reason for Khadafi being at Shawnay's house for one day, let alone three.

I remembered the day that one of the homies in Beaumont went to the Captain's office and stayed in there for about an hour. When Chico and the other big homies told the dude that he had to get off the compound, I didn't understand why. Ameen pulled me to the side and said, "What in the hell did the homie have to say to the Captain that would have taken a whole hour to explain? *Nothing*. He should have taken one of the other homies with him to avoid suspicion. We don't know if he said anything that wasn't proper, but now we'll never know. The suspicion of an impropriety is sometimes worse than the actual impropriety itself."

I thought about the lesson I learned that day and applied it to the one I was now faced with. Khadafi was inside Shawnay's house and, according to Kemie, he'd been there for three days. In my heart, I didn't want to believe the reality that I was now faced with, but my head told me that it was real. Khadafi had to be fucking Shawnay. And if that was the case, he was all the way out of pocket.

THE ULTIMATE SACRIFICE

Everything that happened since I got home came to mind. The scene and the murders at the Masjid, the murders out Maryland at the house, talking to Boo before him and his family were murdered and now the ultimate betrayal. My mind was on overload and I needed to talk to somebody about it. As I pulled away from the curb on 56th Street, I knew that the person I needed to talk to was Ameen.

.CHAPTER FORTY-TWO.
AMEEN

The knock on my cell door woke me up. I wiped the sleep outta my eyes and focused on who was at the door. "What's up?" I called out.

"Felder, somebody in your family just called the institution and asked that you call home. They say it's a family emergency. I'm going to get the phone off of D range and then I'm gonna bring it back here. So be ready in a few minutes," Seg. Lieutenant Russo said and left.

A family emergency? What the fuck? I threw my feet over the side of the bed and sat up. My heart raced as I waited for the cop to come back with the phone. "If something happened to one of my daughters, I'ma kirk out in this muthafucka."

My biggest fear in prison is that one day the Chaplain is gonna come to my door and tell me that one of the people that I really love is dead. To lose a child or the one woman that I love with all my heart is unthinkable. I would definitely need some psych medication.

"Somebody in your family called the institution and asked that you call home."

I stood up and paced the floor as the fear of the unknown overwhelmed me. Where the fuck was Russo with the damn phone? The next thing I know, the food slot on my door opened. I went to the door and saw the range officer plugging the cord into the wall.

"Aye, C.O., did Russo say who called the institution? He said call home, but he didn't say who to call."

As the cop passed the phone receiver through the slot, he said, "Naw, Felder. He didn't tell me shit. All I was told was to bring you the phone. Let me ask him." The officer got on his walkie-talkie. "Cordero to Lieutenant Russo."

"Go for Russo," the voice on the other end said.

"Aye, Lieutenant, do you know who Felder is supposed to call. He needs to know."

"Let me check. It says here that his uncle Harold called and left the message. I guess he needs to call him."

"You heard that, Felder?" the C.O. asked me.

"I heard it. Good looking out."

It didn't take me long to figure out who my uncle Harold was. I didn't have any uncles and nobody in my family was named Harold. The only Harold I knew was Umar. By leaving a message to call him and saying the name Harold told me to call him.

I dialed the number that I had for Umar. He answered on the second ring.

"Hello?"

"This is a prepaid call. You will not be charged for this call. To ref--beep Umar?"

"Assalaamu Alaikum, ock."

"Walaikum AsSalaam. What's up, slim? What's the family emergency?" I asked getting straight to the point, curious to know what was up.

"I don't know where to start, ock. First things first. There was a beef going on out here with Khadafi, Boo, and some other dudes that they brought a move. The same day I got home, the dudes came to the Masjid and laid on us. As we were walking out, they, well, *he* opened fire on us. Did you hear about all the people that got killed coming out of the Masjid about two weeks ago?"

"Naw."

"It was all on the news and in the papers. But anyway, the dude was tryna hit Khadafi and Boo. Khadafi saw one of the dudes and recognized him. We went on a move to get at one of the dudes and a few people got crushed. That made the news, too. Everybody went into seclusion. Then yesterday, we lost one, ock."

"We lost one? Who did we lose?"

"Boo. Boo got killed yesterday evening, I was —"

"Naw, slim! Don't tell me that shit! My man ain't dead." I exploded into the phone.

"Not only him, his grandmother and his daughter, too. They killed his peoples first. Boo must've come home later and found them. He called me and told me about it. He was hysterical on the phone, ock. The killer left him a message and everything. Then all of a sudden, I heard gunshots. Boo got quiet. A voice comes on the phone and tells me that Boo was dead and that me and Khadafi are next. Then he hung up on me. I'm thinking Boo on some bullshit, so I go over to his house to check it out. When I got there, the cops and the meat wagon were already there. I saw them bring one of the bodies out."

"Somebody killed Boo and his family? That's what you're telling me?" I asked. I couldn't believe what I was hearing.

"Yeah, ock. But that ain't the half. You gotta sit down for this one. I thought about not telling you for a few minutes, and then I decided that you needed to know."

"Needed to know what? What's up?"

"After I confirmed that Boo was at least hit, I tried to call Khadafi and couldn't reach him at no number. So I thought that something might've happened to him too, you know? I drove to his house and banged on the door until Kemie opened it. I was relieved to see that she was there and that everything was cool. I asked for Khadafi and Kemie told me that he hadn't been home in days. She said she hadn't heard from him, either. She gave me an address to a house that she said she followed him to one day. She suggested that it was where he probably was. I went to the address and he was there. At least, his truck was parked outside."

I was confused now. Why was Umar telling me to sit down to hear that? So what? Kemie and Khadafi were going through something. Couples did that all the time. "And what? He was at that address and what?"

"Not what, but who. Ask me whose address it was."

"Whose address was it?" I asked already knowing the answer in my heart.

"The address was Shawnay's, ock. Khadafi has been staying with your baby mother."

Most people don't believe in love at first sight, soulmate, and real live spiritual connections, but I do. I couldn't come out and explain to Umar that I had a feeling in my heart that Shawnay was fucking somebody. I can't explain it to myself, but I felt it. I knew that something was going on with her. I just didn't know that the person she'd decide to be with would by my man.

"Ameen? You still there, ock?"

"I'm here, slim. That's a serious blow and I can't even swing back. Maybe he was just hiding out there? Maybe he needed a place to chill and Shawnay let—"

"The suspicion of an impropriety is sometimes worse than the actual impropriety itself. Remember you told me that, ock?" Umar said.

"I remember. Listen, slim, you just dropped a nuclear bomb in my lap. I need some time to get my head together. Tomorrow, I'ma call you on the straight out joint and tell you what I want you to do, a'ight?"

"A'ight, ock. Call me tomorrow and you be easy. Don't hurt nothing. Assalaamu Alaikum."

"Walaikum AsSalaam." I hung the phone up and slid down the wall by the cell door.

I don't know what hurt me more, Khadafi's betrayal, Shawnay's infidelity, or Boo's death. The pain was indistinguishable. Deep inside, though, it all felt the same. I covered my face with my hands and cried. It was all I could do under the circumstances. The knot in the middle of my chest restricted my breathing and I felt like I had asthma. The tears that fell down my cheeks came from the wells in the depths of my soul. My heart cried for me. My tears each told their own story of what I really felt inside.

How could everything go so wrong, so fast? In the span of ninety days, my whole world had just changed. Khadafi was like my brother and he betrayed me. Shawnay was the only woman I ever loved and she knew that. I never expected her to be celibate for the rest of her life. I prepared myself for the Dear John letter telling me that she had found another lover. I would've understood and eventually moved on with my love and my life. But to find out that she's fucking my friend, that hurts a lot. Why couldn't she find somebody other than Khadafi to give the pussy to? And vice versa? They were both all the way out of pocket. They crossed lines that never were supposed to be crossed. I cried even harder at that point.

My younger partner Boo was dead. He was just alive and doing well. Sixty days ago he was here with me and now he's gone. He went home and stayed sixty punk ass days before Allah took his soul. I cried for his family. For the beautiful little girl that he had. What was her name again? Shakira. I thought about all the photos I had seen of Boo's daughter and thought of my own eight year old. Who would kill an old lady and a baby? Then I thought about Lil Cee's mother and little sister that Khadafi had killed. The person who killed Boo's family had the same fire inside him that Khadafi had. I picked myself up off the floor and walked over to my bed.

"Felder, are you finished with the phone?" the C.O. asked me.

I had to struggle to recover quickly and speak because I didn't want anyone to see or hear my weakened state. "Yeah. Aye, C.O.?"

"What's up, Felder?"

"I need to see the case manager tomorrow morning. Can you let Mr. Durant know that and that it's important. I need him to pull me out tomorrow."

"Okay, Felder. I got you."

Laid out on the bed, all types of images rushed across my mind. Graphic images of Khadafi making love to my woman wouldn't leave me alone. I couldn't shake the vivid images of her face as she had an orgasm. I saw the way her body responded to touch and heard her moans as she was stroked in the right way. My mind held me captive and showed me acts of copulation between my comrade and my woman. Both had crossed the line. I dried my eyes and then took off my tank top. I wiped my eyes and nose with the t-shirt. A plan of action formed in my head and I knew what had to be done. As I wiped at the last few tears that formed in my eyes, I vowed to myself to never ever again in life shed a tear. Those were the final tears of my existence. I would never allow myself another moment of weakness. And I would never allow myself to love another person, male or female. To be betrayed is like facing a certain death. I laid in my bed and decided that Khadafi and the woman that I loved more than life itself were my enemies. And it was only fair that my enemies share my pain and suffering.

The next morning, I got up early and worked out real heavy. My body was weary due to sleep deprivation. I had not slept for more than an hour all of yesterday and last night. I worked out for six hours straight until my mind, body and heart ached. At lunchtime, I reminded the cop to tell the case manager that I needed to see him. Case manager Solomon Durant came to get me at a little after one in the afternoon. I shot my spiel about a death in the family and that I needed to make a call on the straight out phone in his office. I knew that if he said yes, he would leave me alone for a few minutes to speak to my family in private. After laying the bullshit on extra thick, he let me make the call. And just like I knew he would, he left me alone in the office. I picked up the phone and dialed Umar's cell phone.

"Hello?" Umar answered.

"Umar?"

"Yeah, it's me, ock."

"I'm on the straight out phone in the case manager's office, so we can speak freely without the conversation being monitored. I don't have much time, though, feel me?"

"I feel you, ock", Umar responded.

"I been thinking about what you told me yesterday and I know what I want you to do. But first, let me ask you a question."

"Shoot."

"Do you love me, slim?" I asked.

"No doubt, ock. With Allah love and dunyah love."

"That's what I needed to hear. Do you remember the last time I saw you?"

"Of course. It wasn't but thirty days ago."

"Do you remember how excited you were to be going home?"

"Yeah."

"Do you remember how you felt when the plane finally touched down in D.C.?"

"Most definitely."

"Do you remember how it felt to get your first piece of pussy?'

"Hell yeah."

"I asked you all of that for a reason, slim. I will never be able to feel all the things you felt. My life will forever be devoid of all those good feelings. I'll never be able to hug my children, take a bath, drive a car or go shopping. I will never answer a phone again or make love to a woman. I'm hit like good weed. You follow me?"

"I'm with you, ock."

"I didn't have to be stuck, slim. I still had avenues available to me in the courts. But me being the dude that I am, I gave all that up for y'all, for you. I hate to put you in this position, but right now you're all I got. You always promised me that you'd hold me down. Remember that?"

"How could I forget?"

"Holding me down can mean a whole lot of things, slim. You gave me your word that whatever I needed, you'd do it. Well, guess what? I need you now. I'm calling in all my markers. Umar, the Islam we believe in gives us the laws of equality, right?"

"Right."

"That means that if a person kills your cow, whether by mistake or on purpose, then that person owes you a cow or you have the right to slaughter one of his cows"—"

"But it also says that it's better for you to just forgive that man."

"I know that, slim, but I am not Allah. I cannot forgive that easily. Allah is the most forgiving, the most merciful. Not me. My fear is not that high yet. I committed the ultimate sacrifice for my men, for Khadafi, for Boo, and for you. I am the sacrificial lamb, slim. I gave my life so that others shall live. The Christians would say that I'm similar to Jesus. Had I not made that sacrifice, things would be different right now, and we wouldn't he having this conversation. You'd be here somewhere in the S.H.U., Khadafi would have never been able to cross me, and Boo would be alive. I am devastated inside about Boo dying out there, but I still don't regret the decision I made for y'all. I love the fact that you are able to enjoy so many luxuries. But sometimes those luxuries come with a price tag. You are the realest one in the group, slim. You have always kept it real. Boo needed the right guidance and he didn't get that from Khadafi. Khadafi is the worst kind of man. And I'm fucked up that I never saw it in him. He has no honor, no principles, and no respect for loyalty and friendship. I gave him his life and in return he killed me on the inside.

He was never supposed to cross the lines he crossed. To go home and fuck my baby mother, he put a knife in my back and twisted it. Shawnay is a bad muthafucka, slim. A temptation to any man. But his love and loyalty was supposed to keep him from giving in to that temptation. He betrayed me, Umar, and what does our law say about betrayal?"

"It's worse than slaughter. Betrayal is worse than slaughter."

"Exactly. I would rather be slaughtered than betray one of my men. The penalty for betrayal is what?" I asked.

"Death"," Umar replied." The penalty for betrayal is death. That's something that Khadafi always said."

"It was the reason why Keith Barnett was killed in the first place, because he betrayed his man. Is it fair that the rules don't apply to him as well? And Shawnay, too?"

"I feel you on Khadafi. But Shawnay? She's not a part—"

"Shawnay is not a part of what? The life? The game? What? She knew the rules, slim. I taught 'em to her. She was in the life through me. And none are a part of the game, because this shit ain't no game. This is real life and the rules apply to everyone evenly. At times of war, the rules of engagement apply to civilians as well as combatants. There's no difference. And this is a time of war. It's my war against those who betrayed and abandoned me. Just as Khadafi did in jail and in the streets with the lives of those that crossed him, now I do the same. Him and Shawnay are both guilty in my eyes and I sentence them to death. That's where you come in. I can't carry out those death sentences, but you can."

"Come on, ock. I can't," Umar started.

"Come on, ock, what? You can't what? Kill? We both know that you can kill, slim. Remember before the Islam and the moral conscience? Remember when Good Hope Road and 14th Street was beefing? Remember when your little brother got hit and put in the wheelchair? Remember how you felt before you went on Good Hope and started putting the most work in? Remember all the dudes you stood over and closed their eyes forever? "

Umar sighed. "I remember."

"I know you remember. I'm talking to Lil Harold right now, not Umar. I need Harold to step to the plate and hold me down. Shawnay and Khadafi gotta pay." As the words left my mouth, it was like a stranger inside of me was speaking. I knew that what I had asked Umar to do was something I'd regret later.

"What about your daughters, ock? Don't they need their mother?"

I gave what he said some thought. "Everybody needs their mother, but sometimes things happen and we have to adjust. My daughters will be raised by their grandmother. They will be all right."

"What about the Islam? Khadafi is still Muslim," Umar argued. "His blood is sacred."

"Sacred to who? You? Isn't Boo dead because of him? What about all the Muslims that died at the Masjid? Wasn't their blood sacred? He didn't shed it directly, but he was the direct cause of the bloodshed. Shawnay's body was sacred to me and he desecrated it. So, to me, Khadafi's blood is no longer sacred. I know how you feel right now, slim, but it is what it is. I need you to hold me down by killing the two people who have betrayed me. I know that you don't wanna do this, but you owe me. I made a sacrifice for you; make a sacrifice for me. Can you do that?"

"I pay my debts, ock. After I do this, then what?" Umar inquired.

"After that you can do whatever you want to, but your debt to me will be paid in full."

"I'll get in touch with you when it's over."

"I need...Umar? Umar?" I sat holding the receiver and realized that he had hung up on me.

I knocked on the door loudly to signal the case manager.

"Is everything okay, Felder?" Durant asked.

"Now it is," I replied and walked quietly back to my cell.

.CHAPTER FORTY-THREE.
KHADAFI

"We only got about thirty minutes", Shawnay said, stepping out of her heels. She walked over to her office door and locked it." "I usually go to lunch with my co-workers, but for you, I'll make an exception."

I leaned against the file cabinet on the wall and watched as Shawnay lifted her dress and pulled her panties down. We had just been together that morning before she left to go to work, but I couldn't get enough of her. In a sick, twisted kind of way, I could see why Ameen was so gone off of her. "Thirty minutes is enough time."

"Well, come and get it. Lunch is now being served." Shawnay laid back on her desk and spread her legs.

I saw the brownness of her skin part in the middle and the pink appear. In seconds I covered the space between us and dropped to my knees. I started at the base of her pussy and slowly moved upwards. Shawnay tasted like vanilla as I ate her.

"U-m-m-m-m. Uh..h-m-m-! This feels s-o-o-o good! Damn! You eating the shit outta me!"

"You want me to put this dick in you?"

"Yes, please!"

I unzipped my Envisu jeans and pulled my dick out. Rubbing the head all around her lips, Shawnay begged me to fuck her. I grabbed both of her feet and held on to them as my rock hard dick slid into her.

"A-a-a-r-r-rrg-ghh! Don't put it in too deep, it's gonna hurt!"

"I'ma go slow"," I assured her.

"O-o-o-w-w-w! Put my legs down some! You got too much dick in me!"

I stopped mid-stroke and pulled out. "Get up."

"Why you stop?" Shawnay asked me as she got off the desk.

"Bend over the desk."

After Shawnay bent over. I put the dick back in her and had her climbing imaginary walls.

After I killed Money's mother and father. I had to sit back and reflect. I was emotionally drained after that night. So I called Shawnay and asked her could I come over. She said yes and that's where I ended up spending the night. My timing ended up being perfect because every year around this time, Shawnay sent her daughter to stay with her grandmother for a week. So Shawnay and I had the house all to ourselves. I cut my cell phone off and never turned it back on. I needed some time to myself away from everybody but Shawnay. She was my guilty pleasure and although making love to her was wrong in some eyes, it was right in ours. Why deny the physical attraction if it was strong?

Every now and again I would think about Kemie and how angry she must be at me. I haven't called her or anything. I went home twice to grab a few things when I knew that she wouldn't be there. She had to know that I'd been there and was probably crushed because of my behavior, but fuck it. I gotta do me.

I picked up the *Washington Post* newspaper to check out the obituaries. If my calculations were correct, there would be something in the Metro section about Money's parents and nephew. The good thing about living in the city was that if somebody dies, the local paper would announce that death and give you a place where people could go and pay their respects. It also gave you the time and day for the service. When I got back to Shawnay's house, I looked through the paper and came across the Crime and Justice section in the Metro. What I read crushed me to the floor....

D.C. Police have identified the bodies of three people killed on Wednesday. The bodies were discovered in a row house in the 400 block of W Street in Northeast. Acting off an anonymous tip, authorities went to the house and found an elderly woman, a small child, and a man dead from apparent gunshot wounds. The elderly woman has been identified as Elsie C. Dammons. The male was identified as Vernon Dammons (27). The child was identified as Shakira Danelle Dammons (8). D.C. Police are asking that anyone with any information about this crime. Please contact Crime Stoppers at 202-234-3647. There has been a $75,000 reward posted.

The paper dropped from my hand. Tears came to my eyes as I realized what was now a reality. Losing my uncle was one thing, but to lose a partner that was like a brother, that was a whole different feeling. Marquette was my uncle. He was my blood. The blood of my slain mother. I loved him for that alone. But the love I had for Boo was a love of a different kind. He was with me at all levels for almost seven years. He was my brother from another mother. We had been through the storm together and conquered it with no rain coats whatsoever. I felt responsible for his death and the deaths of his grandmother and daughter.

Why had someone killed...? The answer came to me before I could even finish my thought. They were killed because I had killed Money's parents and nephew. No one had been spared, just as I had spared no one. The anger in me rose and I had to struggle to contain the beast in me. I needed to be rational at a time like this. My enemy was outthinking and outmaneuvering me. I was acting off emotion and my enemy was using his head. He had to be in order to find Boo and his family so fast. I quickly grabbed my cell phone and checked my messages. The voicemail box was full. The majority of the messages were from Kemie, a couple were from Marnie and a few of from my men. One message was from Alex at the car dealer and two were from Boo. I pressed the button to play Boo's first message that was recorded four days ago...

"Where are you, slim? I had nightmares like shit last night. Get at me when you get this message. Death before dishonor...."

The next and last message from Boo came the day after the first one. It was recorded at 5:38p.m.... "Slim, what the fuck is up with you? Where the hell are you? Kemie been calling my phone asking for you. You need to call her, slim. She said you never came home the night of ...... well you know what I mean. Holla back and let a nigga know what's up with you. Tomorrow, I'ma start looking for your ass. One love, slim. Death before dishonor......"

My man had been trying to reach me and I had ignored him. Now he's dead. I stood up and walked around the living room. I needed to clear my head and think. My next move had to be my best move or I'd end up in the Metro section as well. I wasn't trying to go out like that, so I decided not to rest until I crushed all my enemies. I picked the paper up off the floor and searched for the info I so desperately needed. I saw what I knew would be there and gave a silent thanks to Allah. The obituaries for William and Deidra Smith were there. But there was no listing for the little boy. There were no memorials for children on the whole page. That could only mean one of two things. The little boy's service would be held on a different day and would be in the next day's paper or Umar didn't kill the little boy like I told him to. The more I thought about it, the more I like the second answer better.

I had tried to make Umar into something that he wasn't: a natural born killer with no conscience. I should've handled it myself and now I feel cheated. I would have blown little shorty's little brains out and kept it moving. Umar had to have helped the little dude escape. And that means he lied to me. I asked him that night about the little boy and he said that he hit shorty twice in the head. Lies and mistrust were issues that could never be tolerated amongst men. I decided right then and there to deal with Umar at a later date. Right now, the fact that Money was one up on me in the number of victims on each side had me disturbed. I think it's time I even the score.

207

.CHAPTER FORTY-FOUR.
UMAR

"**A**ssalaamu Alaikum wa rahmantuallah," I said facing my right shoulder and then repeated the taslimah facing the left. I cupped my hands in front of me and said, "He is Allah. There's no God but He. The living, the self existing, the eternal. No slumber can seize him nor sleep. His are all things in the heavens and the earth. Who is there that can intercedeth in his presence except as he willeth. He knows what appeareth to his creatures, before or after or behind them. Nor shall they encompass aught of his knowledge except as he willeth. His throne does extend over the heavens and the earth and he feeleth no fatigue in guarding and preserving them. He is the most high. The supreme in glory. Oh, Allah, forgive me for all the wrong I've done in this world. Forgive me for the wrong I will do in the future. Have mercy on me. You are the most forgiving, the most merciful. Amen."

Rising from the position that I sat in, I stretched my arms and legs. Offering the Janaza salat for Boo was hard for me. I kept crying as I recited surahs from the Qu'ran. I still couldn't believe that Boo was gone.

"......*Khadafi is the direct cause of Boo's death......him and Shawnay are guilty in my eyes and I sentence them to death......*"

I replayed the conversation between me and Ameen in my head over and over again. I heard every word he said as if he was stabbing me directly in the heart. I had given Ameen my word that I'd hold him down and now I am in a hell of a bind. When I became Muslim almost four years ago, I gave Allah my word that I'd never kill another one of his creatures again. I vowed to myself to stick to my word. That's why I couldn't kill the little boy. Now I'm faced with a serious dilemma. Who do I keep my word to? The Creator of all the worlds that can kill me, body and soul, or my friend, buddy, and brother? My loyalties were divided.

At some point I decided that I would do what Ameen asked of me and try to make it right with Allah. Ameen had become my sacrificial lamb. He was right about that and I would never forget that. I had to do what he wanted me to do.

I walked over to my dresser and picked up the Ruger 9mm. I turned it over a few times in my hand and then checked the clip. It was full. It would crush me emotionally to kill Khadafi and Shawnay, but I gave Ameen my word. I had to honor it. A man's word is all he has in this world. I would rather give my life before my word should fail. Grabbing my keys off the dresser, I went to find Khadafi. Just like Ameen had said, I was Harold again.

.CHAPTER FORTY-FIVE.
MONEY

"In the sweat of thy face shall thou eat bread, till thou return unto the ground; for out of it was thou taken; for dust thou art, and unto dust thou shalt return", the preacher said.

I stood beside my mother's casket and stared at the photo of her on top. It was a beautiful picture. It was taken by my father a few years ago when they vacationed in Paris, France. My mother's smile lit up the whole 8x10 photo. I tried to be strong for my family, but I couldn't keep the pain inside. Behind me my sister's wails and screams cut into the morning air and seemed to echo.

Since the house was set on fire, my parent's remains were unrecognizable. Inside the coffins was what was left of them. I glanced at the photo of my father and remembered the day that I snapped it. It was the day he became principal of Banneker Sr. High School. It was his crowning moment. That was five years ago and now he's dead. My desire for revenge is still unquenched. It did make me feel a little better that the dude with the dreads, Boo, was dead. He was gone and so was his grandmother and daughter. They thought that by sparing my nephew, I'd be lenient. They thought wrong. I purposely ordered Cochise to kill any children there. I wanted to send them a message.

The hunt for Khadafi and Umar continues. At times, I think about Mrs. Jones. Ever since her murder, every law enforcement agency has been scouring the street to find her murderer. Well, fuck her and the day she was born. She was the reason my parents were dead in the first place. I don't regret killing her at all. Next up would be Khadafi's father, old man Fuller. And Cochise was hard at work finding him.

"William and Deidra Smith were both pillars of the community and staples in the church. They would have wanted us to celebrate their homegoing," the preacher proclaimed. "Why are you crying for me?" They would have told each and every one of us. The Bible says that every soul shall taste death, Ecclesiastes 12:17 reads, Then shall the dust return to the earth as it was; and the spirit shall return unto God who gave it."

I heard somebody scream suddenly and then people were running in all directions. Startled, I looked to my left and stood paralyzed with fear. The masked man dressed in all black was less than four feet away from me and approaching fast. Instinctively, I reached for my gun and felt an empty waist.

Shit!

I saw a flash of light and then nothing.

.CHAPTER FORTY-SIX.
KHADAFI

From my position behind the tree, I could see the whole cemetery. But what interested me the most was the large gathering at a gravesite not far from where I stood. I had carefully done my homework and paid a groundskeeper to show me the spot where their plot of ground was. That was yesterday. Today, I stood and watched Money release about a hundred or so doves from a box. The gravesite at Harmony Cemetery was packed with people, but I didn't care. The morning sky was clear and my mission to destroy Money was carved in stone. It was my destiny to crush him.

The minister was still speaking as I pulled down my mask and crept up on the gathering. Nobody paid me any mind until I was within feet of my target. I heard a sudden scream and then all eyes were on me. But I was determined to make my move and I didn't care how many people were out there. I created exactly what I wanted, pandemonium. In the midst of that pandemonium, I found Money. He was alarmed and confused. His eyes searched for the cause of the screams and found me quickly rushing toward him. Our eyes locked in a mental embrace. I saw him reach for his waist as I aimed the Calico and fired. At that proximity, I couldn't miss. All around me, people were out of control, but I didn't care. They were invisible to me. The only person that mattered to me was on the ground leaking blood. I ran up on him and stood over his fallen body.

"I'ma make sure you dead this time."

I fired the Calico over and over and watched each hole appear in Money's head. Once I was satisfied that he was dead, I ran. I ran back the way I came and then hit the hill. Running through the woods, I focused on finding the tree that I had marked. At that tree, I knew that I needed to make a left turn. I spotted the tree and turned left. I kept running until I saw a path that led out the woods and onto Sherrif Road. I pulled the mask off and used my hoody to conceal the Calico as I exited the woods. Across the street from me was a 7-11 convenience store. I dropped the mask in the trash receptacle outside the store. Then I went inside the store. I stuffed the Calico and hoody behind several loaves of bread in aisle five. Catching my breath and trying to remain calm, I purchased a slurpee and walked out of the store. I saw several police cars and an ambulance racing to the cemetery.

"It's too late for all that," I said to myself and walked around the corner to my car. I got in the car and turned on the radio. The sound of Young Jeezy blasted through my stereo.

"…..I put on for my city (Southside)/… put on, I put on…/……coming from where I'm from. Call me Jeezy Hamilton/ riding down Campbellton/ so fresh…so clean/ on my way to Charlene's…"

The cat and mouse game between me and Money was finally over. It felt good to stand over him and watch him take his last breath. Then I remembered the dude that Money had bringing me the moves. I needed to find him. As small as D.C. is, the dude is bound to surface somewhere and I never forget a face. I'ma barbecue his ass for jumping out there. I promised myself that I would find him, but first I needed to lay low for a while. The heat behind all the recent murders would have the police geeking and I didn't want to get caught up on a humble. My thoughts were interrupted by my cell phone vibrating. It was Kemie. "Hello?"

"So you finally decided to answer your phone, huh?" Kemie asked.

I braced myself for a tirade that never came. "Kemie, a lot of shit been going on. I can't tell you everything over the phone. I need—"

"Redds, stop the bullshit! I know exactly where you been."

I wanted to stop Kemie before she got on a roll. "I'm not about to sit here and do this with you over the phone. I'm on my way home. Meet me there. We can talk then."

"Home? What home do you have? You don't have no home. At least not at 1736 Woodlawn Drive, you don't. I packed all your shit up. You can take your ass back to 56th Street and I'll make sure you get your shit."

"Kemie, let's not go there. You know me, cuz. You know what the fuck I'll do to you for playing with my shit. Don't get it fucked up," I said nice and calm.

"Fuck you, nigga! You got the nerve to be threatening me and you the one that ain't been home in damn near a week. I'm not scared of your ass. All those other niggas in the street might be, but not me."

"Say that shit to me when we get close to one another, a'ight?"

"Fuck you—"

I hung the phone up on Kemie and checked my messages. One message was from Umar, although I saw that he called my phone several times. I listened to his message and told myself that I'd call him last. Two messages were from Shawnay. I called her at work. She picked up after four rings.

"Administration. This is Shawnay, how can I help you?"

"What's up, boo?"

"Hey! I called you a coupla times and got no answer. So I just left you a message."

"I'm hip. I been handling some business and that took all my attention. I was gonna call you as soon as I finish."

"I don't like the way you sound. But I'm not gonna lecture you about your business. Just do me a favor and be safe. Have you talked to Antonio lately?"

"Naw. You?"

"Naw. That's what's so strange about it. He usually calls."

"Knowing him, he must be in a situation where he can't call home. He a'ight, though. I know that."

"When am I gonna see you again? You know the girls come back home tonight, so we gon' have to go in the basement."

"That sounds good, but give me at least another day to get everything in order. Then I'm coming to lick you up and down until you say stop."

"I never say stop ," Shawnay said.

"We'll see tomorrow. I'ma call you later on today, a'ight?"

"Okay. Be safe out there. Bye."

I was tired and horny. As bad as I wanted to go see Shawnay at work, I knew I had to deal with Kemie first. I dialed Umar's cell phone number and waiting for him to pick up. "Hello?

"Assalaamu Alaikum, ock."

"Wa laikum asSalaam. Cuz, what's up?"

"Where have you been? I been calling you ever day since the night we went on that move," Umar said.

"I been laying in neutral. I need some time to clear my head. You heard about Boo?" I asked.

"Heard about Boo? Ock, I was talking to him when he got killed."

"You was talking to him when he got killed?"

"Yeah. He called me and told me he found his grandmother and daughter dead. He was talking real fast and I couldn't understand everything he said. Then I heard gunshots and he got quiet. I kept calling his name, but he didn't answer. Finally, a voice that I didn't recognize came on the phone and told me that Boo was dead and that you and me were next."

"The voice said that you and me were next?"

"Yeah."

"But, why would he say you were next? What does he, they, know about you?" I asked vexed.

"I don't know. All I know is that the dude said that you and me was next. I thought Boo was on joke time, so I hopped in my truck and went to his house. When I pulled up, the police and meat wagon was already there. That's when I starting calling you."

"Cuz, that's my bad. I should've been there for you, for Boo. I should've left the phone on. I was wrong and I admit that. I failed y'all, but I handled the situation. Boo didn't die in vain."

"What do you mean?"

"I found out about Boo in the newspaper. In that same paper, I got the address to the church where Money's people would be memorialized at and the name of the cemetery. All I can say is that the dude Money is resting peacefully. You feel me?"

"Yeah, I feel you. So what do we do now?"

"I haven't figured that out yet. I'm about to go home and see Kemie about some stuff. Give me a few days, I'll call you so that we can meet up and talk."

"That's a bet, ock. Assalaamu Alaikum."

"Wa laikum, AsSalaam, cuz. I'm out."

When I pulled up to the house, I saw that Kemie's Land Rover wasn't parked outside. I had beaten her home. I used the calm and quietness before the storm to take a shower and get my head together. Inside the shower, I turned the nozzle to the hottest temperature. I wanted the water to soothe my aching muscles and my broken heart. The gravesite at Harmony reminded me of two of its residents—my mother and my uncle. As the tears welled up in my eyes, I thought about Boo and the fact that he would also reside at Harmony in a few days.

Fed Ex field is the home of the Redskins/ Harmony Cemetery is the home of my dead friends.

The verse that I wrote several years ago came to mind as the water ran down my face and washed away my tears. I lathered myself up and reminisced about everything that had happened over the last four months. Everything had gon' extremely wrong. I scrubbed my body as if I could wash away the smell of death. All the lives that I had taken had me smelling like death followed me around. Killing Money had brought me no relief other than the fact he was dead. I hated sensitive moments like the one that was overtaking me now. Because of one fatal mistake, I had caused the deaths of so many. My uncle is dead. Boo is dead, and so is his family. Bean, my right hand man is dead. And Umar is distant. Our bond that we shared was injured the day the gunman killed all those Muslims at the Masjid. It died the day I ordered him to kill the little boy and he couldn't. And what about Ameen? When was the last time I had spoken to him? Sent a picture, a letter or some money? It had been a while and deep down inside I knew the reason why. I knew that I crossed the line. At the time, I just didn't care. I can't lie to myself. If nothing else, to my own self I have to be true. My ego in conjunction with a little greed and lust fueled my desire to cross that line.

Why didn't Shawnay resist me? Didn't she know that we were both wrong? Was she more to blame than me? But didn't she deserve to be happy, even if that meant being with me? Wouldn't Ameen want her to be in good hands with a dude like me? Just as the soap rinsed from my body and entered the drain, so did the answers in my head that came and went. Woman has been man's greatest vice since the beginning of time. Every great man's defeat was precipitated by a woman. And 2008 was no different. Visions of Shawnay popped into my head. Her pretty feet and toes connected to a beautiful set of hairy legs. Her caramel vanilla complexion. Her apple bottom shaped ass and shaved pussy. Her face, her hair, her breasts. Everything about Shawnay was like that. She was the fruit that Allah warned Adam about. And just like Adam, knowing that it was forbidden, I took a bite.

A sound in the next room caught me off guard. I strained my hearing to see if I had heard something or I was just tripping. I heard a noise again. Always on point, I grabbed one of my spare guns out of the cabinet underneath the bathroom sink. I purposely left the shower water running as to not alert the intruder that I had heard him. Slowly, I opened the bathroom door and pointed the .45 in front of me. As the person stepped into view, I almost pulled the trigger. But I recognized Kemie's face underneath a black National baseball cap.

"Keep on creeping around the mutherfucka and your ass gon' get shot," I said and dropped my gun on the bed. I walked naked back into the bathroom and resumed my shower.

Kemie walked into the bathroom and went off. "Nigga are you sick, insane, or just plain cookoo? Who do you think you are, Redds? Huh? You left this mutherfucka six days ago and you never came back. You didn't call a bitch or nothing. What's up with that, huh?"

Whenever Kemie called me Redds, I knew that she was pissed off. As I stepped out of the water and grabbed a towel to dry off, I noticed how sexy she looked when she was mad. She was wearing tight jeans that hugged her pussy and a Moschino shirt that accentuated her breasts. I had almost forgotten just how sexy Kemie was.

"Can a man just take a shower in peace?" I asked as I walked past her into the bedroom.

"Hell no! Especially when that man hasn't been home in days. Answer my question, Redds. What the fuck is going on with you?"

The more I stared at an irate Kemie, the more hornier I became. Without saying a word, I walked up on her and grabbed her.

"Get off me, boy!" she protested.

I paid her no mind as I found her neck and kissed it. Kemie struggled for a while to get me off of her, but I held her tight. I held her and kissed her lips. I licked all over her face, ears and neck.

"Stop it, Redds! Get off me!"

I ignored Kemie completely as I undid her jeans with one hand and squeezed her nipples one by one with the other.

"Don't do this to me! Don't touch me—"

"Be quiet. You know you like it," I said as my hand found her pussy. I bit down on Kemie's neck at the same time that I put my finger in her. Kemie continued to struggle against me, but it ended up working against her. The more she wiggled, the deeper my two fingers went inside her.

"Stop it!"

My free hand reached under Kemie's shirt and found her breast. I lowered myself to it and sucked on it like a child. Soft moans escaped Kemie's mouth as I took turns kissing and sucking each breast. I pushed Kemie back against the wall.

"Get offa me, Redds."

My fingers were soaking wet. I pulled them out of Kemie's pants and licked the juices off of them. Then I kissed her stomach and navel. I tugged at her jeans and pulled them down as Kemie submissively wiggled to make my job easier. Once the jeans were at her ankle, I kissed my way back up her legs until I was at that box. Slowly, I licked circles around Kemie's clit. She reached down and guided my head deeper into her so that my tongue would reach farther. I stuck my tongue inside of Kemie and it drove her crazy.

"O-o-o-o-o-h s-s-s-h-h-i-t! E-e-e-e-a-a-t this p-p-p-u-u-s-s-s-y!"

I took my right thumb and rubbed the clit while I was eating the pussy. The combination of both stimulations had Kemie cumming in seconds.

"I'm-m-m c-u-u-m-m-ming! Damn! I'm c-c-u-u-m-m-ming!"

Never letting up, I still used my tongue like a sword and stabbed her pussy over and over again. I eased down to the base of her pussy and tried to put a passion mark on it. Kemie was openly hollering now. I continued to ignore her as I stepped up my assault on her. I nibbled on Kemie's clit and had to endure her soft punches to the top of my head.

"You gon' make me cum again!"

After bringing Kemie to another screaming orgasm, I went down and pulled each of Kemie's Hermes tennis shoes off, one by one. Then I pulled at the jeans that huddled at her ankles until they were off as well. I found the fact that she wasn't wearing any panties very appealing. I stood up erect and pulled Kemie's shirt over her head. We locked lips and the kiss was surreal. Electric sparks shot through me as I guided my dick to her pussy. I felt like I had popped an E-pill or something. I rubbed the tip of my dick around the opening before I pushed into Kemie. She gasped and moaned at how good and tight she felt. Kemie wrapped one of her legs around my waist and locked her arms around my neck. I pumped myself deeper and deeper into her and enjoyed every minute of it.

"Damn, girl! This pussy is a torch!"

We dipped and stroked, dipped and stroked. I felt like a contestant on "Dancing with the Stars." The way Kemie moved her body like a snake had me sweating and struggling to keep up the pace. She used her muscles in her pussy to grip my dick and coax the cum out of me. "I'm 'bout to cum, Kemie!"

"Cum for me, boo!" Kemie shouted.

I couldn't hold back any longer. I came deep within Kemie for what seemed like an eternity. Kemie pushed me back a little and dropped to her knees. She took my semi hard dick and put it in her mouth. I felt my dick roll around her tongue as she sucked the last few drops of cum out of me. Kemie kept sucking me long and deep until I rose again. I put both hands flat on the wall and leaned over Kemie. The sight of my dick disappearing all the way into her mouth had me ready to explode early. I threw my head back and decided not to watch in an effort to control my desire to cum again. Kemie worked her magic on me until I had to stop her flow and change directions. Lifting Kemie up off her knees, I headed toward the bed and took her with me. "Get on the bed and assume the position. You know how I like it."

I watched as Kemie climbed up onto the bed on all fours— doggy style. She dipped her back low and grabbed the covers.

"Why are you grabbing the comforter?" I asked her.

"To bite down on because it hurts too much. I'm not gonna give you the satisfaction of hearing me scream."

"I just heard you scream a few minutes ago."

"Two totally different screams. I always scream when you eat me. Fucking me is something different. Go ahead and put it in. You like fucking me like this because you think you can control me. Today I'ma show your ass that you ain't controlling shit."

I laughed at the stupid ass shit that Kemie had just said. But it did make me more determined to hear her scream. I slid my dick in Kemie and grabbed her waist. After building a rhythm, I pressed down on her back and forced every inch of dick into her repeatedly.

Kemie tried her hardest to bite on the covers, but her moans and screams, although muffled, still came through. I pounded the dick in her and broke down all that bullshit she was talking moments ago. "I thought you was gon' show me that I wasn't in control of shit?"

"Fuck you, Re-d-d-s! F-f-f-u-u-c-c-k you!"

"Fuck you? You want me to fuck you, huh? Okay." I stopped mid-stroke and turned her over onto her back. I grabbed her legs and pressed them back as far as they would go. Then I put her feet on each of my shoulders. My dick slid back into her on its own. I hunched down on her so far that her toes were touching the headboard of the bed. I grinded the dick as far as it would go as Kemie scratched my back and called out to the heavens. I did exactly as she asked me. I fucked the shit outta her. Then I fell asleep.

.CHAPTER FORTY-SEVEN.
UMAR

The sun was starting to set and I was starting to wonder if Khadafi was gonna come back out at all. I sat in my truck across the street from where he lived and watched the front door. I saw the Infiniti truck and his Cadillac parked outside, so I knew that he was in there. After talking to him earlier, I rushed out to Takoma Park. He told me on the phone that he was going home. I decided to be more proactive in my quest to kill Khadafi.

I was starting to tire of the wait. I pulled away from the curb and drove two streets over to Riverton Road and parked the truck. Dressed in an all black Squash All Beefs jumper and black Nike boots, I made my way back to Khadafi's house. I took the back way all the way there. When I got to Khadafi's street, I walked down an alleyway until I reached his back door. There was a fence about four feet high around Khadafi's backyard. I hopped the fence and crept through the grass to the side of the house. I crouched down low and looked out from around a bush. I had a perfect view of the driveway where Kemie and Khadafi's vehicles sat. I looked at my watch. It read 7:47 p.m. I decided to give Khadafi another hour before I called him and forced him to come out of the house. And when he did, I'd fulfill my promise to Ameen.

.CHAPTER FORTY-EIGHT.
KHADAFI

It was becoming harder to breathe by the minute as it felt like a large weight was placed on my chest. I opened my eyes to find Kemie sitting on my chest completely nude. She had tears falling down her face and a gun pointed at my forehead. I felt the tip of the barrel as it bore into my skin a little bit at a time. My heart raced as I tried to figure out a way to keep Kemie calm. "Kemie, get that gun outta my face," I said in an effort to remain completely calm.

"Did you fuck her like you just fucked me? Huh? Have you been eating her pussy like you just ate mine? What the fuck did she do to you to make you stay with her for six days? Answer me, muthafucka or I swear to God, I'ma blow your head off."

"Put the gun down, Kemie." I said again.

"You think I'm bullshittin', don't you?" Kemie said and chambered a round into the handgun that I had dropped on the floor earlier." You think I won't kill your ass, huh?"

"Kemie, I'm not gonna say it again. Get that damn gun outta my face. Let's talk this out like a man and a woman."

"A man? You ain't no muthafuckin' man. You a bitch hiding behind a rack of guns. Now the rabbit got the gun and that shit don't feel right, huh? Bitch niggas do the type of shit you do. How you gonna call yourself a man? You weren't man enough to call me and tell me that you had pussy on the side that you needed to service. I know that a bitch's pussy wasn't that good to make you forget where home and the phone was. I been calling your ass for days and you wasn't man enough to just answer the phone. Now you talking about let's talk like a man and woman. Nigga please! I followed you to 56th Street, Mr.

Man. I knew that you were there and that some bitch lived there. Now you ain't even man enough to keep it real. You're a bitch, Redds!"

"Kemie, it wasn't what you think. Put the gun down and let's talk," I pleaded.

"You gon' sit here and lie in my face, huh? As good as I have been to you. This is how you feel about me? Just lie in my face, right?"

"Ain't nobody lying to you. Stop acting like a kid and be a woman. Put the damn gun down, Kemie."

"This is the thanks I get for doing ten years with your ass? I have been putting up with all your wild ass ways. All the robbing sprees and the killing. I'm in danger every day by staying with your wild ass, but I do it. I stayed because I love you. I continued to put myself in harm's way for you. Isn't that some crazy shit? And now you got the audacity to prance up in here and try to wash away all the evidence of your infidelity. Why you didn't shower at that bitch's house, nigga? Huh? I'm the crazy one for loving you so much."

"Fuck it, Kemie. Go ahead and shoot me if that's what you want to do. But don't keep sitting here talking about how much you love me. Did you love me when you was fuckin' with that nigga Phil? When you was writing me and sending me naked pictures that he probably took? Did you love me then? That nigga is the one that taught you all the wonderful things that you know about sex. Did you love me while class was in session? When he was teaching you how to suck dick and swallow cum? Did you love me then? When I left you, you wasn't taking no dick in your ass. Phil taught you that, too. Did you love me, then, too? When he fucked you and turned you out, did you love me? When you got dumped by him and you fucked Omar and Bean, did you love me then? Did you?"

"I...I...I uh—"

"What's wrong, Kemie? Cat got your tongue?" What I said struck a nerve and discombobulated her. I saw the pain register in her face. Her body sagged slightly and she took her eyes off of me. That was the break I needed. In one split second, I reached out for the gun and knocked Kemie off of me at the same time. The gun went off, and Kemie fell onto the floor and balled up in the fetal position. I got off the bed and leaned over her. I pulled Kemie's hair until her face was showing and smacked the shit out of her about five times. The sight of her blood made me thirsty like a pit bull. I grabbed the gun and put the barrel to her head. "How does it feel, Kemie? Does it feel good to have a gun pointed at your head? I should kill your stupid ass. "I pressed the gun into Kemie's cheek. "Since you got so much to say, give me one good reason why I shouldn't kill your ass right now." When Kemie didn't respond I said, "That's what I thought."

I left Kemie there on the floor as I got dressed. Ten minutes later, somebody knocked on our front door. I crept to the door and looked out the peephole. My face drained of all its color. There were two cops at the door. I silently raced back into the bathroom and put the gun back into its stash spot. I went to Kemie and said, "Kemie, the police are here. Go answer the door."

"Fuck them and fuck you. Leave me alone."

The knocking became more persistent. I knew that the cops wouldn't leave until somebody answered the door. The cops at the door were local cops and I hadn't committed any crimes in Takoma Park, Maryland, so I was straight. I walked to the door and opened it. "May I help y'all, officers?"

"Sir, we have a report of shots fired from this residence. Are you the owner of this house?" The tall heavy set white cop asked.

"No, I am not. My girl owns this house. There's been some kind of mistake. There were no shots fired from this house."

"Can I speak to the woman that owns this house, please?" The second officer asked.

"She's not here. She—"

"Sir, the caller that called us said that the woman of the house drives that Land Rover parked in the driveway and that they saw her go into the house several hours ago."

"She never left, sir," the heavy set cop said. "We are not going to leave until we have spoken to her, sir."

I was stuck. I didn't know what else to do, so I called Kemie to the door. After what seemed like forever, Kemie came down the stairs and stepped to the door. One look at the bruise on her cheek and the busted lip told the story. A deep scowl crossed both officers' faces.

"Sir, please keep your hands where we can see them and turn around and face that wall." I complied with the cops. "You have the right to remain silent...."

.CHAPTER FORTY-NINE.
COCHISE

The sound of a gunshot jerked my head in the direction of the house that I had watched Khadafi's girl go into. What the hell happened? I checked my watch and determined that I had been sitting here for about five hours. I put a little money out there down Capers and came up with a hit. It never dawned on me to look for Khadafi's woman instead of Khadafi. I found out a long time ago that his girl's name was Kemie and that she was from Capers too. I got a call from somebody early this morning telling me that Kemie would be at a house on the street in about an hour and that she would be there doing somebody's hair for a few hours. I went to the address that I was given and sure enough a gold Land Rover was parked out front. After waiting about two hours, Kemie came out of the house and got into her truck. I followed her to this address where I am now.

On the way here, I heard a breaking news bulletin on the radio about a man being gunned down at a gravesite at Harmony Cemetery. Although the news people didn't release any names, I knew in my head and in my heart that the victim at Harmony was Money. It was too much of a coincidence. Money had called me yesterday and told me that his parents' memorial service was being held at Harmony and that they'd bury his folks there. Somehow, Khadafi had found out about the service and went there to get his man. Nothing has been confirmed as of yet, but all attempts to reach Money have failed. So I proceeded as if Money was still here. I'll pour out a little liquor for him at a later date. Right now, its rabbit season and I'm trying to catch a rabbit.

Kemie never paid me any mind as I stayed two cars behind her. My first thought was to snatch her and get inside the house and then wait or make her get Khadafi to the house. But that was too gung-ho for me at the moment. Somebody was sure to spot me bringing the woman and alert the cops. I decided to be smart and sit it out. No matter how long it took, I knew I had to get Khadafi now. If he was in the house, I'd get him. If he comes to the house, I'll get him. Either way, I'm not moving until I get him.

I heard the sounds of sirens approaching in the distance, but I didn't think anything of it until I saw the two police cars pull up in front of the house that I was staking out. From the darkness of my new Mazda van, I watched the officers go to Khadafi's front door and knock.

To my surprise, a man answered the door, a man that looked just like Khadafi. My stomach did flips as I realized I was looking at the man that I had come to kill. So he was home the whole time? I didn't know what was up with the cops, but I hoped that they'd hurry up and leave. I needed Khadafi to come out of the house to accomplish my task.

Out of the corner of my eyes, I detected movement. I saw a head peep out from around the corner of the house. I couldn't believe my eyes. I shook my head and refocused to make sure I was seeing what I thought I was seeing. The street light that illuminated enough light to keep the house out of the shadows allowed me to see the person's face. I recognized the face immediately. The beard was unmistakable. The face that I was staring into was the face of the next victim on my list, Umar. What the fuck was he doing on the side of Khadafi's house, lurking about like a burglar? I couldn't believe my good fortune. I had stumbled upon my other prey. Or did he stumble upon me? I kept an eye on Umar as he regressed back into the darkness on the side of the house and watched the scene unfold at the front door all at the same time.

The cops were arresting Khadafi. Shit! I took my fist and hit it on the steering wheel. Maybe my luck wasn't so great after all. But justice delayed, didn't mean justice denied. I'd have to wait until another time to get Khadafi. Knowing exactly where he lived made that task that much easier.

As I watched the police walk Khadafi down the walkway, I saw his woman behind the cops pleading with them. They paid her no mind as they put Khadafi in the back of the patrol car. On the side of the house, Umar peeked his head out and watched the officers pull away from the curb with Khadafi in the back seat. Then he disappeared from my sight. A couple of minutes later, Umar emerged from the darkness, from the alley behind the house and jogged what appeared to be two blocks and turned down a street. I started the van and drove past the street that he turned on. I saw the black-clad figure getting into a truck of some kind. The headlights and taillights on the truck lit up the block as he pulled out of the parking space and drove down the street. I waited for a few seconds to pass before I went after the truck. I caught up with it on Cherry Hill Lane. As always, I stayed two to three car lengths away and followed the truck to wherever it was headed.

.CHAPTER FIFTY.

UMAR

What the hell had happened? I kept asking myself all the way to my truck. I heard the gunshot go off inside the house, but it was easy to explain that right away. Khadafi could've been cleaning or loading one of his guns and accidently discharged it. I never thought that he or Kemie had shot one another. I never even thought that the shot would bring the police, but it did. I guess that was one of the drawbacks of living in a residential neighborhood that's way too quiet for its own good. Or had Kemie called the police? I shook to dispel that thought. Khadafi would have never allowed Kemie to make it to the phone if there was really a problem. So why had the police locked Khadafi up? And why did he go so willingly? Knowing Khadafi like I do, he would have never submitted to them people if they had him on some serious shit. It had to be domestic. In the state of Maryland, you got a slap on the wrist for domestic shit. Kemie and Khadafi were probably fighting and somehow a gun went off. I could almost visualize the whole thing. The cops came and locked Khadafi up because Kemie must've had a mark on her that was visible. She didn't want him arrested, that much was shown by the way she followed the cops to the car and pleaded with them to let Khadafi go.

I was mad a little but overall, I took Khadafi's arrest as the will of Allah. It just wasn't his day. But who's to say that tomorrow won't be? Or whenever he gets out. I couldn't stand there and cry over spilled milk, so eventually I left. Now, on the way to Shawnay's house, I'm wondering if she's going to be as fortunate. The drive to 56th Street was about twenty-five minutes from Khadafi's house. I parked on 58th Street by Evans Jr. High School and got out of the truck. I won't lie and say that I wasn't nervous as I walked the two and a half blocks to my destination. I ran from the back of the house to the front door. I saw that lights were on inside the house and could hear the sounds of a TV on. I rung the doorbell and waited. Seconds later, I heard a female voice say, "Who is it?"

"Harold. Ameen told me to come by and check on you and the kids." Before I could finish my sentence, the door opened and there stood Shawnay Dickerson. She looked just like all the photos I had seen of her in Beaumont.

"When did you speak to Antonio?" she asked.

"Yesterday. He sent you a message."

"He did? And what's that?"

I had the gun out, but it was hidden behind my back. "He said to tell you that betrayal is worse than slaughter. And the penalty for betrayal is death." I pulled the gun and pointed at Shawnay. But just as I started to pull the trigger, a small face appeared.

"Mommy, I need you to—" the little girl said. I looked at her as her mother screamed and recognized her instantly. She looked just like Ameen. I kept the gun pointed at Shawnay and willed myself to shoot her, but I couldn't. I lowered the gun and ran. As fast as my feet would take me, I ran. I ran back through the yard and hopped the gate. I jumped the gate of a yard behind Shawnay's house and ran to the front of that house. With the gun still in hand, I ran back to 58th Street. I had failed. Ameen would have to understand. I had Shawnay right there and I couldn't kill her. I slowed myself down as I approached the truck. Just as I put the key in the driver's side door, someone popped up from the front of the truck. My eyes grew as large as plates when I saw that it was the same man that was shooting at us at the Masjid. His gun was already drawn and aimed before I could react.

"I told you, you were next."

I heard those words, saw a flash, then heard nothing else.

.CHAPTER FIFTY-ONE.
KHADAFI

Three Months Later...

"*Mr. Fuller, I will accept the terms of your plea agreement and respect the fact that Ms. Bryant adamantly states that she started the fight. Since the government decided to pursue the case, I have no other resource but to sentence you to six months of incarceration. I will suspend all but ninety days and give you credit for the time you've already served. In the future, Mr. Fuller, you and Ms. Bryant need to find a non-physical way of dealing with your problems. And please do not let me see you in my courtroom again. If I do, believe me when I say, that the next time I will not be so lenient.*"

I laid in my bunk and replayed Judge Peter's words in my head. I had caught a break and I knew it. Now, I can only hope that the supervised release people would see things the same way. When I was released from Beaumont, I knew that my judgment and commitment order from my original judge stated that I had to do three years of supervised release. Supervised release is just like being on parole, only it's a little bit more lenient. I came home and saw my supervised release worker one time. He was a young black dude named Mr. Roberts. He told me that I didn't have to report into his office. I had to call once a month. I haven't spoken to him since being held at the Seven Locks Detention Center in Montgomery County, Maryland. I'd see him tomorrow, though, when the board came to let me know what they decided to do in my case. They could either let me go since my time was up on the misdemeanor domestic abuse case, or they could send me back to jail for up to three years.

I thought about doing three years in jail and instantly got sick. I needed to be in the streets. I still had business to attend to. I glanced at the freshly inked tattoo on my right forearm. There were doves flying and unfurling a banner that said "In Memory of Vernon" Boo" Dammons and Harold "Umar" Howard." Then there were tombstones that protruded awkwardly out of the earth that had both of my men's birth and death dates. I got up off the bunk and went to the mirror. I turned around and looked at the tattoo on my back. There were two portraits inked on my back. One of my mothers and one of my uncle. They both stared down at an image of me on my knees as I prayed to Allah to forgive them for their sins. I laid back down and reminisced about all the people that I had loved and lost. Alone in my cell, after I found out about Umar getting killed, I broke down and cried for hours. The next day and every day thereafter, I tried to call Shawnay, but received no answer every time. She was avoiding me and I didn't know why. The only person that I could depend on was Kemie. She never left my side, mainly due to the fact that she felt responsible for me being back in prison. But my thoughts still took me back to the last time that I had fucked Shawnay.

We were in her office at work. I thought about the way she had ended the lunchtime quickie session by eating my dick like it was a Coney Island hot dog. I can never forget how she swallowed all of my cum, burped and then said, "Thanks for lunch." Before I even knew what I was doing, my hand was in my pants and I was pulling out. I thought about Shawnay and beat my dick until I came all over the cell floor.

The Supervised Release Board ended up giving me a twelve-month hit. They cited the new criminal conduct as their reason for doing it. With credit for the three and a half months that I'd already been in jail, I was scheduled to be released in March of '09. One week later, I was sent back to the Feds.

The van carrying eleven of us to Harrisburg Airport in Pennsylvania pulled onto the tarmac not far from the runway. There were several other vans just like ours parked on the tarmac as well. Having taken the trip before, I knew that somebody on the van was gonna get on the Feds' big raggedy-ass white airplane. Breathing a sigh of relief, I knew that I wasn't getting on the plane. With only eight months left to do on my hit, I figured I'd be staying on the East Coast for sure. An hour later, the Fed plane landed and steered its way toward us.

"Airlift. When I call your name, step to the front of the van. Butler."

I watched the dude next to me named Gunsmoke get up and say to me, "Take it easy, joe."

"Simpson," the Marshall called out next.

My partner B.F. from Barry Farms stood up and said, "Marshall, where they got me going to?"

The Marshall looked down at his paper and said, "Simpson, you're going to USP Pollock. Next man, Winston."

I watched my man Whistle from down the Valley get up and off the van.

"Last man, Fuller."

"Who did you just call, Marshall?" I asked, not believing what I had just heard.

"Luther Fuller."

I was devastated as I rose to go to the front of the van. "And where am I going, Marshall?"

"Beaumont. USP Beaumont."

"Luther Fuller, you're back, huh?" Rose, an overweight black C.O. that ran receiving and discharge grinned and said. "Strip, Fuller."

I ignored the fat bastard as I stripped out of all my clothes.

"Don't wanna talk to me, huh? It ain't my fault you couldn't stay free for a year. Take your ass over there and stand on the black line. You know the drill. Time for a few photos."

After I was processed back in, the Captain came to see me.

"Welcome back, Fuller. I knew you'd fuck up in the free world. It says here that you only got eight months to do before we have to let you go again. Let's see here...domestic abuse, huh? You never get enough, huh, Fuller? Beating on women makes you feel tough?"

My disdain for Captain Garcia was well established between the both of us. "You know how I get down."

"I sure do, Fuller. You're such a tough guy that I'm afraid of you. I'm so afraid of you that I don't want you around me. So you'll be doing that eight months in Special Housing. Is there anything that you'd like to say before you go?"

"Yeah," I answered. "Fuck you."

Captain Garcia smiled a wicked smile and said, "Naw, Fuller. Fuck with me and watch how fast I send that team up in your cell to beat your ass. Rose, call somebody in S.H.U and tell them to come and get this piece of shit."

.CHAPTER FIFTY-TWO.
AMEEN

I was on 670 burpies when Green Eyes, my Pensacola, Florida buddy, came to my door and gave me the good news. Hearing Green Eyes at my door, I stopped working immediately, knowing that he was the S.H.U orderly and that someone had sent me something.

"What's up, Green Eyes?"

"It's your birthday, my nigga."

"Yeah?" Knowing that my birthday was in June and it was now October, I was confused. "Why you say that?"

"Guess who just came in the door downstairs?" Green Eyes asked.

"Who?"

Green Eyes smiled a big smile and said, "Khadafi."

I thought that my buddy was bullshittin' at first. Then he added, "He came back on a violation. He got eight months to do. Captain Garcia says he gotta do it in the hole."

"Oh yeah? Good looking out, baby boy."

I waited for Green Eyes to leave the tier before climbing up on the toilet and hollering through the vent. "Big Tee?"

"Yeah, what's up, ock?" Big Tony Coleman answered. "Remember that package I told you I was waiting for about two months ago?"

"No doubt."

"It just arrived today. Send me your line over. I got a kite coming to you."

"It's on the way, ock."

I jumped off the toilet and grabbed a pencil and paper. Then I put my man next door down with what I was trying to do.

237

.CHAPTER FIFTY-THREE.
KHADAFI

Laying awake in my bunk the next morning, I wondered when I'd finally see Ameen and what I'd tell him. I knew that he'd be disappointed in me because I let Umar and Boo get killed. I'd explain to him that I killed all of the people responsible for their deaths, except one, and he was living on borrowed time.

"Rec! Who wants to sign up for rec?" an officer shouted down the tier. "Don't let me pass the door. If I pass by you, you're hit. Be at your door to give me your name. Rec call!"

Climbing down from the top bunk, I made it to the door just in time. "Five cell wanna sign up for rec, CO."

"Both of y'all want rec?"

I woke my celly up. "Yusuf, you going out?"

"Naw," he said, turned over and went back to sleep.

"Just one, C.O. Fuller."

"I got you, Fuller."

I got back on the top bunk and thought about what my celly, Joseph "Yusuf" Ebron said to me last night. He told me about how much the compound had flipped over while I was gone. He said that the S.I.S. had rounded up the homies La-La, Champ, Buckeyfields, TJ, Player, Mansoo Cain, and Scoop and shipped them all over the country because the D.C. car was too strong in Beaumont. He also told me that the whole Detroit car was gone, too. They had gotten rid of Dee, Bam, Omar, and all the rest of my Detroit partners. He told me that Ameen was still waiting to go to trial on that body and that he was on A-range, still on a three-man hold.

"C- range, get ready for rec!" the C.O. called out. I jumped off the bunk and brushed my teeth.

Twenty minutes later, I was handcuffed and led to the rec cages.

"Fuller, where you tryna go?" the rec cop asked me.

"Put me with my D.C. homies," I replied.

"That'll be right back here then." I was led to the rec cage in the back of the rec yard. The cop opened the rec door and let me into the cage. I recognized two of the homies in the cage, but not the other two. I got the cuffs taken off me and then I gave Kevin "Twin" Tinsley and Billy "Dolla" Richardson a hug.

"Khadafi, this is the homie Big Tony," Twin said. "He just got here from Colorado. And that's the homie Fice. He came from Big Sandy."

I spoke to both men, but my eyes settled on Big Tony. The dude was huge. He had to be like six-four and 280 pounds. He did pull-ups off the fence while everybody else talked to each other. A few minutes later, the cops brought Ameen out and put him in the cage next to us. I waited until the cops were gone before I went to the fence and hollered at him.

"Assalaamu Alaikum," I greeted Ameen.

"Wa laikum AsSalaam," Ameen said, returning the greeting. "What happened out there, slim?"

"It all started with my uncle." I ran the whole story down to Ameen about the beef in the street and the dude Money.

"Well, if you killed Money that morning, who killed Umar that night?"

I gave Ameen my theory on that and then rested my case. "Cuz, shit got hectic real fast. But on my mother's grave, I'ma get the dude that killed Umar."

"It's something you're not telling me, slim."

I stared at Ameen with a quizzical look on my face. "What are you talking about, cuz?"

"Shawnay," Ameen replied.

"What about Shawnay?"

"You promised me that you'd take care of her, slim."

"I did take care of her, cuz. You didn't hear about that?"

"Oh, I heard about *it* all right. You took real good care of her, slim. You took such good care of her that you fucked her, right slim?"

I was suddenly afraid. I looked back over my shoulder and saw the dude in the cage with me still engaged in various acts of working out. "It wasn't like that, cuz. I don't know who you been—"

"Talking to? You gave me your word that you'd take care of my family. I didn't mean fuck my girl, slim. You violated the trust and bond that we had. I—"

I watched Ameen reach into his jumper and pull out a nine-inch shank that was sharpened to perfection.

"Was my brother's keeper," Ameen continued. "But my brother didn't keep me. I made the ultimate sacrifice for you and you fucked my woman. You stopped writing. You stopped answering your phone. What happened to all the flicks I asked you for?"

"Cuz, I"...I..." I stammered.

"Fuck that shit, slim. Forget I even asked you that. But answer this for me. Did you ever consider us brothers?"

Just as I was about to respond, I felt strong arms reach under my armpits very quickly. The hands attached to those arms locked themselves behind my neck and pressed me up against the fence. Pain set in as I realized that somebody had me in a full nelson head lock. "Ameen, we brothers, cuz."

"And just like Cain killed Abel, I'm about to kill you, brother. Did you really think that I was gonna let you get away with everything you did in them streets? Did you really believe that I was that forgiving? If you did, you thought wrong."

Ameen walked up to the fence and plunged the shank into my stomach. The pain was indescribable.

"This is for Boo," he said and stabbed me again. "His daughter and grandmother."

I felt the knife enter my chest deeply. I tried to speak, but my words came out garbled.

"This is for Umar," Ameen spat as he pushed the knife repeatedly into me. "This one is for Shawnay."

I felt blood rise up in my throat and start to choke me. My life was slowly leaving my body and there was nothing I could do about it.

"And this one here is from me."

I coughed one time and spit blood on Ameen. It was over for me and I knew it. The arms that held me captive released me. Then I heard a voice scream out, "Felder, drop the knife!"

As I hit the concrete, for an instant my whole life flashed through my mind. I saw all the people that I loved alive again. They called out my name. I gave in to the darkness.

TO BE CONTINUED...

READING GROUP DISCUSSION QUESTIONS

THE ULTIMATE SACRIFICE

1) Was Kemie right or wrong for staying with Khadafi, knowing that he hadn't been home 30 minutes and killed two people? What about after she learned that his victims were a woman and a little girl?
2) How do you feel about Khadafi's uncle Marquette saying that he loves his nephew, but still put him in harm's way by sending him to rob and kill people?
3) Could you have made the sacrifice the Ameen made for his friends?
4) Would you describe Khadafi as mentally insane because of all the murders he committed or would you call him a product of his environment?
5) Do you believe that Boo was too loyal to Khadafi?
6) After he was robbed, shot and left for dead, should Money have been thankful to be alive and left the situation alone? Or was he right for going after Khadafi and company? Was the end result worth it?
7) Was Khadafi wrong for crossing the line and sleeping with Shawnay?
8) If you were Money's father, would you have given up Money to save the lives of your wife and grandson?
9) Was Ameen wrong for telling Umar to kill Khadafi and Shawnay?
10) How do you feel about what Ameen did to Khadafi in the end?

MEET ANTHONY "BUCKEY" FIELDS

After being sentenced to fifteen years in prison for attempted murder, Anthony Fields discovered his love for the written word. Born and raised in Washington, D.C., a desire to rise above his conditions caused him to pen his first novel, Angel presented by Teri Woods. Having watched that book receive critical acclaim and staying on the Essence Magazine Bestsellers list for months, Anthony was inspired to pen and publish his debut novel "Ghostface Killaz". He also co-wrote "Bossy" with Crystal Perkins-Stell. Now signed to Wahida Clark Presents Publishing, Anthony hopes to broaden his fan base and give the people great street tales to read. When he's not writing, he spends his time mentoring younger inmates and helping them to attain their dreams of becoming published authors.

Anthony Fields currently resides in a federal penitentiary in Pollock, Louisiana.

ON SALE NOW

National Bestselling Author of Payback with Ya Life
WAHIDA CLARK
W•CLARK
PUBLISHING
A STATEMENT IN LITERATURE
A Novel
THUG LOVIN'

AVAILABLE NOW
WAHIDA CLARK PRESENTS
CHEETAH
ALWAYS BE AHEAD OF THE HUSTLE
MISSY JACKSON
W•CLARK
PUBLISHING
A STATEMENT IN LITERATURE

ON SALE NOW!
WAHIDA CLARK PRESENTS
KARMA
With A Vengeance
TASH HAWTHORNE

COMING SOON

COMING MAY 2010
WAHIDA CLARK PRESENTS
THE MADAM
Blood Secret
DION JONES

www.ingramcontent.com/pod-product-compliance
Lightning Source LLC
Chambersburg PA
CBHW070614310726
48982CB00001B/81